All Lori w**r own arms** ~~never~~ let go.

"I like how you're always thinking," he whispered and pressed his forehead against hers. "Smart girls are hot."

Tears prickled the back of her eyes, tightened her throat. Why did he do this to her? Make her want the one thing she knew would only hurt her in the end? Why did he let her believe in something that could never be hers? "So are men in uniform," she said before she could stop herself. "But you know what?" With more strength than she thought she possessed, she planted her hands flat on his chest and pushed herself away. "Friends don't kiss friends like that."

"No." Matt caught one of her hands before she could pull free. "No, they don't. But maybe I'm on my way to earning another chance at being something other than friends."

Dear Reader,

Welcome back to Butterfly Harbor.

When I "met" Lori Bradley, she was one of those solid background characters I knew would pop up occasionally. So, thinking she'd be in the shadows, I made her a little like me. Okay, I made her a lot like me, which means this is probably the most personal book I've written to date. I think if you ask, a lot of authors will admit to putting bits of themselves into their characters or, if they don't, they put other people they know into them. It's the nature of the art. The fun part of the story was finding her "match." Lori isn't the only woman who falls for Matt Knight. I kinda did, too.

Matt Knight made his first appearance in *The Bad Boy of Butterfly Harbor*. Like Lori, he was really just supposed to be a one-scene walk-on, but when he arrived he was so much more. Burly, a touch of Southern good old boy and a former soldier who has seen more than his share of tragedy. He's as honorable as they come, sometimes to a fault.

For me, this story proves you never realize who you truly are until you see yourself through someone else's eyes. When someone else believes in you, challenges you, that's when you become who you're meant to be, which is precisely what Matt and Lori do.

I hope you enjoy their story, and the stories still to come. And yes, before you ask, Kendall will be getting her own story soon.

Anna J.

HEARTWARMING

Always the Hero

—

Anna J. Stewart

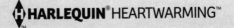

HARLEQUIN® HEARTWARMING™

Recycling programs
for this product may
not exist in your area.

ISBN-13: 978-1-335-63355-2

Always the Hero

Copyright © 2018 by Anna J. Stewart

Printed in U.S.A.

Bestselling author **Anna J. Stewart** can't remember a time she wasn't making up stories. Raised in San Francisco, she quickly found her calling as a romance writer when she discovered the used bookstore in her neighborhood had an entire wall dedicated to the genre. Her favorites? Harlequins, of course. A generous owner had her refilling her bag of books every Saturday morning, and soon her pen met paper and she never looked back—much to the detriment of her high school education. Anna currently lives in Northern California, where she continues to write up a storm, binge watches her favorite TV shows and movies, and spends as much time as she can with her family and friends...and her cat, Snickers, who, let's face it, rules the house.

Books by Anna J. Stewart

Harlequin Romantic Suspense

Honor Bound

Reunited with the P.I.
More Than a Lawman
Gone in the Night

Harlequin Heartwarming

A Dad for Charlie
Recipe for Redemption
The Bad Boy of Butterfly Harbor
Christmas, Actually
"The Christmas Wish"

Visit the Author Profile page
at Harlequin.com for more titles.

For Victoria Curran

Whatever comes next is because you said yes

CHAPTER ONE

Deputy Matt Knight sat at his desk and stared at the divorce papers that had taken him three years to have drawn up. He stared at the black on white print, the familiar words blurring behind tired eyes.

"Just sign the thing already." Even as he muttered to himself, his fingers tightened to the point of going numb. What on earth was stopping him? It wasn't as if divorce was some big taboo these days. He certainly wasn't holding out hope for a reconciliation. How could he when his soon-to-be-ex had made it perfectly clear—well before Matt's discharge papers from the army had been processed—that she'd moved on. There was no ill will. There were no feelings at all. It only made sense. If he was serious about moving on with his life, serious about becoming a father to an abandoned troubled teen, it was time to cut ties and start over.

His stomach knotted. Signing his name was the right thing to do. For everyone. And yet…

If only signing the decree didn't mean admitting he'd failed. Matt had spent a good portion of his thirty-two years determined to avoid anything close to failure. He couldn't shake the deadening sensation that writing his name only proved his father right.

He leaned forward, set his jaw. How messed up did he have to be to give credence to anything his long-dead father would have thought, especially when it came to what constituted failure? It was time to make this final break and move on with his life. If he didn't owe that to himself, he certainly owed it to Kyle Winters. What kind of example would he be setting for the kid if Matt couldn't put his own past aside? Besides, there were bonuses to starting fresh.

Bonuses like Lori Bradley.

His lips curved as an image of the lush, generous, quiet brunette with eyes as green as spring grass appeared in his mind.

The tip of the pen hovered.

"You can stare at that piece of paper as long as you want." Deputy Oswald "Ozzy"

Lakeman's voice drifted across the small station house. "Whatever it says, it's not going to change."

Matt clicked his pen shut, tossed it onto the desk. He sat back in his creaking spring-loaded chair and swore he heard his divorce papers laugh at him. He looked over and found Ozzy grinning at him before he snapped his teeth through one of those mini carrots he'd been munching on of late.

"I thought you were taking Fletch's patrol this afternoon," Matt said.

"I am." Ozzy leaned back and looked up at the station clock. He clicked his tongue. "Still have a few minutes to bug you. How am I doing?"

"At bugging me? Stellar performance, as always." The banter came easily, as it had when he was in the army. The soldiers he'd served with had been his friends, his family. At times, he had to shake off the guilt that he had a new family now, a new group of friends while his fellow grunts... He swallowed the bitterness and grief.

Chances were Ozzy appreciated the downtime as much as he did. With Butterfly Harbor's annual Monarch Festival less than a month away, the entire township was flitting around, prettying up store windows, touching up paintwork, finalizing sponsorship plans and making certain the soon-to-arrive tourists were given the best show possible when it came to the Pacific Coast tourist town.

Everyone was too busy to get into much trouble save for the occasional parking and noise ordinance violations. That was just fine with Matt, but he'd lived long enough—and hard enough—to know the quiet wouldn't last. "Do we have an ETA on when Luke's back in the office?"

"Chief's due back tomorrow morning according to Holly," Ozzy said, referencing the owner of the Butterfly Diner and their boss's wife. "We should have a full house again now that Fletch has returned from his honeymoon. Oh, hey, Jasper." Ozzy glanced up at the teen hobbling out of the bathroom on crutches. "I unearthed a new box of files that need to be digitized. When you're caught up."

"On it." Jasper O'Neill clicked his way over to the desk they'd given him last month and dropped into his chair. "Can't wait to be off these things." He leaned over and set the crutches against the wall before logging back on to his computer.

"It's been almost six weeks." Matt couldn't believe that much time had passed since the teen had nearly gotten himself killed playing amateur detective. That Jasper had been the prime suspect in the string of increasingly disturbing break-ins and vandalism had been a driving factor. The kid hadn't done himself any favors by dressing like death and taking pleasure in making people feel uncomfortable. But when the smoke cleared, the sheriff and his deputies had decided to take Jasper on. The boy's determination and cleverness couldn't be ignored. The part-time position with the police department allowed him to continue with his forensics studies, stay out of trouble and earn some serious résumé references.

"Only ten days to go." Jasper swiped his hand over too-long bangs that covered dark eyes. "Then you guys will have to start taking me on patrol with you."

Matt grinned. "We'll see about that." Personally, Matt was hoping Jasper would be up for renewing his friendship with Kyle. Jasper could be a good influence on him.

Matt pushed his chair back, stretched out his prosthetic leg and waited for the gentle click that, had he not left his actual leg on a dirt road in Iraq, would have felt like a muscle easing into place. "With Luke and Fletcher both out, I guess that means I'm on deck for the town council meeting tonight." Matt barely resisted the urge to groan. What a way to spend a Friday night. He'd seen the setup coming for weeks; his coworkers' planned absences that would ensure he'd be the one to make the final push for the sheriff's department's contribution to the Monarch Festival. The annual fall event was, at least until the new butterfly sanctuary was built, the town's biggest claim to fame—and its biggest tourist draw. From the Butterfly Diner, to Harvey's Hardware, to the Flutterby Inn, businesses were snapping up sponsorships and initiatives like nobody's business.

While his boss and fellow deputies agreed they needed to participate, they'd also decided to focus on a job that would be of benefit beyond a week's worth of events and activities. He pinned Ozzy with a determined, hopeful stare. "Unless you'd like to—"

"Not on your life." Ozzy held up his hands

as if shielding himself from a radiation blast. "Not on my life. Not on anyone's life."

Jasper chuckled as he tapped away on his keyboard.

"As long as you're sure," Matt mumbled. "You could at least come with me." It made sense. Despite living in Butterfly Harbor for almost three years, Matt was still considered a newcomer. Before becoming a deputy, he'd mostly kept to himself having moved here alone after his separation. Not that he hadn't piqued his neighbors' curiosity, but he kept his private life private. As far as anyone in town knew, he was an unencumbered bachelor. Ozzy, on the other hand, had been born and raised here, which meant everyone knew his business. "I could use the backup."

"No offense, but the only way I'd voluntarily attend the Mayor Hamilton show is if it was a direct order from my boss." Ozzy visibly shuddered. "Lucky for me, that is not you."

"But you're good at throwing me under the bus," Matt said.

"Yep. You don't have a history with Gil." Ozzy ducked his round face out of sight at the mention of the mayor. "And it's not as if he'd take anything I have to say seriously anyway. I know what he thinks of me."

Matt flicked his thumb across the stack of divorce papers as anger simmered low and hot. "And what's that?"

"That I'm a drag on the department." Ozzy flinched as if speaking the words out loud hurt. "Word is he's planning on instituting physical fitness requirements for all of us in the department. Like what they do over in Durante."

"I bet Luke will have a thing or two to say about that." When Ozzy didn't respond, Matt prodded deeper. "Is that what all this diet stuff's been about, Oz? You worried about keeping your job?"

"No."

"Oz." Matt used the same tone with the younger deputy that he had with new recruits. Granted, Ozzy wasn't about to walk into a war zone, but sometimes the same medicine worked on different ailments. "What's going on?"

Oz shook his head. "It's not a big deal, Matt. You know how Gil is."

"Yes, I do." One of the reasons Matt wasn't overly fond of their mayor. If it wasn't for

Ozzy's tech know-how and efficient computer skills, they'd still be typing on Selectric typewriters and stuffing the wooden filing cabinets to the point of overflowing. "I'll tell you something right now, Oz. If you're looking to lose weight to appease anyone other than yourself, it won't work in the long run. Short term, maybe."

"I know. At least I'm feeling better." Oz shrugged in that casual way he had of trying not to call attention to himself. "And I'm up to a mile-and-a-half run in the mornings. Well, I can do that much without wanting to puke. Mostly." He looked at the carrot in his hand. "I'm getting really sick of these things, though."

Personally, Matt was surprised the deputy hadn't turned orange. "Don't let anyone else determine how you live your life, Oz. You want to lose weight, you do it for yourself. Not because some jerk like Gil Hamilton's bullied you into it."

"Word," Jasper muttered.

"I hear you." Ozzy nodded. "And I know you're right. Anytime I think about quitting, I remember that day Charlie got trapped in the caves down at the beach. I should have been able to help Fletcher more than I did. They both could have drowned."

It wasn't the first time Ozzy had made mention of the near-catastrophic event. There also wasn't any mistaking the hint of self-loathing and disappointment that came with letting the people you care about down; or worse, believing you had. That day had been rough on all of them; the idea that eight-year-old Charlie might never have made it out of those caves if it hadn't been for her now step-father's actions and the support of most of the town still made his gut clench.

"No one believes you let anyone down." Matt chose his words carefully. "Not Luke, not Fletcher and not me, who by the way, took three times as long getting down the beach as you did." He slapped his hand against his prosthesis. "If we don't blame you, there's no reason to blame yourself."

"Yeah, well." Ozzy shook off Matt's attempt to placate him and returned his bag of carrots to the mini fridge under the coffee station. "I'm not going to let anything like that happen again. I want Luke to know he can count on me for whatever might happen.

That all of you can. And if the mayor does institute physical tests, I'll be ready for them."

"As long as you're doing it for yourself, too."

"Funny how times change." Ozzy looked genuinely surprised. "You know, back in high school, word got around my mother had put me on a diet. Some of the guys on the football team loaded my locker with those cream-filled sponge cakes. Ruined my first edition copy of *Hitchhiker's Guide to the Galaxy*."

There was little Matt loathed more than bullies. "Any of those jerks carry a gun and get a patrol car with spinning flashing lights?"

Ozzy grinned. "Nope."

"Then you win. Speaking of winning." Matt gestured to the clock on the wall. "Patrol started five minutes ago."

"Oh! Geez." Ozzy spun around, checked his belt for his weapon and phone, dived for his jacket and stumbled to the door. "Thanks, Matt. I'll see you later. Oh." He poked his head back in the office. "If you want something to look forward to tonight, Abby told me Lori is going to be representing the Flutterby Inn at the town meeting. You know, in case you want to say hi or something."

Matt wadded up a piece of paper, chucked it at him and yelled, "Be grateful I don't have a Twinkie!"

But Ozzy had made his point. Just the mention of Lori was enough to take the sting out of Matt's obligation for tonight. There was something about just laying eyes on Lori that made his day better. He'd been careful with her, slowly building up their casual friendship despite his desire for more. Lunch. Coffee. A couple of small town events. He couldn't let himself get too interested, too tempted, as long as he was still officially married, and the truth was, he was both—interested and tempted. He enjoyed the time he spent with her, felt the dormant fire inside of him light up when she looked at him, smiled at him. Laughed at his stupid jokes. It took a special woman to get his sense of humor. Which was why, in the last few weeks, since soon after Holly and Luke's wedding, he'd been avoiding her.

Matt Knight was all about doing right by people. Especially those he cared about. But there wasn't any moving forward, not with his life, not with Lori, as long as he was still anchored to the past.

The phone rang. Before Matt could reach for the receiver, Jasper answered. "It's for you, Matt. A Chris Walters?"

"That's Kyle's caseworker," Matt said as he picked up his extension. "Chris? Kyle okay?"

"Doing well, actually." The social worker's encouraging words belied the tension in his voice. "We're still on track for an early release. For now at least."

"What's that mean?" Matt squeezed the receiver so hard his fingers tingled. "What's going on?"

"The judge in charge of Kyle's case is retiring. His replacement is reviewing all the cases ahead of time and, well, since we're jumping beyond fosterage to adoption, she has some concerns about your living situation."

"What's wrong with my living situation?" Matt asked. "I've got a room ready for him, he'll have a part-time job with the sheriff's department, and most importantly he'll have more stability than he's known in years."

"I'm on your side, remember? You don't have to convince me. She's not denying your petition, Matt, but she has suggested a female influence in the house wouldn't be a bad thing for Kyle. And given your marital status…"

"That's about to be resolved." Matt looked down at the papers on his desk. "I filed the divorce papers and am getting ready to sign them as we speak."

"Okay. We'll have to see how that plays with the judge."

"Given Kyle's last female influence was too hopped-up on prescription meds to give him a second thought, I wouldn't think this would be any judge's first concern." Matt hated to speak ill of Kyle's mother, but the truth was the truth.

"It's a concern, Matt. And the judge only suggested it would be in your and Kyle's best interest if there was someone in your life to help bring a bit of balance. Even if it's just a girlfriend, which brings me to what we talked about before. She's going to want to call Lori as a character witness."

"Lori? How does she know about Lori?" The last time his heart had pounded this hard he'd been dodging bullets.

"Because I listed her in my report. You

said you were dating her, that you thought it was getting serious. Are you telling me something's changed?"

Changed? Other than Matt all but ignoring her the last few weeks while he got his head on straight and cleared the emotional deck? "No, nothing's changed," Matt blurted before his brain could catch up with the panic seizing his chest. He'd made a promise to Kyle, and Matt Knight never made a promise he couldn't keep. "We've been seeing each other for a while, off and on." Most recently off. All the more reason to remedy that. "She's completely on board with me taking Kyle in."

"So you're okay with her listed as a character witness? She'll back up your statement should the judge want to call her in during Kyle's hearing?"

"Yeah, of course." Matt swallowed the lie. Well, it wasn't a lie exactly. Lori did know about Kyle but Matt's current relationship with her might be a bit, well, up in the air. "Have they set a date yet for the hearing?"

"Um, yeah. Hang on, I've got that right…" The sound of shuffling papers scraped against Matt's ear. "Three weeks from Monday. Looks like the judge has us penciled in for two in the afternoon."

Matt scribbled the date on his calendar, noting that was the same day as the big welcome dinner that opened the Butterfly Festival. That would take some juggling given it was all hands on deck in town for the department. "I'll be there." Somehow. "I thought I'd come up and see him in a couple of weeks. Need to figure out my days off."

"You're on the visitor's list for anytime," Chris said. "I'm glad you told me about Lori. This will go a long way with this judge in approving Kyle's placement."

"I hope so." With Kyle's troubled past, the only other placement option for him would be a group foster home or to extend his stint in the detention center he currently resided in. "Let me know if there are any more changes."

"You got it."

Matt hung up. Why was it, even when he had the best of intentions, he ended up messing things up? At least now he had even more of a reason to apologize to Lori. As much as he wanted her back in his life, he needed her. Kyle needed her. Unease settled in his gut like a stone. He hated lying. To anyone. But especially to Lori Bradley.

"Everything okay?" Jasper asked. "Is Kyle still getting out?"

"He sure is." He picked up his pen, clicked it open and scratched his name.

A few seconds later, he set the sealed envelope on the counter, where it would go out in the afternoon mail.

CHAPTER TWO

"LORI, THANK GOODNESS!"

Lori Bradley glanced up from behind the registration desk at the Flutterby Inn as Beth-Ann Bottomley swooped in like a redheaded designer bird of prey. A Butterfly Harbor native who had returned home after the death of her senator husband, BethAnn was one of those people you crossed the street to avoid. Somewhere north of fifty, she had the uncanny talent of turning any compliment into an insult. Today's campaign-worthy suit was the color of summer cherries. The look in her eyes? Seek and destroy.

"You have got to help me!" BethAnn dropped a stack of boxes on top of the registration desk and draped herself over them in exhaustion. "Esther Kravatz's arthritis is acting up and she totally forgot about these invitations. If I don't find someone reliable to send them out, the entire welcome dinner could fall apart! I'm so glad you're on the committee."

Esther Kravatz's arthritis had been flaring up a lot since BethAnn had returned to Butterfly Harbor after more than a decade away. In the past, the welcome dinner had always been a casual affair, certainly nothing like the big to-do BethAnn had in mind.

"Actually, I'm not on the…" Lori trailed off as she stood, pulled to her feet by the breathy desperation in BethAnn's voice. A sinking sensation swept over Lori as she tucked a strand of hair behind her ear and brushed a self-conscious hand down the front of her blue-and-white-striped maxi dress. "How many are there?" Lori's chest tightened as she did a quick mental count.

"Five, six hundred, give or take. We're not expecting that many to show up, of course, but they might be up for donations to our charity gift baskets. You can take care of it, right? I'd do it myself, but I'm just so busy getting sponsors and making delivery arrangements. It shouldn't take too long. Just have a glass of wine, pop some corn and get to stuffing."

Lori's smile stretched almost as wide as

her patience. Some things never changed. People rarely said no to her, if only to get BethAnn off their backs.

"No one else on the committee can help? What about taking them to the youth center and asking the kids…"

"Oh, well, we can't trust children with something this important, can we?" Beth-Ann waved that dismissive hand of hers in the air. "And as far as the committee, apparently not everyone's taking this kickoff event as seriously as I am. It's vital we make a good show of things if we're going to draw a higher level of clientele."

Lori bit the inside of her cheek. Higher level of clientele was BethAnn code for her rich "friends."

"We've already got multiple television stations coming," BethAnn went on. "Which means we're going to be front and center. And then I remembered you and how you've always been tip-top when it comes to responsibility and volunteering. I have to tell you, Lori." She pressed manicured fingers against her chest and tapped where most people possessed a heart. "While I was honored you all elected me to lead the charge on this event,

I had no idea how much work would be involved! Thank goodness for all my worker bees."

Elected? Lori pressed her lips into a hard line. More like the committee had been too intimidated to argue when BethAnn announced her intention to take over the event. Lori sighed. Most of the "work" BethAnn referred to had been completed and locked in place thanks to Lori securing the caterer. All that was left was to figure out furniture rental, decor, and, well… She looked down at the invitations.

Clearly BethAnn's desire for the spotlight hadn't diminished in her years away. As happy as people had been to see her go, just like a Monarch, she'd found her way back.

"Buzz, buzz, buzz." BethAnn clapped her hands together as if wishing a fairy back to life. "Oh, and these all need to be mailed by the eighteenth."

Lori's hand froze as she flicked through the addressed envelopes. "You're kidding? BethAnn, that's—"

"I know it's short notice, but I have every faith in you, Lori. Drop me an email when they're done so I can mark it off the list. I have tons to do before the town council meeting tonight. Stay tuned! There's going to be a big surprise! Ta!" BethAnn flicked a wave over her shoulder and hurried to the door before any malevolent plans could take hold in Lori's mind.

"Unbelievable." There went her free time. Lori grabbed the top box and stuck it on the floor out of sight. She wasn't up for another lecture from Abby Manning—her friend and boss—about what a pushover she was. She didn't want to hear how she should be living and enjoying her life instead of hiding behind a desk or holing up in her greenhouse of a sanctuary. Or getting sucked into jobs that weren't her responsibility.

As if on cue, Abby stepped out from behind the sliding glass doors of Flutterby Dreams, the inn's now-award-winning restaurant, and turned her perky nose to the ceiling to sniff. "I smell desperation and condescension. BethAnn's been here, hasn't she?"

"She just left." Lori chuckled and pushed the box farther under the desk with her foot. BethAnn's signature perfume certainly caught people's attention. "Did you want to say hi?"

Abby rolled her eyes and stepped into the lobby, the flouncy pink skirt of her dress bouncing around her knees. Looking like a cross between a 50's carhop and a sprite one might find in Lori's meticulously maintained flower garden, the longtime manager of the Flutterby Inn narrowed laser beam blue eyes on the boxes in Lori's hands. "What are those?"

"Invitations for the festival kickoff dinner." Lori had almost pulled them out of reach when Abby's hands locked around her wrists.

"Why do you have them?"

Lori's cheeks warmed. She shrugged and shifted on her feet, wishing there was some way to become invisible under her friend's penetrating stare. How did someone so petite make so many cower? "Because I'm reliable and responsible." Lori knew how important the festival was to the continued financial recovery of the town. If it meant a few extra hours of work, so be it. "BethAnn was saving me some time by delivering."

"Uh-huh." Abby shook her head, clearly not believing her. "And she couldn't possibly have found someone else to do it or done the work herself. We talked about this, Lori. You have to stop letting people take advantage of you."

"You take advantage of me," Lori teased.

"I pay you. There's a difference."

"These don't have to go out for a while. It'll be fine." Given the expression on Abby's face, Lori scrapped plans to get a jump start during her downtime at the inn. "I can get a good start tonight—"

Panic rose in Abby's eyes. "You're covering for me at the town hall meeting tonight, remember? I have that dinner with Jason's partner. If he hadn't flown in from New York…"

"No, I've got it. It's okay." Darn it! She'd forgotten she promised to go. "It's no big deal. I'll make it all work."

"Whew. Thanks. Jason's super nervous about the meeting. I need to be there for moral support. And to pour the wine. Keep your ears open in case our good mayor throws a festival curveball."

"What kind of curveball?"

"I wish I knew. Don't worry. You just need to be the face of the inn. Since we agreed to host and sponsor the BBQ cook-off and food market with Calliope—"

"You're not participating in the cook-off, are you?"

"No." Abby scrunched her mouth and released Lori's hands. "Geez, I set off half a dozen fire alarms in this town…"

Lori sank into her chair after settling the boxes in their not-so-hidden hiding place. Abby Manning inhabiting a kitchen was one of the reasons smoke detectors had been invented.

"You'd think the fact I'm marrying a chef would have earned me some points by now," Abby huffed.

"When are you doing that, exactly?" Lori asked in the hopes of keeping Abby off her case for a while longer. "Getting married?"

"Oh." Abby blinked, and then a slow, dazed smile stretched across her features. "On Christmas Eve."

"*This* Christmas Eve? Abby!" Lori leaped out of her chair and wrapped her arms around a vibrating Abby. "You finally decided on a date! That's great! Oh, a Christmas wedding." Lori's mind exploded in images of blossoming poinsettias and frosted trees decked out in twinkling golden lights and shimmering ribbon. Was there anything more beautiful? "Where?"

"Here." Abby stepped back and clutched her clasped hands against her chest. "This will be Jason's first Christmas in Butterfly Harbor and I want to go full bore. Total fantasyland here at the inn. I've already talked to our new owners and they want to make it part of their travel promotion next year, which gives me some fun financial numbers to play with." She hesitated, bit her lower lip and raised uncertain eyes to Lori. "I'm about to become a complete hypocrite."

"But it's coming with a warning. I appreciate that."

"Is there any chance you'd help me with the wedding? The flowers and decorations I mean. I could hire a florist, but you're so good with the arrangements we put in the rooms and on the table. We get so many compliments." She gestured to the exploding bouquet of autumn buds and full-blown sunflowers on the side table courtesy of Lori's greenhouse habit. "And you're organized, which we both know I need. If you'd be up for it I'd be in your debt forever!"

"You don't even have to ask." Excitement struck dead center of Lori's heart, tempered by momentary worry at the idea of letting her friend down. She hadn't tackled a project as big as a wedding before, even if it was just the flowers and decor. She'd helped with Holly's nuptials earlier this summer and then there had been Paige and Fletcher's spur-of-the moment ceremony a few weeks ago, but nothing along the scale of what Abby no doubt had in mind.

Still. Lori bit her lip, unable to stop the smile from forming. She could do this. She *wanted* to do this. Even as she tried to convince herself, her hands shook. She had to do this. Abby was counting on her. "I'm honored, Abby. Truly. Whatever you need."

"Well, that's a relief. I know it won't be easy with you playing double duty as a bridesmaid—"

"Wait, what?" Lori's pulse flatlined. She touched trembling fingers to her suddenly dry mouth. "Abby, you don't want me as a bridesmaid. That's so public. And you're so…" She waved her hand up and down Abby's short, petite frame. "And I'm so…" It took her twice as long to indicate her own body.

"You're so what?" Abby's eyes sparked and narrowed.

"I'm not bridesmaid material. Next to you I'll look like the Jolly Green Giantess." The fat, frumpy Jolly Green Giantess. She tugged at the waistline of her dress, felt her fingernails dig into her palms through the fabric. "Good heavens, the photographer will need a special lens to get us both in the same picture."

Abby planted her hands on Lori's shoulders and shoved her into her chair. "You know I hate it when you do that."

"Do what?"

"You know what. Put yourself down, make a joke out of something I don't find funny. I can almost understand it with people you don't know, but we've been friends long enough. Stop it."

"But this is different." Those pictures would be…forever.

"The only thing that's different is it's my wedding. I want you standing with me and Holly and Paige, and I'm not taking no for an answer."

Lori swallowed hard. Because the idea of standing next to beautiful Abby wasn't humiliating enough, being caught among Butterfly Harbor's version of Charlie's Angels made her nauseated. Not to mention there were bound to be reporters and news crews covering the event thanks to the popularity of Abby's celebrity chef fiancé Jason Corwin. Top that off with the publicity department from the hotel… That meant cameras, and cameras, as everyone knew, added ten pounds. At least. Maybe if she went back on that liquid diet she could lose enough to— she took in a shuddering breath.

"Lori, stop." Abby bent down and grabbed hold of Lori's hands. "This isn't the reaction someone's supposed to have when they're asked to be a bridesmaid. There's at least supposed to be a smile in here somewhere."

"How's this?" She pointed to her overwide smile.

"You look like you're being tortured by a winged superhero. Knock it off. When are you going to stop letting numbers on a scale define you?"

Lori hesitated. When she could look in the mirror and not immediately see a fat girl. When she didn't feel as if she was the biggest person when she walked into a room. When she didn't hear her mother's voice asking her "how much do you weigh now, dear?" When she could look back at a particularly nasty few weeks in high school and not feel like a complete idiot.

"It's an automatic reaction." Lori knew Abby was right. For the most part, she didn't dwell on the fact she was, well, larger than most women. But then there were times—like being asked to be a bridesmaid or when a lifetime of insecurities and criticisms flooded back at her like a tidal wave—that she couldn't withstand the pressure. "I'll think about it," she offered.

"Good." Abby nodded as if it were a done deal. "And since Jason plans to ask Matt to be a groomsman, you've got your escort all... arranged. And what's with that look?" Abby circled a finger in front of Lori's face. "You got a funny expression on your face when I mentioned Matt."

"Did I?" Lori resisted the urge to squirm. If only she could crawl under the desk with the envelopes and invites.

"You did. What's going on? I thought you and Matt were—"

"Well, if we were, we aren't now." Lori

hated the defensive tone in her voice, but this was yet another conversation she didn't want to have. "I mean, yeah, we hung out for a while." The idea was almost humiliating that at twenty-six she'd finally had her first—second if she was being honest with herself—date. But whatever she thought was going on with Matt, she'd clearly been wrong. Sometime in the last few weeks, he'd stopped returning her calls, didn't answer her texts. If she hadn't seen him walking or driving around town on patrol, she might have worried something had happened to him. "We're friends. That's all."

Did friends miss each other the way she missed him? Obviously she'd come across as overeager, even desperate, and scared him off. Big surprise. She thought she'd done her best to keep her feelings and hopes to herself. "It doesn't matter. Stop looking at me that way, Abby."

"What way?"

"Oh, poor Lori. Friday Night Popcorn Queen. Scares off a man who carries a gun for a living."

"Stop feeling sorry for yourself. I never

took Matt Knight for an idiot, but I've been known to be wrong before. I'm sorry."

Lori shrugged. "No big deal," she lied. "I'm more a status quo kind of woman anyway." If there was one thing Lori knew about it was how to be alone. Then again, she wasn't alone. She had Winchester. Her cat.

"So we'll make different arrangements for the wedding. Get you a different escort."

"I don't think—"

"You think too much." Abby gave her hands a hard squeeze before she stood. "I know you'll do a great job making my wedding beautiful. But I'd be lying if I said I wouldn't be disappointed to not have you standing beside me when I get married." She walked to the restaurant doors, stopped and looked over her shoulder. "Someday I hope you stop letting what other people might think matter so much. As far as I can tell, the only person judging you, the only person standing in your way, is you."

CHAPTER THREE

BEFORE HE'D SIGNED on as a deputy in Butterfly Harbor, Matt could count on one hand the number of town council meetings he'd attended. Politics wasn't his game; watching it play out in front of him like bad theater really wasn't his game. There was, however, something to be said for small town personalities in a confined space that provided an unpredictable concoction of gossipworthy entertainment.

The makeshift City Hall—the original one had been shut down last year due to code violations—loomed over the edge of town like a ghost from the past. The old Checkerspot Pub now housed the mayor and a good portion of city staff, or so the brass plaque beside the double glass doors decreed. The weathered two-story building had always reminded Matt of an old-time saloon with its wraparound porch and second-story overhang. All that was missing were wooden swinging doors creaking in the evening breeze and the tinny sound of an untuned piano.

"Evening, Matt." Harvey Mills, all belly and overly round eyes, headed from where he must have trekked from his hardware store on the opposite end of Monarch Lane. "Good turnout tonight?"

"Looking that way." Matt gestured toward the door where the cacophony of voices continued to rise. He peeked inside the window. "Best grab a chair while you can." Nerves prickled the back of his neck. He glanced at Harvey, who didn't look any more eager than Matt to head in. "Everything okay?"

"I'm hearing rumblings our good mayor is about to pull the rug out from under us where this festival is concerned."

Matt waited. Mrs. Ellison might have cornered the market on town gossip, but when it came to reliable information, Harvey was the go-to man. There was something about men gathering in a hardware store—which also housed the town's post office annex—that turned the business into Butterfly Harbor's version of a confessional. The fact Harvey had lived here his entire sixty-two years also added a layer of authenticity that kept Matt's interest piqued. "Any rug in particular getting pulled?"

"Details, much like our mayor's intentions, are scarce. Best be prepared for anything."

"I usually am when it comes to Gil." Matt took a long, deep breath. "Jasper get you that list of tools and supplies we'll be needing to get those houses in shape?"

"Ordered and mostly received." Harvey gave a firm nod. "Got you a good deal on some replacement windows. You'll need to pick them up over in Durante, but they were a steal since they've been discontinued. Way too many empty houses around here have gone to rot. Your idea to get at least the exteriors fixed up, get those yards under control before the festival starts? It's a no-brainer if you ask me. I've still got some feelers out on gardening supplies. Might have some donations coming your way."

"Plus it makes for a nice tax write-off for you," Matt joked.

Harvey grinned. "Not going to complain about that. Those volunteer lists you've got around town look to be filling up. 'Bout time we get more people involved. Make them feel more a part of things. Community center kids getting involved, too?"

"That's the idea." Matt would have given his right arm for a teen community center like the one Luke Saxon had opened soon after becoming sheriff. He'd wanted a place where kids could take classes, hang out, get tutoring and, most importantly, stay out of trouble. Having Luke's predecessor—and current father-in-law—running the place made the idea something the mayor hadn't been able to argue with. "Way things are going, the center will outgrow that building on the beach by the end of the year." Faster if houses started selling again.

It was a problem Matt was anxious to have, which was why he was scoping out new locations for the community center every chance he got. "All that being said, it would be a great promotional push come festival time. Gil wants to get buyers in here, year-round and seasonal. If visitors see us as a tight community that takes care of our own, that can only be a positive."

"Well said," Harvey agreed. "I can see why Luke trusts you with this."

No need to erode Harvey's faith in the department by stating he was only a stand-in. This project was Luke and Fletcher's baby. "When I was in the army, word had it I could sell sand in the desert." A pang of grief struck low and hard at the memory of his friends who were gone now. Only two of them had made it back and he hadn't heard from Hack in at least a year. "My platoon leader called me Superstar."

Harvey chuckled. "You shouldn't be giving me information like that, Matt. You never know where or when I might use it." Harvey patted Matt's arm as he headed inside. "If the mayor starts slinging, you don't back down, hear me? We need people like you and Luke who put this town and not your personal agendas first."

"Understood." Matt started to follow, then came up short as a flash of blue caught his attention coming down the hill. Lori.

His entire body felt lighter just seeing her. He tugged at the hem of his jacket, flexed his hands as he watched her approach. She'd lightened her hair, added subtle red highlights that caught in the late setting sun. He loved that rich, doe brown that curled subtly down and around her shoulders and framed her round face. She tended to wear the same type of dress, long and flowing around the ankles, almost covering the flat shoes she wore. He caught a quick glimmer of surprise shining in her bottle-glass green eyes when she spotted him. She glanced away long enough to tie a substantial knot in his belly.

Even if he didn't need her help with Kyle, he'd been anxious to see her again, to explain why he'd disappeared on her. Funny. He hadn't had any problems facing down insurgents with grenade launchers, but the idea of facing Lori after all these weeks of silence left him almost petrified.

"Hey." He tried to sound as casual as possible even as his heart pounded hard in his chest. "Ozzy said you'd be here. Long time no see."

"I know." When she stepped up beside him, she could almost look him directly in the eyes. It had been one of the first things he'd noticed about her—one of the first things he'd liked. She didn't turn simpering smiles or bat overactive lashes to get what she wanted. She didn't look to him to rescue or placate her. She was straightforward, honest and, most importantly, fun to be around.

He'd missed her.

"I suppose I owe you an apology." The second the words were out of his mouth, he wanted to take them back. He supposed?

The corners of Lori's eyes twitched. "For what?"

She was going to make him say it. "For not returning your calls or your texts. I've had, well…" Oh boy. He'd rehearsed this and yet none of the words seemed to be waiting for him. "I had a lot of thinking I needed to do. Some decisions I had to make and—"

"You don't owe me any explanations, Matt." She shrugged as if they were discussing something no more important than the weather forecast. "We're friends. Well, acquaintances really. Nothing to worry yourself over. We're good."

"Okay." Except it wasn't okay. He could feel all his plans, everything he wanted to say to her fall through his fingers like water. "But I would like to talk to you. Maybe tonight, after the meeting—"

"I have a lot of work to do when I get home. Maybe some other time." She reached for the door handle at the same time he did. His fingers brushed the back of hers. She snatched her hand away as if she'd been burned.

He moved in, lowered his voice and inadvertently brushed his lips over her ear. "I should have called. Or at least told you what—" She jerked away, her face flashing with anger before she eased her expression. Matt almost gulped. As big a heel as he felt before, he felt like an even bigger one now.

"Stop making this out to be something it wasn't, Matt." Was that irritation in her voice? "You have your life, I have mine. It's not surprising there's not a lot of overlap. So while there's nothing to apologize for, I'll just accept it so we can move on. Sound okay?"

"Move on as friends." Definitely not the direction he needed to go.

She glanced away and nodded, but not before he saw a flash of disappointment in her eyes. A flash that gave him the thinnest thread of hope to cling to. "I think we'd better get inside, don't you? Sounds like there's a lot on the agenda and I need to take notes for Abby in case anything's been changed."

"Yeah, sure. Of course." This time when he pulled open the door, she gave him another smile and stepped in ahead of him, only to skid to a halt. "What's wrong?"

So much for thinking a lot of residents were avoiding the meeting. Matt hadn't seen a turnout of Butterfly Harbor folks this large since the food festival last spring. He saw plenty of familiar faces—most of the members of the Cocoon Club, an expanding group of the more senior members of town—but also people he couldn't put names to. He recognized homes and buildings more than he did people.

Empty chairs were few and a number of attendees milled about the long counter along the west side of the room. Others grabbed coffee, water or a soft drink from the other side of the bar, grabbed cookies from the plastic silver trays someone had brought.

"Are you okay?" He couldn't help but notice Lori seemed caught between paralyzing nerves and shock.

"I'm fine." Lori tugged at the sides of the short sweater she wore, pulling it tighter across her chest. "Just more people than I expected."

Matt spotted two chairs in the front. "How about up there?"

She shook her head, her gaze skittering around the room until she let out an audible sigh of relief. "There's Calliope. Over there by the window. I'll just join her."

"Sure. Yeah." Frustration crashed through him. He'd really blown it. He should have been honest with her from the start, but he hadn't been able to find the right words to say he needed to slow things down so he could decide what to do about his divorce papers. Telling her, not telling her—neither was honorable, but he'd chosen to keep quiet to protect her. Instead, he'd hurt her. Far more than the truth ever would have.

"Hey, Calliope." Lori slipped onto the metal folding chair beside the closest person Butterfly Harbor had to a spiritual guru. Thankfully the row of chairs against the wall was far enough away from the main throng she could melt into the scenery.

"Lori." Calliope turned a friendly smile on her. The light dusting of freckles across her nose reminded Lori of a doll she had as a child. The beads and tiny bells laced through Calliope's waist-length red hair tinkled above the din of the crowd and managed to soothe

Lori's frazzled nerves. "How are those hollyhock seedlings I gave you working out?"

"Beautifully." Lori rested her notebook on her legs and locked her ankles together. "I don't know what you do to plants, Calliope, but I'm grateful for your touch. I should have fully grown plants back to you in a few weeks."

"Lovely. Just in time for the fall harvest." Calliope tapped a long finger against Lori's arm. "It's been a relief to have someone willing to take over the less edible offerings my customers enjoy. And I think it's you who has the magic touch. Something tells me those flowers will be splayed across Butterfly Harbor sooner than later."

Lori smiled. While she loved her job at the inn—most days—her real love was horticulture, especially when it came to nurturing seedlings into fruition. Plants didn't judge, they didn't speak, they either grew or they didn't. Now that Duskywing Farm had become quite the tourist attraction, partly because Chef Jason Corwin had talked up the organic farm in a number of his interviews, Calliope had to expand both her crops and her business plans. The weekend farmers' market and open field policy—it wasn't every town that had its own "pick your own food" option—was something everyone agreed to promote. That Calliope had asked Lori to oversee the plants and flowers she sold felt like an honor.

"How are you set for poinsettias?" Lori asked.

Calliope's eyebrows shot up. "What a coincidence. I completely overordered last year and they're outgrowing their space. Care to come take some cuttings?"

Lori didn't believe for a second the excessive order was coincidence. Calliope had always possessed a special "sense" when it came to the needs of Butterfly Harbor residents. "I can't say why, but yes. We're going to be needing quite a few this holiday season. For the inn," she added, for fear of ruining Abby and Jason's surprise.

Calliope turned her attention back to the town council moving toward the makeshift stage. "I look forward to Abby and Jason's official announcement."

Lori's chuckle was cut off by Matt taking a seat beside her. "Don't mean to interrupt." His Louisiana accent drifted over her like warm honey out of Calliope's hives. He shifted and straightened his jacket as Lori crossed her arms over her chest. "Not a lot of seating choices."

Obviously. What Lori wouldn't do to be able to control the flush of heat to her cheeks. She avoided Calliope's knowing glance as she tried to focus on the board members moving onto the stage at the front of the room. She'd felt accomplished when she'd managed to hold a somewhat normal conversation with Matt outside. It wasn't easy talking to a man who had gone out of his way to avoid her for the last few weeks.

Hopefully, whatever come-hither vibes she'd been transmitting a few weeks ago had gone dormant. She certainly didn't want to push herself on someone who clearly wasn't interested, or worse, thought her pathetic and only talked to her out of pity. Nor did she want Matt thinking she'd locked herself away and was pining over him when it was clear he didn't want to be anything more than *friends*.

She squeezed her arms tighter against her body, wishing not for the first time that the action would make her shrink.

Matt Knight was the type of man who conjured images of late-night beach fires and hands entwined beneath the stars. She could almost smell the flame-kissed pyre, feel the crackling sparks. Not so long ago he'd worn his dark hair shaggy, a bit unkempt, which accentuated the beard he'd had since he'd first moved to town. The beard was gone now; his hair tamed. Gold-flecked espresso brown eyes that glinted in the light shouldn't have any effect on her, but they did. As tempting as he was to lean into, to give in to, Lori stopped herself. She was doing just fine on her own. She didn't need a relationship or a boyfriend to complete her. She didn't need a man to make her life meaningful.

But that didn't change how she felt about him. She liked him.

A lot.

As if feelings like that had ever led her anywhere good. Good heavens, what was the matter with her?

"Is it me, or does the council look as surprised at the turnout as we were?" Matt motioned to the group that included town veterinarian, Dr. Selina Collins; accountant, Kurt Murphy; and Cocoon Club members Oscar Bedemeyer and Delilah Scoda. Lori returned Delilah's enthusiastic wave with a shy smile. The former hairdresser had "dated" Lori's late grandfather years before and earned a place in Lori's pantheon of friends.

Lori made an "uh-huh" response as she caught the lightning flash movement of Beth-Ann Bottomley taking a seat in the front row. Perched on the edge of her chair, BethAnn craned her neck and scanned the crowd. Her surprised gaze landed on Lori. She opened her red-painted mouth in silent question. She probably assumed Lori had chained herself in her house until she finished with those stupid invitations.

As if she'd even started them yet.

Gil Hamilton, only five years Lori's senior, strode onto the stage, his khaki slacks and button-down white shirt looking more catalog chic than small town mayor. Thick, beachy-blond hair swept over sharp, hawk-like green eyes. He took his place behind the tabletop podium and banged the gavel every Butterfly Harbor mayor had wielded for the past half century.

In an almost-Pavlovian response, Lori reached into her purse for a pen and opened up her notebook as the room fell silent.

Matt's arm brushed against hers as he shifted in his chair. He stretched out his leg with a wince. Lori bit the inside of her cheek. Matt was never one to complain, not even when it was obvious his leg was giving him problems.

"Did you call your doctor about that new prosthesis they want to fit you with yet?"

He looked startled at her question. Maybe he was shocked she'd remembered their conversation about his leg more than a month ago. "Not yet, no." He turned a tense jaw toward her and focused on the mayor. "Haven't had time."

She should have kept her mouth shut. It always confused her how he seemed perfectly fine with the fact he'd lost his leg in the war; there wasn't a self-conscious inch of him. But when it came to his treatment or discussing advancements in lost limbs, he shut down faster than... Lori smirked. He shut down faster than Lori did when she was asked to be a bridesmaid.

"Calling this meeting to order." Gil banged his gavel again and reminded Lori of when he'd been senior class president. The Hamiltons were as close as Butterfly Harbor got to royalty. Fourth-generation ruling class, his great-great-great-grandfather—or was it only two greats, Lori could never remember—was one of their founding fathers, had been chosen to govern. How her grandfather had gone on about the Hamiltons and rarely in a good way. Something Lori was certain Gil was more than aware of.

The rules of order were recited, the board members called attendance, the minutes approved. Lori struggled against the pull of boredom and swirled her pen over the paper, letting her imagination take hold.

There were times over the years she'd felt sorry for Gil, like when his father died. But those times were easily overshadowed whenever Gil declared a bit too vociferously that he had the town's best interests at heart. If ever there was a flashing red warning sign…

Then again, Gil couldn't do any more harm to Butterfly Harbor than his own father had. The previous mayor had nearly bankrupted the town, certainly sent the family banking business into a tailspin, and as a result, a mass exodus had ensued. The decreased population had put everyone's lives on hold as they hoped and prayed things would right themselves once more.

Which was why this year's Monarch Festival was so important. With stability came pride and there was nothing her fellow townspeople liked more than showing off their beloved home. Especially before the start of the monarch migration season.

"I swear, if they verbally itemize the budget report…" Matt mumbled.

Lori refused to laugh, but inside, she grinned. She knew Matt well enough to know attending an event like this was tantamount to torture. "I thought Luke usually came to these things."

"He's on a field trip with Simon." Matt's response earned an irritated look from a flannel-clad Cyril Walters across the aisle. "He's taken being a stepfather very seriously. You here for Abby?"

"She had a dinner meeting with Jason." Before Cyril could glare at her, she threw the middle-aged crank a smile and ducked her head. "Sorry you got stuck."

"I'm not." Matt shook his head, his gaze falling to the notebook she scribbled in. "I got to see you."

Lori's pen froze in midstroke. She jumped when Gil banged the gavel again. "Someone needs to disarm him."

"Overcompensation comes in many forms," Calliope said. "He's stressed. I can see it coming off of him in waves." She shivered as if those waves crested over her head.

At Cyril's "shhhhhh" the three of them fell silent.

"I'd like to make one announcement we've been anxious to share." Gil's theatrical voice echoed in the room. "The board has finally approved an architect to design the new butterfly sanctuary. Xander Costas of Costas Architecture out of Chicago will be arriving in the next few weeks to get things underway. He'll be touring the town, talking with folks in an effort to give us the perfect design. Keep in mind, we'll be looking for a community liaison to work with him and ensure the design he comes up with reflects who we are."

Out of the corner of her eye, Lori caught Calliope's hand tighten into a fist.

"At least they moved the proposed site," Lori whispered. The original location had been less than a half a mile from Calliope's farm, which hadn't sat well with most people, Calliope in particular. Rumor had it Lori's brother, Fletcher, was instrumental in ensuring the new project would be built on the secondary location, halfway between the farm and the decrepit old Admiral's Lighthouse on the edge of town.

"I see dark clouds approaching," Calliope murmured with that familiar dazed look in her eyes. "Dark, dangerous clouds."

Lori pursed her lips, looked back at her notebook. The idea of the butterfly sanctuary being anything close to ominous seemed a far stretch even for Calliope's eccentric tendencies.

As the meeting dragged on, Lori scribbled meaningless notes. The sound of Gil's voice became a distant hum. She found herself sketching the exterior of the inn, filling in the seasonal garden roundabout with poinsettias and twinkle lights, making notes as she went. An arbor would be nice, maybe with hanging votive candles… She made a note to ask Abby if she was planning a nighttime wedding, which would be something completely different. Would people want to spend their Christmas Eve at a wedding, though? Hmmm…

Brainstorming Christmas ideas and words, crossing out what didn't feel like "Abby." The page filled up as her imagination took hold. It wasn't until Matt reached over and covered her hand to pull it away that she blinked back to the present.

"What?" Had she missed something?

"That's beautiful." He kept his voice low, but his warm breath brushed against the side of her face. She tightened her fingers around her pen, resisting the urge to look into the blue eyes that not so long ago she'd considered drowning in. "You worked a lot on the landscaping upgrades at the inn, didn't you?"

Lori nodded. "Abby doesn't know a daisy from a carnation. She lets me play."

"You play well."

She glanced at him long enough to see his brows knit. Was that confusion? Surprise? Disapproval? Just what was going on with him anyway? A few weeks ago, he'd slammed the dating door in her face. Tonight, was he attempting to open it again?

Hope—as unwanted as it was—pounded

unevenly against her ribs while fear of being hurt again quickly steamrolled over it.

"Which brings us to the Monarch Festival committee proposals." Gil reached for a bottle of water and drank. "I'm happy to say the board has agreed to approve most of them. But before we get into all that, there's one topic I need to address." He cleared his throat. "With all I have going on at the mayor's office, it's been brought to my attention that I won't have as much time to dedicate to overseeing every committee's actions."

"What a shame," Matt said.

Lori clicked her pen shut. Abby had been right. One curveball coming their way. "Wait for it." Lori sat up straight and braced herself.

"Wait for what?" Matt asked.

"As most of you know, town board member Bobby Singer has submitted his resignation," Gil said. "As it's within the authority of the remaining members to elect a substitute to serve the remainder of his term, I'd like to welcome BethAnn Bottomley to the board. BethAnn has also generously offered to oversee all of the community project committees and she'll be acting as my personal go-between to make certain we're putting our focus and finances in the right places. BethAnn?"

"That." Lori deflated as she joined in the muted applause. No wonder BethAnn had been so anxious to offload those invitations on her. She was clearing her own schedule so she could shine and claim as much credit for the festival as possible. Not that Lori cared about credit. But she didn't like the idea BethAnn would steal other people's accolades.

BethAnn hopped out of her chair and practically two-stepped her way onto the stage where she swooped in front of the mayor to stand at the podium.

"Thank you, Mayor Hamilton," BethAnn said. "And thank you, all of you, for welcoming me so warmly. It's so nice being back in the town I called home once upon a time."

"Tell me again who this is?" Matt leaned over and whispered.

"Trouble with a capital *T.*" Lori could feel the plans already made for the festival decidedly tip. She noticed the other board members casting uneasy looks at one another, while Delilah, board secretary, tapped restless manicured nails on the table beside her laptop.

"Looks like the town council is about ready to bolt," Matt said. "Harvey was right. I sense fireworks." He sat forward in his chair, hands clasped with an expression of near giddiness on his face.

"First," BethAnn said, "I want to thank everyone who has stepped up to volunteer to make this year's Monarch Festival the absolute best yet. You all have had some fabulous ideas and I look forward to implementing them all with you."

Murmurs of grudging agreement rumbled through the hall.

"I also want to say that while the proposals we've received at the mayor's office are all excellent ideas," BethAnn continued, "we've had to take a hard look at finances and time frames, especially in regards to the sheriff's department's beautification proposal."

Lori glanced at Matt in time to see his right eye twitch.

"As many of you know, the sheriff's department—"

"Has already procured most of the supplies and donations we need to complete the project on time." Matt got to his feet. "We are ready to move full steam ahead as soon as we have a completed list of weekend volunteers."

The room, as a whole, turned in their chairs. Lori swallowed hard as dozens of eyes landed on her before shifting to Matt. She clenched her fists, determined not to sink in her seat.

"I think we can all agree how important it is that Butterfly Harbor look its best for all the visitors we're expecting in a few weeks," Matt continued as if he'd prepared a speech ahead of time. "The three areas in question are all very visible cul-de-sacs, homes and yards everyone who drives in will see. As they look now, people are going to wonder if they're in the right place. Not only are they eyesores, they're also a testament to this town's past economic problems." Matt shifted his gaze to Gil. "Something I'm certain we don't want to advertise."

Lori's eyes went wide. Did he really just call Gil out on his father's illegal banking practices in front of the whole town? She covered her mouth with her hand.

Gil shouldered himself in front of BethAnn. "Deputy Knight, I'm not sure this is the right time—" Gil attempted to cut through the murmurings rippling through the crowd.

"I am," Matt said. "While I applaud all the events and plans this festival will include, surely everyone in this room can agree we need to put some attention to long-term goals. What we are proposing takes more man— and woman—power than money. But the payoff in the long run could be beneficial to every resident. While we want visitors to enjoy everything we have to offer, we also are hoping to entice some of them to stay."

More than just murmurs of support rose from the crowd. Some began to cheer. Gil's jaw pulsed. "I can see the need for more discussion is in order as far as this project is concerned."

"No, it's not!" Harvey Mills shouted from the back of the room. "I've already received most of the supplies needed to complete the project, a lot of which was donated by businesses outside of Butterfly Harbor in exchange for advertising. Are you suggesting we let those supplies just sit in my storeroom and collect dust?"

"Of course I'm not," Gil said as he banged

his gavel to call for silence. "It was agreed on by the board—"

"Not unanimously," Delilah interrupted. "I'm in complete agreement with Deputy Knight. This is a project that needs to happen. What good is some fancy dinner spotlighting our main thoroughfare if the houses nearby look like bombed-out shacks?"

More nods of assent, more cheers and applause.

"I'm not trying to be difficult," Matt said when the voices calmed. "And I'm not trying to be disrespectful. But I think Mrs. Scoda raises a valid point. We need all of Butterfly Harbor to shine, not just the areas we guide people to. We have more than a dozen volunteers ready to spend the next few weekends hard at work. I, along with some of the other deputies, will be spending our off time on the properties. This isn't something we plan to do piecemeal or only when it suits us. And this is just the beginning. There are a lot of other homes that need attention but their owners simply don't have the means to improve the curb appeal. If we do this right, this could become a way of life here. If we want to build up our community we need to start with our community."

BethAnn opened her mouth, but was stopped by the enthusiastic applause and shouts of approval echoing in the room.

"I'm sorry. Forgive me, as we don't know each other." BethAnn raised her voice and peered down her upturned nose. "What is your name again, Deputy…?"

"Knight. Deputy Matt Knight, ma'am. It's a pleasure to meet you. I've heard a lot about you."

Lori snorted behind her hand.

Matt flicked a quick look at her. His lips curved.

Lori's cheeks warmed.

"I wonder if you could answer a question for me, Deputy Knight, since the board needs to determine where best to spend our…its money," BethAnn said. "As I recall, when Jake Campbell was sheriff, his deputies were spread pretty thin. Are you stating that's no longer the case despite the rise in criminal activity since his retirement?"

Lori closed her eyes shut and shook her head. *Oh boy. Here we go.*

"I don't think that's a topic we need to

get into—" Gil practically dive-bombed the podium.

"Beg your pardon, BethAnn." Jake Campbell, the town's previous sheriff, stood up from the middle of the seated crowd and leaned heavily on the cane that had helped him walk for the last fifteen years. "Seeing as you haven't lived here in a while you might want to check your facts on how my term ended and the current statistics."

The room went dead silent. Lori's ears pounded as she looked around the crowd. Jake Campbell was beloved in Butterfly Harbor. His dismissal from his job was still a source of controversy for some despite their acceptance of Luke Saxon as his replacement.

"If you're attempting to imply that the crime issues we've been experiencing are directly related to a change in oversight," Jake said, "I'd like to point out the new sheriff is my son-in-law and he has had my support from day one. I was, in fact, the one who recommended him for the job. I can assure you the safety of this town has been his foremost concern since he pinned on his badge. Have there been issues? Yes. Will there continue to be issues? Yes. But we also see this project as a way to stave off these issues and, if we're lucky, eliminate them altogether. They're a capable, smart team of deputies. They can make this work. All they need is this town's support."

Matt shifted on his feet, as if suddenly uncomfortable.

Lori reached up, touched her fingers to his arm and felt him jump. He glanced at her before returning his attention to the dais.

"We understand the undertaking, Mrs. Bottomley," Matt said. "And I can assure you we will not be shirking our responsibilities. This project is simply an extension of our current positions."

BethAnn gave him a smile that might have frozen a fresh-caught fish solid. "That might address any issues we have with the home repairs and refacings. I see where you have some construction experience from your time in the armed forces, but nowhere on your proposal do you list a landscaping expert. As much as we'd love to contribute town funds to the project, I'm certain I speak for the rest of the board and the mayor in saying we don't like the idea of a short-term solution.

We want this done right from the start. We don't want to be replacing and redoing areas ad nauseum. Which to me means bringing in an actual expert."

Calliope nudged Lori with her elbow.

"What?" Lori leaned over, torn between fascination and revulsion. How could Beth-Ann not see how important a project like this was to the entire community?

"You know what." Calliope nudged her again. "You are an expert in landscaping."

"I am not," Lori protested.

"You're the closest thing we've got other than me, and I'm already committed." Calliope turned calm, considering eyes on her. "Unless you'd rather spend the next few weeks acting as BethAnn's gofer. Take an escape, and an opportunity, when it's offered."

Oh. Lori bit her lip. She glanced up at Matt as the audience rumblings grew louder. She looked at the stage, to where BethAnn turned a satisfied smirk on the mayor, who looked as if he were ready for the evening to be over. Lori caught Delilah's eye and the old woman nodded as if giving her approval.

"I can do it." The words came out of Lori's mouth on their own.

"There you go." Calliope patted her arm.

"What?" Matt looked down at her.

"I can do it." It was barely a whisper, as if she needed to bolster herself to commit, but the more she thought about it, the more it made sense. The thought of getting her hands in the dirt of all those yards, of deciding on color and plants and decor and… Her pulse raced. First Abby's request to help with the wedding, and now this?

"I can do it!" Stronger now, louder. Loud enough to catch the attention of those sitting around her. Loud enough to bring a wide, eye-brightening smile to Matt's handsome face.

She set her notebook on the floor and stood up.

Matt stuck two fingers in his mouth and whistled, the shrill sound blasting through the rising conversation and felling it to silence.

"Something else to add, Deputy Knight?" Gil asked with something akin to hope in his eyes.

"Lori Bradley has agreed to oversee the landscaping portion of our project." Lori's heart expanded as Matt's chest puffed with pride. There were times he did seem to be in her corner. "I think we can all agree she has the expertise and talent to make this project work."

"But she can't." It was then Lori saw panic in the normally controlled BethAnn's face. "She's already committed to the welcoming dinner committee—"

"No, I'm not." Lori didn't want to take pleasure in the statement, but she did.

"I don't understand," Gil said. "Given you're an employee of the Flutterby, I assumed you were helping Abby with the barbecue and food market."

"I am. I have been," Lori said.

"Along with the welcome dinner?" Gil frowned at BethAnn.

"I never volunteered for that, actually." Lori wiped her damp palms on her hips. The last time she'd spoken in front of this many people had been in her high school speech class. It wasn't any less terrifying now. "I only offered to take the minutes at the first meeting since it was at the inn. No one ever took me off the email loop."

"Well, then clearly you need to choose," BethAnn challenged.

"I already have," Lori said. "There are more than enough committee members to make the welcome dinner happen, especially since most of the arrangements have already been made. I'd be thrilled to work with the sheriff and his deputies on this project. If they'll have me."

"We'll have you," Matt said in a way that had Lori's cheeks burning and the audience chuckling.

"That's settled then!" Delilah, acting in her role as council secretary, plucked the gavel off the table and struck it once, hard. Beth-Ann jumped. "Motion passes. Let the committees, all of the committees, commence."

CHAPTER FOUR

MATT WASN'T KNOWN for making Hail Mary passes, but when he threw one, he tended to score. Success, however, might be measured differently this time around. Given the shell-shocked expression on Lori's face once Delilah banged the gavel, he was betting she'd need some time to digest what had taken place.

A wave of residents rushed forward to swallow them into congratulatory circles of backslaps and handshakes. He had a little trouble processing what had just happened himself, but that Lori would be working on this project with them, with him, inflated that tiny bubble of hope that had been bouncing around inside of him. To have this time to repair their relationship, get his personal life on solid footing so the judge considered him a more acceptable candidate as Kyle's father? It was an opportunity he couldn't pass up. Add to that, Lori might finally see for herself how well liked and appreciated she was by those living in Butterfly Harbor.

While he didn't have much trouble navigating the crowd, he caught an occasional glimpse of panic in Lori's eyes. Probably a reaction to making such a public declaration. Maybe a tinge of regret, but he was grateful for whatever bolstered her volunteering. He should have thought of it himself given he'd been watching her sketch in that notebook of hers, seeing images of the inn take shape behind the explosion of flowers and plants, details she plucked out of thin air. He knew she was the secret weapon he'd been looking for. Of course, she was the perfect solution.

Now, as cochair, she wouldn't have any choice but to work with them. Uh-oh. Matt made forgetful conversation with his neighbors as he realized he had only come tonight as a substitute voice; this wasn't his idea or his project despite his willingness to be a part of it. Now he found himself in the uncomfortable position of having taken the lead on something his boss and fellow deputies had devised.

He certainly didn't want them thinking he

was taking credit for their idea or work. That said, if he hadn't, he wouldn't be witnessing what he could only define as a sudden blooming of Lori Bradley.

She hadn't pulled into her shell, hadn't dipped her head or lost eye contact with anyone coming over to congratulate and thank her. Instead, while she seemed a bit flummoxed, he thought for sure he caught something akin to excitement shining in her eyes.

Typical Lori, with a smile that brightened an already-pretty face. She had no idea how people reacted to her, that she had a way of making whoever she was with feel as if they were the most important person in the room.

She looked over at him and her eyes sharpened, as if she wasn't quite sure what to make of him and the entire situation.

Whether she realized it or not, Lori Bradley made him happy. Now it was his turn to return the favor.

"You going to need protection on the walk home?" Fletcher slapped a hand on Matt's already-bruised shoulder.

"They're leaving," Matt looked back as the crowd filed out.

"Wasn't talking about them." Fletcher's

normally amused eyes held a hint of seriousness. "I meant protection from my sister. I've been on the other end of that look, pal. She hasn't made up her mind what she thinks about this situation yet. She's not the only one."

"Yeah, sorry about usurping the project like that." Matt winced. "Luke said you wouldn't be here."

"Wasn't supposed to be," Fletcher said. "And things turned out the way they were meant to. No worries on my part."

"Or mine." Paige Bradley ducked in under her husband's arm and tugged her long brown ponytail free. She'd come a long way from the shy, secretive person she'd been when she'd first arrived earlier in the year, but she'd made a new start—and a home for her and her daughter in Butterfly Harbor. "This is exactly what Lori needs. She spends too much time cooped up at work or at home. This project is perfect for her. And if she's worried about Abby not having enough help with the food market, I'm happy to lend a hand. Holly's already working with her, so it makes sense. And—" Paige craned her head to look up at the stage where the board members were filing out "—you managed to tick off BethAnn Bottomley. I bet that'll be worth a free mocha shake from Holly next time you come by the diner."

"Our good diner owner isn't a fan of our new town council member?" Matt asked of his boss's wife. As he was clearly not as up on town gossip as he should be, a trip to the hardware store this week might be in order.

"I don't know the particulars other than BethAnn burned a lot of bridges on her way out of town. Something to do with Holly's mother?" Paige shook her head. "I might be able to pry it out of her on our next girls' night."

Fletcher looked down as his stepdaughter, Charlie, ran over to grab his hand, her red pigtails sticking out crookedly on either side of her head. "What's going on, kiddo?"

"I want to help plant the new flowers with Aunt Lori." She swung her arm high and back as she bounced on her heels.

"You mean you're going to abandon me along with your mother?" Fletcher teased.

"You can help, too," Charlie said with an exaggerated eye roll that was all her mother. "Besides, Mom said I could start my own garden if I learned what to do. Do you think Aunt Lori will mind teaching me?"

"I can speak for Aunt Lori." Finally free of her crowd, Lori bent down to retrieve her belongings and stayed low to meet her recently acquired niece eye to eye. "I would love to have you as a student and a volunteer. After your homework gets done, though. And after all your chores are finished. And you've checked with Mrs. Hastings to make sure you're caught up with her."

"Yeah, yeah, I know." Charlie leaned so far over to the side she nearly tipped over. "Mom, I'm going to need a calendar like yours."

"No one has a calendar like your mom's." Fletcher pulled Paige close and pressed his lips to her forehead. "Always the busy bee. Must run in the family."

"I'm going to head back to the inn, talk to Abby. Fill her in on…things." Lori seemed to be looking at anyone—and anything—other than Matt. "Paige, I'll give you an update on the inn's plans as soon as I do some rearranging with my schedule."

"How about I walk you back?" Matt offered.

"Not necessary, thanks." Lori looked across the empty room to where BethAnn was having a pouting session with a less than sympathetic Gil. "She's actually taking this pretty well all things considered."

"She just assumed you'd do her bidding on helping to organize the welcome dinner, didn't she?" Fletcher said.

Lori shrugged. "I am helping on a few things."

"Oh, Lori, you aren't." Paige sighed. "Why didn't you say no?"

"Because she doesn't like disappointing anyone," Matt said before Lori could respond. She glared at him, but didn't argue.

"What did she rope you into?" Fletcher asked.

"Nothing much. Just mailing out her special invitations. I can do it one night after work. Or two. It'll be fine." Judging by her tone, however, Matt could hear an unfamiliar trace of resentment in her voice. "It's the last thing I'll do for BethAnn. Promise." She held up her fingers like a Girl Scout swearing an oath.

"Uh-huh." Paige rolled her eyes. "As one

people pleaser to another, I'm going to hold you to that."

Lori smiled. "Deal."

"I don't like her. She's rude," Charlie declared. "Mrs. Hastings called her a snob." Charlie's eyes were big as saucers as she slapped a hand over her mouth. "Oops. I wasn't supposed to repeat that."

"Mrs. Hastings would probably know the details about BethAnn," Fletcher agreed. The former high school principal had become a surrogate grandmother to Charlie. "She definitely made a name for herself around here before she married into politics. Perfect bedfellows, our grandfather said. But now you don't have to worry about her, Lori. You'll be working with Matt here, instead."

"Hmmmm." Lori's lips thinned as she said her goodbyes and headed to the door. "Lucky me."

"Seriously, man, I wish you luck." Fletcher pushed Matt behind her. "Just don't forget, she's my sister."

"Ease up, Fletch," Paige ordered. "Charlie, let's say you and I check in with Calliope about our fresh produce deliveries for tomorrow?" She held out her hand, and mother and daughter scampered off, leaving Matt and Fletch alone.

"What's going on with you and Lori?" Fletcher asked Matt before he could get away. "A bit of on-again, off-again?"

"Yeah." Matt fought the urge to wince. He didn't need to be reminded how badly he'd handled things with Lori. It had definitely bitten him in the backside in more ways than one. "That's on me and it was a mistake." He reached for his baseball cap and tugged it on. "One I plan on fixing, believe me. But since you brought it up. You good with this? With me and her?"

"Are you asking my permission to date my sister?" Always one to make a joke, Fletcher's usual levity didn't quite break through. Matt's fellow deputy was known for his easygoing nature to the point of being a pushover at times, a family trait, obviously. Fletch definitely wasn't the disciplinarian in the recently formed Bradley household, which was why Matt took the stern glare in Fletch's eyes to heart.

"Lori hears you ask that, I won't be the only one in need of protection," Matt said. "I like her, Fletch. I like her a lot and I'm being straight with you when I say I know I screwed up." Not that he was about to admit how he'd screwed up. On the one hand, he probably shouldn't have kept his marital status a secret. On the other hand, Matt hadn't cared enough to talk about it. Not that anyone had asked. They'd just assumed. That said, it probably wasn't the best idea for Fletcher to know that, technically, he was a married man. Or that he needed to get things back on track on the off chance she was called to testify at Kyle's placement hearing.

"And if I say no, that I want you to stay away from her?" Fletcher asked.

Matt could only imagine how protective he would be if he had a younger sister, so he cut his friend some slack. "I'd say I'm sorry you feel that way, and tough. I want… I need to see where this can go." After three years of uncertainty and self-doubt, he was finally feeling as if he was back on solid ground. And honestly? He had Lori to thank for that. Being around her had pulled him out of the quicksand of his past. Now that he was out, he didn't have any intention of sliding back in.

Fletch turned, looking to where Lori stood just outside speaking with Willa O'Neill.

"Getting past me isn't your problem," he said. "She's locked a good part of herself away, Matt. There are walls I've never been able to scale and I lived a lot of the same things she has. What went down with our parents, for instance. We only turned out the way we did because our grandfather stepped up and took us in. She puts on a good show, but she doesn't trust easily. Nor should she with the wounds she has. Just be prepared. And be careful. As much as I want her to be happy, I don't want her hurt."

"On that we agree." Another hurdle passed, Matt bade his goodbyes and pushed through the door to outside. The laughter in Lori's eyes faded when she saw him. "Ready when you are. Hey, Willa. How's Nina doing?"

"Mom's better, thanks." Willa pushed her hands deep into her sweater pockets and rocked back on a pair of thick-soled practical shoes. "The experimental treatment she got into in San Francisco seems to be working and I was able to bring her home sooner than expected. Did you hear Paige is going to start doing home care here in town? Once she gets her nursing license anyway. We're on the top of her patient list."

"I knew she'd been studying for a big test," Matt said. "You know your house is on the list for the beautification project, right?"

Willa's silver-gray eyes showed genuine surprise. "It is?"

"If it's okay with you," Matt added, realizing how presumptuous he sounded.

"I've been so preoccupied with Mom and Marley I haven't really thought about it. Other than installing the wheelchair ramp, we haven't had the money—"

"This wasn't Matt criticizing," Lori broke in, and it was then Matt realized his error. "If Fletch hadn't put your house on the list I certainly would have considered it. It's about time we started taking care of our own around here."

Matt caught the well of tears in Willa's eyes. "It would make Mom so happy. She used to love gardening before...well, before everything happened."

"How about we get in touch when we finalize our plans and schedule?" Lori wrapped an arm around Willa's narrow shoulders and squeezed. "Maybe we can even keep it a surprise in some way for her?"

Willa nodded. "That sounds wonderful.

Thank you so much. I can't wait to tell Marley and Jasper."

"Your brother already knows," Matt said. "Who do you think put your name on the list?"

"Of course he did." Willa swiped at the single tear that plopped onto her cheek. "You all have been so good to him, this seems almost like it's too much. He's started looking into colleges thanks to you."

"Yeah, well, he's earning his keep at the station," Matt assured her. It was extra handy having someone with the talent for basic forensic tests in-house, which ended up saving enough money on the budget to afford to pay him.

Selfishly, Matt hoped once Kyle was released from detention, Jasper would renew their wayward friendship—and provide another example of how someone dealt a bad hand in life could turn things around.

"I didn't handle that particularly well, did I?" Matt asked Lori as Willa headed off on her walk home.

"You've done worse," Lori said with enough spark in her voice to reignite Matt's guilt over how he'd shut her out. "I can't be-lieve I did that."

"What? Volunteered? I can."

"Well, in private, sure, but in front of the town?" She fanned her face. "I haven't been that terrified since I had to give a speech senior year in high school. Had nightmares about it for a month beforehand."

"You did great," Matt assured her as he fol-lowed her down the stairs. "And I bet we'll work well together."

"We'll see about that." Her flat shoes slapped against the plank boards. "Do you need me to talk to Luke or are you going to?"

"I'll do it." If Fletch's reaction had been any indication, their boss wasn't going to have any issues about Lori working with them. The evening breeze kicked up with its normal ocean chill. "I'm just glad we're finally alone so we can talk." He followed Willa's lead and pushed his hands into his pockets as he caught up to Lori. "I want to explain about why I didn't return your calls. Why I disappeared—"

"Contrary to popular belief, I don't need coddling, Matt. You apologized. I accepted. We don't have to discuss it anymore."

Matt reached out, caught her arm and pulled her to a stop. "Would you please slow down? I don't move as quickly as I used to."

"Oh, I'm so sor—" The instant sympathy on her face faded when she lifted her gaze from his leg to his face. "Really? You played *that* card?"

"Desperate times." Matt let go, not liking the tension in her arm. When he saw her shiver and pull her sweater across her chest, he shrugged out of his jacket, hesitating briefly at the guarded look in her eyes. "You aren't going to slug me for this, are you?" Before she could respond, he draped the coat around her, grateful for the excuse to step closer. He loved how her hair smelled, like flowers and vanilla. "Just give me a few minutes, please. That's all I'm asking. Believe me it won't take much longer than that to admit what a complete idiot I've been."

Lori's eyebrow arched. "So the universe is wrong? Men are fine admitting when they're wrong?"

"Some of us are." It wasn't his favorite pastime, but he knew when he was due for a mea culpa. "I meant it earlier when I said I had some things to work out. Some things I've been carrying around since before I got out of the service. Then you and I started getting close and I realized I was out of time."

"What on earth are you talking about?" Lori's eyes went blank.

Matt sighed. Maybe this wasn't the right time and place after all. The sun was nearly gone for the night. The lighted streetlamps caught the red highlights in her hair, the silver flecks in her eyes. Or maybe he was stalling because telling the truth would make him look like a bigger idiot than she probably already thought him to be. How he wished she could read his mind so he didn't have to explain. But that wouldn't erase the skepticism and the hurt that had been haunting him all evening.

"Matt." She reached out, almost took hold of his arm, then seemed to think better of it and snatched her hand back to clutch at his jacket. "Matt, if we're nothing else, we are friends, remember? Whatever it is you have to tell me, whatever it is you think you need to—"

"I'm married."

"MARRIED." SHE BLINKED SO quickly and so fast her vision blurred. "You're…married." Her pulse couldn't decide whether to race or stop altogether.

"Was married. Until today," he said as she took a step back. "I signed the divorce papers. Today. This morning. It's been years since I've seen her, spoken to her, and then after you and I started getting closer, I realized I needed to figure out—"

"Wait a minute. Stop." The odd ringing in her ears made her blood pound. She barely recognized her own voice, and when she held up a hand, her fingers trembled. "You're married? As in." Her gaze dropped to his hand as an invisible curtain dropped between them. "You have a *wife*?"

He scrubbed his hand across his bare chin. "Look, I know how this sounds, how it looks—"

"I'm not sure how it could sound or look any other way." How was this possible? How had she not known? How could he not have told her?

"I should have told you from the beginning. The truth is—"

"The truth?" She didn't know what else to do. She laughed as she shoved his hands away.

"Okay, yeah, I deserve that. The truth is my marriage to Gina was over before I got back home from Iraq."

"You've been home for three years, Matt. That doesn't sound over to me."

"I don't know if I can explain… I can't quite explain it to myself," he said, and for a moment, the desperation in his eyes struck her like an arrow to the heart. "Admitting I failed at something, it's just not easy. But, it was time. I did sign the papers."

"Today." After weeks of talking to her, spending time with her, letting her believe there was more than just friendship going on?

"Yes, today, because I can't move forward as long as I'm stuck in the past. I loved Gina. She was the first girl I ever loved, the first girl I ever…well, she was the first for a lot of things…"

"Please, spare me the details." She slipped one shoulder free of his jacket and welcomed the chill. "I don't need to know all this, Matt." She didn't want to know. He'd lied to her. From the first day they'd met. He'd deceived her.

The past hit her like a wave crashing against the back of her knees, threatening to drag her under, back to when she couldn't breathe.

"But you do need to know," Matt said. "Don't you see, I signed them because of you. I want to see where things can go. With us."

"You should have saved yourself the ink." She looked down at her hands. How many nights had she spent wishing she could go back and stand up for herself, say what she felt, defend herself against those who had hurt her down to her very soul.

Never did she think she'd get another chance. Tears pricked the backs of her eyes. Never did she think she'd have to do so with Matt. "You know how hard it was for me to even let myself think about dating someone. How scared I was, but you promised we were worth the risk. I could have accepted you changing your mind about me. I expected it, honestly, but hearing now that you've been lying to me from the start? You're married, Matt. *Married.*" For the first time in months, years, maybe her entire life, her thoughts and feelings were clear. And her heart hurt more than it ever had before. "I appreciate the faith you've put in me with this project—"

"You're still going to help, aren't you?" The hope that had disappeared from his face flared to life.

"Given I just gave my word in front of the entire town, I don't exactly have a choice, do I?" Would that she could relive the last couple of hours. Working for BethAnn was preferable to working with a liar. "Of course I'll do the work. But as far as moving forward with us?" She unwound his jacket and pushed it into his hands as she gave up more than she ever thought she'd have to. "I might not be the most confident of women—I may even be a coward, but I deserve respect, Matt. And I deserve to be with someone I can trust. I'm sorry, but hearing this, knowing you lied to me from the start? That person definitely isn't you."

CHAPTER FIVE

WITH A FINAL sip of coffee and silent thanks for a rare weekend off, Lori ended her mile-long trek to Duskywing Farm Saturday morning on a sigh of relief. After a sleepless night, the fresh air and quiet of a Butterfly Harbor morning arrived with squawking seagulls and playful stereophonic ocean waves. It was the reset she needed, a reminder that wallowing wouldn't do anyone—herself especially—any good.

Besides, nothing worked off a good mad better than a long walk.

She'd staged her own rebellion last night after getting home and hadn't touched the boxes of invitations—something she'd probably regret at some point. She was used to manipulative people, used to the snark and passive-aggressive machinations, but this time had been one time too many. One Beth-

Ann smirk too many. Lori had taken a stand and, for once, done something unexpected.

And it felt great.

Her time, her abilities weren't any less valuable than anyone else's. Why did she continue to spend her life worrying about what other people thought about her? Abby was right. There was more to her than numbers on a scale. There always had been. Time to start acting like it.

That she'd started by ending any potential romantic involvement with Matt Knight before it had ever really gotten started seemed a tad overkill.

She should have known allowing herself to dwell on all those romantic ideas she'd never let herself entertain would come back and bite her. Besides, if things had gotten serious with Matt, she had her own confessions she'd have had to make about what the future did—or in her case didn't—hold in store. So maybe this entire situation was a blessing in disguise.

Maybe she just needed the reminder that she would be okay on her own.

She had her friends, her family, a new niece and, knowing Fletcher's desire for a big family, there would be more kids for him and Paige in the future.

She should feel relieved that Matt was officially out of her life—and she would be if she didn't have to deal with the whole beautification project. Story of her life. She'd finally taken a chance on something, grabbed hold of what she really wanted and in so doing exploded another part of her life.

She'd needed a reality check. She'd needed to get her head out of the clouds. She needed to remember that reality had crashed over her the summer she'd turned ten. Had continued to crash for years after.

With parents who had blamed rather than comforted, criticized instead of encouraged, the child Lori had been disappeared the day her little brother had died; whoever she'd been meant to be had been washed out to sea along with Colin, leaving a shell of a little girl desperate for someone to cling to; to grieve with. And when Fletcher and her grandfather hadn't been enough, or when she couldn't bear to cry one more tear, she'd turned to the one comfort that would never let her down.

Which was why, at two this morning, she'd

found herself heading out to the greenhouse in her backyard rather than falling back on old habits to rummage through the refrigerator and cabinets for something to eat. Dim lamps and welcoming buds were more productive, more welcoming, than a bowl of cereal or a pint of ice cream.

As if she'd been able to leave her disappointment—and disillusionment—about Matt outside.

"How could he not have told me?" Lori asked the question for what may as well have been the millionth time and received the same answer: silence. Funny how it wasn't the being married that bothered her so much as the omission. He could have told her. She probably would have understood, but then again, maybe not. If he'd lied to her about this, what else would he lie to her about? There weren't a lot of things that were important to her, but honesty? That was a deal breaker.

"Meow."

A sleek gray cat leaped effortlessly onto the top of the fence and walked toward Lori, its purr as loud as an engine as it greeted her at the farm gate.

"Good morning, Ophelia." Lori reached out and scratched the cat on the top of her head. Ophelia sat and pushed her head into Lori's palm as if to thank her. "Out and about early, too, I see."

"Meeeeeow!"

The handle of her gardening wagon clutched in her hand, the light fabric of her sunshine-yellow maxi dress caught around her legs in the morning breeze. She pushed through the gate of Duskywing Farm and set the sad thoughts of what might have been aside.

Ahhhhh. She took a slow, deep breath and as she released it, a smile spread across her lips. Walking on this property was like entering another world. A quiet world. A healing world.

A stone cottage reminiscent of Irish perfection sat nestled amidst thriving, expansive and lush acreage. The vegetable patch—an understatement given its size—glistened after an early morning dew dousing and stretched almost farther than she could see. Tiny splotches of color shifted against the restless leaves—butterflies slowly awakening under the growing warmth of the sun. Soon they'd be flitting about as eager and curious as those in the eucalyptus trees growing throughout Butterfly Harbor.

The wooden stall just inside the trellised gate was a recent addition. Along with an old-fashioned metal cash box, the shelves beneath the counter displayed stacks of worn baskets and bundles of reusable totes for customers to fill to their pocketbooks' content.

One of the hidden treasures of Butterfly Harbor, the organic farm boasted an open policy on Fridays and now Saturdays where customers could literally pluck their food from the ground, with gentle oversight of course. Most preferred to drop their list in the painted box outside the gate throughout the week for Calliope to fill for pickup or delivery. Fortunately for Lori, she had been given free rein in Calliope's kingdom but she never wanted to exceed her welcome.

In less than an hour, visitors and customers would begin to wander through the peaceful side gardens, enjoying the Jones's special lemonade or, in the cooler months, piping hot chocolate. Paige and Charlie would be by to pick up their morning deliveries before Paige was off for her shift at the diner.

Which didn't give Lori much time to mark this first item off her To Do list. She'd had enough of crowds last night, and besides, there was something to be said about enjoying the farm in the empty prepublic hours.

The gurgle of water tumbling over stones welcomed Lori and told her the rock garden Calliope and her young sister, Stella, had been working on for the past few weeks had been completed.

Located at the top of Angel Trumpet Way, this stretch of land really did feel as if it had disconnected from the rest of the world and even Butterfly Harbor itself. The distant noise of traffic and the town at the bottom of the hill never reached this far, or, maybe it was just that Lori never wanted it to.

Paradise, Lori mused. There were those with green thumbs, people who possessed a natural affinity for encouraging nature's growth and explosions of color and bounty. Lori happily counted herself among them as she could lose herself for hours in the garden and greenhouse she and her grandfather had meticulously tended from the day she and Fletcher had come to live with him. But as good as Lori could claim to be, there was something, well, magical, about Calliope's way.

Lori stopped on the edge of the herb garden that had been inspired by the manicured English tea gardens thousands of miles away. She closed her eyes, lifted her face to the still-warming sun as it rose to its morning crest and inhaled the scent of lavender, of mint, and the faintest hint of woodsy rosemary.

Late September, while certainly not the heart of growing or blooming season, had Calliope's gardens caught somewhere between the fading affection of summer and the early breezes of fall. Not that the Monterey area saw severe temperature fluctuations. Consistent, enjoyable weather was something to boast about, but it wasn't always the most hospitable for plants, unless of course those plants got their start at Duskywing Farm. It was like a boost of immunity that ensured thriving, healthy results.

The gentle tinkle of bells made Lori's smile widen. Scrunching her toes in her walking sandals, she opened her eyes as Calliope emerged from the front door of her cottage, arms loaded with glass jars filled with rich, amber honey from her recently acquired hives.

Lori's stomach rumbled at the thought of the glistening sugary liquid dripping lazily over a piece of Calliope's homemade, crusty bread or a blueberry scone. She could feel an extra pound grab hold of her midsection just thinking about it. All the more reason for the walk here and back.

"Good morning, Lori." Calliope arranged the Mason jars at the booth where the lemonade would soon be set up. "Here for the poinsettia cuttings already?"

"Need to get them going sooner than later if they're going to be ready by Christmas Eve."

"I have no doubt they'll be brimming with holiday spirit." Calliope's long curls all but disappeared against the deep turquoise of the dress she wore. Ever the epitome of a free spirit, the farmer/businesswoman strode barefoot across her land, motioning for Lori to follow her around back of the cottage.

The wagon wheels squeaked as Lori pulled it over packed dirt and sporadic grass, rumbled as she dragged it over paving stones. The paned windows to Calliope's cottage were filled with various hanging accents, prisms to catch the light, wind chimes that clinked in the breeze. Thick vines of purple and pink wisteria wound their way around the wood-trellised porch that protected a workspace for the pottery wheel Stella, Calliope's eleven-year-old sister, had recently taken over. The small pots and planters that displayed various flowers and plants around the property were the young girl's doing.

"How are your feet not blocks of ice?" Lori asked Calliope as she parked her wagon by the door of Calliope's growing house.

"After all these years I'm used to it," Calliope said with her usual understanding smile as she pulled open the door. "I love the feel of being so close to the earth, to the soil. Makes me feel connected. Speaking of connected, I'm very pleased you decided to work with Matt on this project."

"Mmmm." *Pleased* wasn't the word Lori would use. Not now at least. Thankfully, thoughts of Matt evaporated as she stepped inside what she considered Calliope's treasure house. Flowers and plants in every stage, in every color, sat in their biodegradable pots or more sturdy planters. Window boxes lined the walls along the sills and were filled with herbs from fennel and dill to perennials like bergamot and hyssop. Wild strawberry plants mingled with mint, the bubbles of red settling happily between thick leaves and winding stems. Pansies, yarrow and calendula burst from the soil like fireworks caught exploding in midair.

This place never ceased to amaze her. She'd spent most of her life around plants, around flowers of all kind and she didn't think even she could name all of what she saw.

It was as if she'd walked into a grove kissed by the fairies.

"The PVC pipe is new." Lori motioned to the wide pipe anchored into one of the pieces of wood frame. Calliope had carved out holes large enough for small plants that thrived on air rather than water to thrive and larger ones for the cacti.

"Space is becoming an issue," Calliope said. "And since I'm not in a position to build another shed, Stella's had some creative ideas."

Lori trailed her fingers over the edge of the metal-encased worktable beneath a collection of seedlings, barely there sprouts just emerging from their bed of dirt. "I never know where to start."

"I did some rearranging last night after the meeting." Calliope leaned against the door frame and watched Lori wander between the narrow rows. "And, as always, each plant has been labeled. I'm assuming you have some plans already coming together for the homes and yards Matt plans to beautify?"

Lori nodded. "With the new sanctuary focusing primarily on the monarchs, I want to see what we can do to attract other species of butterflies. Although I'm not sure that's entirely possible given the time of year." Whatever worries she might have had where the mayor, BethAnn or even Matt were concerned paled when she considered the time of year and weather.

"Anything is possible with the right touch," Calliope assured her. "True, most of the flowers you'll be needing should have gone in this spring, but they're sturdy. And with some care and faith, they might be blooming enough to put on a show for our festivalgoers."

"You really think so?" Lori wasn't convinced.

"I know so. There's wild milkweed behind the toolshed. I've been harvesting it for a while and they're hearty enough to survive. They'd make lovely additions closer to the homes."

"Milkweed is the universal butterfly dining experience which makes it the perfect backdrop," Lori agreed. "Do you mind if I just take my time, look at how the colors work with one another, make some notes?"

"Stay as long as you like. You'll find the poinsettias toward the back. Just remember not to dismiss anything because you're afraid it won't survive the transplant. We can work around that."

"Thanks, Calliope. I don't plan to take anything other than the cuttings today." She didn't know many details about the project yet—not the homes they'd be focusing on, not the watering system, or even the condition of the soil. Their budget could very well be eaten up by dirt and drip systems. "I don't want to get ahead of myself. Except…" She did know of one house for certain. "Willa and her mother are on the list. I wanted to do some research on plants and flowers known for aiding in healing and to ease pain and sickness. I thought perhaps you'd have some suggestions?"

"I can put together a selection for you, certainly. Lovely idea. You see? I told you you were the right person for this job." She inclined her head. "I'm afraid I have some early arrivals this morning, so if you'll excuse me. I'll leave you to this."

Lori only nodded, happy to lose herself once again in the flora around her. Plants, flowers, soil, water—they didn't judge. They didn't lie. They didn't do anything but give beauty to the world, even when they needed a little coaxing and care.

Regret bloomed inside of her. Regret that today, had a face; the rugged, handsome face of a man with a slight limp, weary deep brown eyes and a smile that, for a few weeks, made her forget just how lonely she'd been.

CHAPTER SIX

MATT PULLED HIS truck into one of the empty spaces of the Duskywing Farm parking lot and turned to his canine companion.

Big, black eyes blinked lazily into the morning sun as his golden coat glistened and shined. "You and Ophelia going to get along today, fuzz face?"

"Woof." The response was muted, almost as if the retriever resented being asked. Normally Luke's shadow was well behaved, but put him in the vicinity of Calliope's feline friend and, well…

Matt clicked open the latch on the leash and locked it onto Cash's collar. "Sorry, bud. Holly made me promise."

Cash inclined his head and sighed.

"It was either this or you hang out alone at the sheriff's station." Matt slid a finger under his own collar and tugged. "And we both know what happens when you're left alone."

Okay, so leaving a leftover box of doughnuts on the coffee counter probably hadn't been the smartest of moves, but Matt had definitely earned a best friend for life. When Cash wasn't tied to Luke's hip. He liked the pooch and he appreciated that Holly and Luke thought enough of him to call on him for dog-sitting duties even at the last minute. It had seemed a bit strange this morning, however, when Holly had dropped him off. She'd had an odd, dazed expression on her face and a secretive grin he couldn't quite decipher. That she'd bustled out before Matt could ask any questions had him wondering what might be going on at the diner or with the Saxon family.

Fletch had just headed out on patrol while Matt and Ozzy were splitting on-call duty, so it seemed fitting to spend some time outdoors. It made sense. Rumbling around in his large empty house, having little to think about other than the devastated expression on Lori's face when he'd finally told her the truth didn't go very far in keeping Matt's sanity in place.

He knew he'd have to start over with her, but he hadn't thought the admission would destroy all the trust they'd built up. Maybe he should have. Maybe he was just too worried about what would happen if he didn't convince Lori he was worth taking another chance on. He needed her on his side, in his life; Kyle's future depended on it. Matt's future did. He'd already carved out a part of himself to include this boy in his life. Now, somehow, he had to convince Lori to do the same for him.

On the bright side, he didn't have anywhere else to go but up.

He wrapped Cash's leash around his hand and pushed open the door, cringing at the aged creak as the dog jumped to the ground beside him. Last night for the first time in over a year, he'd found himself slipping into the darkness that had the power to consume him. Call it genetics, call it learned behavior, there were times the pull of a bottle promised to ease his mind even as it clouded it.

Most times, one beer was plenty. He could have a celebratory drink, toast with friends, relax after a day at work. But then there were the days when all he could think about was escaping.

Which was why, first thing this morning, he found himself standing over the sink emptying beer bottle after beer bottle down its porcelain throat. He might be many things, but Matt had vowed years before that he would never, ever, turn into his lying, violent, manipulative father.

"Morning, Deputy." Kate Willingham, one of the city's accountants, along with her firefighter husband and three look-alike daughters waved to him as they crested the hill. "Jeff and I were just talking about the beautification project you and Lori are heading up. We've been wanting to get involved with the festival. We'd all like to sign up for what you've got in mind. If you're still looking for volunteers."

"We are always looking for volunteers," Matt said. "We're hoping to get our first full day's work next Saturday. Does that work for you all?"

"Mo-oooom!" The oldest Willingham girl, who was nearing sixteen, crossed her arms over her chest and pouted. "I thought we were going to San Francisco. They're opening that new outlet store."

"We can go to the city anytime, Katie." Jeff Willingham settled his hands on his other girls' shoulders. "And one designer purse for anyone your age is plenty. Matt, feel free to leave flyers or sign-up sheets at the firehouse anytime you want. There's a bunch of us wanting to get this done."

"You got it." The more people they got on board the faster the work would go. Now all he had to do was call a truce with Lori and figure out a plan of action.

Katie's grumbling echoed in Matt's ears as they all headed through the gates. The Willingham girls darted off, heading directly for the lemonade stand. Cash's growl was low and almost imperceptive, but the way the dog strained against his leash had Matt searching for a furry gray feline.

"Ah, there you are, Ophelia." Matt wound his hand around the leash, shortening it to an arm's length as he stayed a few feet away from the cat's chosen perch on the fence. Looking as royal as an Egyptian goddess, Ophelia tipped her chin and pinned unnerving blue eyes on Cash, who, after a moment of staring blinked and dropped his butt on the ground. "Peace in the kingdom after all then?" Matt bent down and ruffled Cash's fur. "I knew you were all bluster."

"Woof."

Whatever response Matt might have had disappeared from his head as he was swallowed up into the activity that was a Saturday morning at Duskywing Farm. It had, in the last year, become a gathering place, one the residents and visitors equally enjoyed. The promise of fresh, organic products along with quirky artistic offerings, it was part farmers' market part craft fair. Laughter and conversation filled the air; the squeals of children and excited cries coming from the depths of Calliope's vegetable patch. He spotted Jasper O'Neill hobbling on his crutches among the rows of kale, lettuce and whatever other greens Calliope had thought to plant. Matt could hear him giving instructions on how to cut certain bundles free, answering questions from inexperienced, amateur farmers.

"Coffee, Matt?" Matt turned and found Calliope Jones standing behind him, a slightly crooked brown porcelain mug in her hands. Steam swirled up and over the uneven lip and he caught the hint of hickory—and cinnamon?

"I thought Saturday morning was lemonade time?" His stomach rumbled at the distant sight of fresh-baked muffins topped with farm-fresh honey. "Since when do you serve coffee?"

"Since certain customers seem to need it. You look a bit peaked." She held out the mug and, even before he accepted, she took Cash's leash from him. "Here on business or just for pleasure?"

"Oh. A little of both. Paige and Fletcher have that big housewarming BBQ next Sunday. I thought I should bring something." He looked at the various tents and market stalls that had been erected, his head spinning. He glanced over to the booth selling homemade pies and pastries but he'd bet Holly had that part covered. "Any suggestions?"

"Always."

"Keeping in mind my talents do not lie in the kitchen."

Calliope dropped to wrap an arm around Cash and buried her hands in his thick fur. "I think you underestimate yourself in many areas, Matt. Even you should be able to put a salad together."

"Yeah, I'm not a big salad kind of guy." He indicated his torso.

She chuckled. "How about you let me worry about what to put in it and you can pick it up next weekend? And in the meantime, take a little time to enjoy your coffee. Relax. There's a nice quiet spot around the back of the house. Near the cuttings shed."

"Um, yeah, sure."

"Wonderful. Ophelia and I will keep an eye on Cash for you. Go on."

Cash seemed to frown when he looked up at her.

"Okay." He did as he was instructed, mainly because he didn't want to see what happened if he got on the wrong side of Calliope Jones. Given that she was currently leading Cash over to Ophelia, he'd bet both cat and dog were about to be lectured on the importance of interspecies truces.

Saturday mornings at the farm were becoming a Butterfly Harbor habit. Every week there seemed to be more tents filled with locals selling home-baked goods and handmade items. Crafters flocked to the weekly events, from Judy Ashley and her handmade purses to Athena Halloway, town crafter extraordinaire, who offered hand-dyed wool yarn and knitting supplies. He could only imagine the crowds come festival time and, for an instant, wondered if perhaps BethAnn had been onto something last night when she'd mentioned the sheriff's department being stretched too thin.

He'd definitely have to talk to Luke about plans to shift schedules and routines in the near future.

The din of the marketgoers faded as he wandered around the side of the house, enjoying the peace and quiet. When he spotted the wood-and-glass building at the back of the property, curiosity got the better of him. Sipping whatever elixir Calliope had fixed him, he approached the wagon parked near the narrow door. Worn wooden crates had been filled with dozens of tiny poinsettia plants, mostly red, some white. A traditional selection, to be sure. He didn't understand the trend of weirdly colored poinsettias.

He bent over, drew a finger over one of the petals.

The door opened.

"Matt!" Lori stood on the other side, eyes wide, cheeks flushed. That mahogany-streaked hair of hers shone against the fluorescent light of the indoor lamps. Her shoulders stiffened, her mouth went tight, as if she'd been suddenly cursed by the tension fairy. "What are you doing here?"

"I was just wandering. Killing time. You know, before I head over to the station."

"So you're working."

Did she have to sound so relieved?

"I will be." He shrugged. "Since I ran into you—" He cleared his throat and wondered when his body had been inhabited by an insecure teenager. What was he so nervous about? He'd already blown it with her, she'd made that perfectly clear last night. Given the guarded expression on her face he was betting his chances at getting her to forgive him were about as good as Cash and Ophelia walking paw in paw through the garden gate. "About the project."

"Yes?" She stepped outside and set the poinsettia plants in the last empty spaces in her crates.

"I'm thinking we should make plans. You

know, go through the list of addresses, check out the houses—"

"The watering systems? Yes, I was thinking the same thing."

She stood up so quickly he had to take a step back to avoid getting knocked on the chin. Not many women rivaled him in height. That he'd always been able to look Lori in the eye had been one of the things he'd liked about her. Equal footing. From day one.

"I was looking through Calliope's flowers. Do you, um…" She tucked a strand of hair behind her ear and flinched ever so slightly. "Do you want to hear some of my ideas?"

Yes! He wanted to shout, do a completely unmanly fist bump. She wasn't scrambling to get away from him, wasn't pushing him aside or glaring at him. All of which on some level he'd expected. He knew how to deal with hostility. What he wasn't so great with was this odd distance between them now. He remained calm, nodded and smiled. "Sure. I'd like that."

"Come on in." She waved him inside. The second the door closed it was like an oxygen mask had been slipped over his face. The air was so clean, so cool and crisp. An oasis.

Back when he was serving in the Middle East, he used to dream of cool breezes and misting sprays even as he surrendered to the reality he might never experience those sensations again. One of the reasons he'd moved so close to the ocean. He appreciated every single day. A touch of humidity kissed the air inside the small building, as if the atmosphere had a mind of its own and was focused on giving the extensive array of plants and flowers exactly what they needed.

Lori cleared her throat. "I was telling Calliope I think we should focus on the butterfly aspect, do what we can to attract even more to the area."

"Okay." What Matt knew about butterflies would fit on the edge of a monarch's wings, but he could fake it.

"I've made a list of flowers and plants that I think would thrive, at least for the short term between now and the end of the festival. I'd also like to see us use as many drought-resistant plants as possible to limit water consumption. We could do those on the lower-lying properties so they can catch runoff. For the higher areas, I'd like to install a drip system."

And stave off any complaints from the mayor. "Considering the watering is going to be done on the city's dime for the foreseeable future, I agree." It was a point of contention Gil and Luke had already run into. "Gil and BethAnn won't be able to argue with anything that saves money. I'd like to consider alternate ground cover, too. Not just grasses and clovers."

She nodded, biting on her thumbnail as she looked down at an array of flowering herbs and thistles. "We might also consider focusing in on some that attract hummingbirds and bees. I'm trying to imagine someone driving down Monarch Lane for the first time, seeing all these winged creatures flitting about the homes. Especially those three cul-de-sacs I'm assuming you're mainly paying attention to at the front end of town."

He appreciated how he didn't have to explain their plan of action. "The entire section is an eyesore and was actually what got this idea off the ground. I don't know that we can do much until we get the facades of the homes taken care of first, though."

"I know." She sighed. "We really need to

start making a schedule of what needs to be done when. And by whom."

"Okay. Have you had breakfast?"

"Have I—what? No." She shook her head, irritation flashing in her eyes. "Why?"

"I just thought we could head over to the diner, get things underway. We're both going to be busy with work on top of this, so it makes sense to use the time we have. Unless you have plans."

"I don't have plans." But she didn't look thrilled at the prospect. "I have these plants I have to get home and under protection. And eating at the diner—"

"I thought you liked Ursula's cooking?"

"Of course I do. I just don't like eating—" She smoothed her hands down the front of her sunny yellow dress and didn't finish the thought as she glanced away. "Never mind."

Matt frowned. Obviously they were still in the redefining aspect of their relationship. "I can drive you home to take the plants since you don't have a car," Matt offered, barging through the verbal opening she'd left for him. "I have to take Cash back to the diner anyway. At least I think I'm supposed to.

Holly wasn't very forthcoming with the details when she dropped him off."

"Luke's due back. Simon, too. She's probably just distracted."

Distracted. Yeah, Holly had seemed distracted all right. Which was what was so strange. Holly Saxon was one of the most levelheaded, controlled people he knew. Granted he hadn't known her all that long, but seeing her, well, flummoxed, set all kinds of bells blaring in the back of his head.

"So what do you say? Breakfast? On me of course. And after we can swing by and take some pictures of the houses."

"You have time to do all that?" She turned skeptical eyes on him. "I thought you were on call today?"

"I am, but I can make a phone call." And offer something of a bribe to Ozzy to cover for him for a few extra hours. "What do you say?"

She pinched her lips together, drew trembling fingers across the miniature daisy peeking out from its surrounding leaves. "I don't know, Matt."

Afraid he might have pushed too hard too fast, he scrambled to salvage the morning.

"It's work that has to be done. I understand this is hard for you, Lori. And I'm sorry for it. But you're the one who said we're still friends."

"I said that before I knew you'd lied to me."

He could see her accusation surprised even herself and while he wanted to argue with her, there wasn't an argument to be made. She was right. He had lied to her. And now he was paying the price.

"So we're not friends?"

"I didn't say that."

"So we are."

She looked frustrated with herself, as if she couldn't believe she couldn't make sense of the situation. Nice to know he wasn't the only one. Trust was a fragile thing. He knew this better than most people, which was why he had to give her some space. If only he had the time to do so.

"It doesn't make sense for each of us to do the work and then have to do it over together. Let's see how this morning goes and we can take it from there." Anxious, nervous and more than a little encouraged, Matt pressed a little bit more. "We can make this work, Lori. I promise."

She looked at him, the question evident in her eyes. Was he talking about the project or was he talking about them?

"Since I gave my word at the town meeting to do my best, I'm locked in."

Matt's hand fisted at his side as the hope swelling inside of him popped. "Is that a yes?"

She nodded. "We have to start somewhere."

"Good. Good." He backed toward the door, resisting the urge to babble. "If you're done loading up your wagon, I can get it settled in my truck. If that's okay with you?"

"I'm done." She sighed, as if she wished she wasn't. "I just need to talk to Calliope before I leave."

"Me, too. I'll meet you by the gate in a few minutes." He grabbed hold of the wagon and pulled it behind him.

On his way to a second chance.

CHAPTER SEVEN

"JUST A TWO-EGG veggie omelet with fruit on the side and coffee, please, Twyla." Lori didn't have to look at the Butterfly Diner's menu to know what to order. It hadn't changed much over the years. While Matt rattled off his choices, Lori busied herself with digging out her notebook, pen and the list she'd scribbled back at Calliope's.

She tugged the edge of her sweater down and squirmed to get comfortable in the booth as the edge of the table all but pinned her against the seat. Wedging herself in was never fun, but the diner was limited to booths and counter seating; neither of which was plus-size friendly. Her insides were already compressing at the idea of shoving herself free once breakfast was over, especially in front of Matt.

Not that it mattered. Why couldn't she think of him as just someone she was having a meal with in one of Butterfly Harbor's oldest businesses?

The throwback atmosphere was one of cheer and goodwill. The black-and-white-tiled floor, the old-fashioned black Formica countertops and orange upholstered stools and booths, all paid silent tribute to the monarchs that flitted through and settled in Butterfly Harbor on their annual migration trek. In recent months, Holly had begun adding various artists' renderings of their patron insect, from kids' drawings to etchings, to photographs that had been framed and placed on the walls between booths and over windows. Personally, Lori loved the oversize, wooden monarchs settled in and around the front door outside, as if one was walking into the perfect butterfly sanctuary—with the best burgers and pies in town.

"You sure that's all you want?" Matt asked as Twyla pivoted on her stick-thin legs, ink-black hair swinging long in a braid down her back, and headed to the kitchen.

"I'm sure." Lori gave him one of her practiced smiles.

Lori flipped open her notebook. She'd been working so hard on putting her issues with food behind her. Stressing over calories only made her want more, so she'd finally learned to order whatever she wanted and eat less of it. Not as easy as it sounded; not when she had that shrill voice echoing in her head—her mother's voice reminding her food was not a friend. It was in many ways her enemy and no matter how hard Lori fought it, it was a battle she'd already lost.

In her mind, she slammed the door hard and fast on the very idea of the mother she hadn't spoken to in almost four years. Life was too short to spend dwelling on a relationship that would never, ever be healthy.

"What's wrong?" Matt rested his arms on the table and leaned in. She could feel the warmth of his breath, feel the heat of his concerned gaze.

"Nothing." She shifted in her seat. "It's… nothing."

"Now who's lying?"

Her chin shot up at his accusation but it was then she saw he was teasing her.

"Come on, Lori. Tell me what's bothering you. You've been acting weird since before we came in here. Are you embarrassed to be seen with me?"

"Why on earth would I—" She took a deep breath. "You're making fun of me."

"How else am I going to disarm you enough to tell me what's going on in here." He reached up and tapped a finger against the side of her head.

"It's not important." Darn it, why did she always let this get to her? Why hadn't she just been honest and told him she didn't want to go to breakfast?

"Given we've spent the last couple of minutes debating that fact, I'll say you're wrong. What is it?"

"I just…" Could her face feel any hotter? "I don't like eating out, okay? There. You got me to confess, copper. Take me to jail." She held out her wrists, palms up.

"Why don't you like to eat out?"

"Oh, for…" She tucked her hair behind her ears and sighed. "It's silly. Stupid even."

"Clearly, it's not. Tell me."

Tell him? Tell him one of her most embarrassing secrets? Tell him about how even her own parents were disgusted by her? Yeah, that should kill off any residual feelings he might have for her. "When I was a little girl and we went out to eat, my mother would constantly criticize me. I shouldn't have that or what will people think, a chubby girl like you eating that. I embarrassed her. And she made sure everyone knew it." All these years later and it still messed with her head. "I told you it was stupid."

"It's not stupid. I'm sorry you had to deal with that." He reached over and held out a hand. She stared at his open palm, heart pounding as she realized how much she wanted to take it. Instead, she pulled her hands into her lap and locked her fingers together. "No child should ever be made to feel less than. For any reason."

"I totally agree. Which is why I haven't talked to her in about a gazillion years." That neither of her parents seemed interested in reaching out to her—or Fletcher—didn't help the situation. It was one thing to be a child and suspect your parents didn't like you; it was another to be an adult and know it to be true. "So, there you go. I don't like to eat out because my mother used to make fun of me for being fat. Bring on the chocolate pudding."

"Have I mentioned how much I loathe self-deprecating humor?" He sat back and pinned her with a stare that made her shiver. "We're being honest with each other now, yeah? Stop making fun of yourself. I don't find the jokes funny and I don't agree with them. What on earth does your dress size have to do with the type of person you are? I like who you are, Lori. I have from the first time I saw you, so suck it up and deal with it. And while you're at it, stop making light of things that cause you pain. It's irritating."

"Yes, it is." She didn't want to take what he said to heart. She didn't want to believe he meant what she'd always wanted someone to say to her; someone who might actually care for her, love her. "It's also the one defense mechanism that's worked for me, so forgive me if I don't bow to your lack of expertise in this matter." She meant for the comment to tick him off, drive him away. Offend him to the point he'd settle her firmly in the friends column. Instead, she watched the anger lines around his eyes ease and the corners of his mouth flicker.

"You'd be surprised what I know about parental disapproval, but that's a conversation for another time. Look at us, getting to know each other. Being honest with one another.

It's almost like we're starting a new relationship or something."

Lori shook her head, wanting nothing more than to walk away and forget that whenever she was with him she didn't want to be without him. He had a way of making her forget everything that shouldn't be important. "What's wrong with you? Everything that should make you angry makes you laugh."

"And sometimes vice versa," he confirmed with a shrug. "You have your coping mechanisms, I have mine. And for the record, I'll give you time to work on that bad habit of yours. Not a lot, but some."

"How generous. Now how about we actually get to work on what brought us here in the first place?" Because this current conversation was going further off the rails than she'd ever be comfortable with. "We're going to focus on the exterior of the houses before we tackle the landscaping issues, right?" Lori clicked open her pen and they got to work. "How many houses are we looking at?"

"There are five in each cul-de-sac," Matt rattled off the addresses from his phone. "And then we have…"

They settled into an easy conversation,

much to Lori's relief. As long as they focused on the task at hand, as long as she had a job to do, things would be fine between them. She didn't have to worry about what she was saying, if she said something inappropriate or misleading, not that she would. Not now that she knew the truth about his marital status.

But the more she thought about that— beneath the anger and the hurt she felt at him lying to her all this time, she had to admit there was a blossoming curiosity about his marriage.

None of your business, she scolded herself.

By the time their breakfasts arrived, they'd made good progress on the project plans, probably because they had similar intentions and work processes. Lori's stomach grumbled as Twyla set one of Ursula's oversize blueberry granola pancakes in front of Matt and followed up with Lori's omelet.

She picked up her fork as a second plate for Matt arrived, this one with scrambled eggs and, sigh, bacon. "My kryptonite," Lori joked as she avoided his gaze. "Why is bacon so tasty?"

"I never ask the whys, I'm just glad it is." He offered her the plate. "You want some?"

She started to shake her head but caught the challenge in his eyes. "Sure. One piece." She reached over and plucked one off his plate.

"I'd say good girl, but I'm afraid you'd slug me."

Lori laughed and glanced outside to where he'd left Cash in the cab of his truck. The retriever had his chin resting in the open window, his dark eyes moving along with the growing crowd milling about in the morning hours.

"You really think Cash is okay out there?" Clearly she was desperate for conversation topics.

"It's not like he's coming in here," Matt said. "He'd scarf up my bacon in about thirty seconds flat."

Lori swore she could see Cash's gaze land on them, as if he heard his name being spoken.

"He looks so sad."

"That's his shtick," Matt said. "Don't let him sucker you. That dog is more than fine."

That the dog was still in Matt's car raised another question. "I'm surprised Holly isn't here." She leaned her head back, searched between customers to see if Holly was behind the counter. "Saturday's her busiest day."

"Like I said, she seemed a bit off this morning. Maybe she's sleeping—" He caught Lori's look of skepticism and stopped. "Yeah, okay, you're right. It is unusual. Poor Twyla's looking a little overwhelmed."

As if on cue, the front door dinged open and Lori's sister-in-law, Paige, came flying through, little Charlie tight on her heels. She maneuvered her way through the crowd and darted into the kitchen.

"Paige usually has the afternoon shifts on Saturdays, right?" She looked back outside and saw Charlie had left her new puppy tied up near Cash and the truck. "I hope Holly's okay." She bit into an underripe piece of cantaloupe.

"I guess I'll just keep Cash with me until I hear otherwise," Matt said. "He'll be a good buffer for us on our house tour."

"Buffer?" Lori almost swallowed wrong. "We don't need a buffer."

"We do if we're going to talk about what you don't want to talk about." He shrugged in silent challenge. "My divorce."

"Really? We just called a truce and you're going to bring up your marriage now?"

"Divorce," he corrected. "And I've never known when to back off." He'd already polished off half his breakfast while she continued to nibble on a grape. "But seeing as I'm not sure when or if another opportunity will arise where you don't have your nose in that notebook of yours, seems as good a time as any. Go ahead. Ask me."

"Ask you what?" She didn't want to do this. Not in public. Maybe not ever. Whatever had been between them was over. It had to be. He'd already lied to her once. It was only a matter of time before he did it again.

"Anything you want. I'm an open book. Now," he added at her unrestrained eye roll. "Now. I'm an open book now. If there's a way to repair what I broke—"

"There isn't." She cut him off but even as she said the words, she knew she was lying. That he was trying to make amends for what had happened meant something. She didn't want it to, but it did. She also didn't want to get her hopes up again. She was tired of having them snapped in half.

"I didn't want to tell you about it until I'd

made up my mind. I liked how things were going with us. We were in a good place."

"So good you decided to leave out the part about you being married."

He flinched. "I was also afraid you wouldn't understand."

"Well, you got that right at least. But I'm not convinced that's why you didn't tell me." It was like her mouth had taken off without her. Did she really want to get into this now?

"What other reason could there be?"

She took a deep breath, set her fork down and cupped her mug of coffee in both hands. "I think you didn't tell me you were married because you were holding out hope there was a chance to save your marriage." She sipped and hid behind her cup. "I think maybe you still love her."

"Love hasn't been a part of my relationship with Gina for a very long time." That he didn't hesitate with his answer earned him a few points. "I'm not sure it ever was."

"On your part or hers?"

"Both."

"And here's our problem." No matter how hard she'd tried to prepare for it, disappointment sliced through her. "I don't know whether I believe you or not."

"Then I guess I'm just going to have to earn back your trust, aren't I?"

"Matt—"

"I hope I'm not interrupting."

Lori held a deep breath, closed her eyes and sighed. "Good morning, BethAnn," Lori lied with a strained smile. Today's all-business attire consisted of a pea-green pantsuit and a chunky gold necklace that reminded Lori of a bicycle chain.

Matt cleared his throat and wiped his mouth. "Mrs. Bottomley."

"Deputy Knight."

Lori sat up straight and braced herself at BethAnn's "I'm on a mission" tone.

"What can we do for you?" If Matt was uneasy about the intrusion, he didn't let on. If anything, he looked relieved.

"I just wanted to check in," BethAnn explained. "I know we all have a lot on our plates what with these various committees and obligations." She clutched what looked like nervous hands around the satchel bag. "I also wanted to let you know, Lori, that anytime you'd like to come back on board to help with the dinner you're more than welcome. If there's anything I can do to accommodate your schedule, please say the word."

"I appreciate that." That warning system that rarely steered her wrong blared like Def Con 3. "But I don't anticipate having a lot of extra free time."

Something unfamiliar flickered in Beth-Anne's ice-blue eyes. "Well, I hope we can still count on you to get those invitations out. You know how important they are to the success of the dinner especially now that we're going in a different direction."

A different direction? Lori did her best to keep her expression neutral even as it almost killed her not to ask. "They'll be done in time, don't worry."

"Excellent. Mayor Hamilton and I also discussed it and we're going to need a planned work schedule and proposed budget for your project." She aimed her laser-like gaze on Matt.

"I see," Matt said. "I take it from the personal notification that we're the only committee who needs to submit one?"

"You have to admit, this is quite an undertaking. We need to make sure every penny is being used to its fullest potential." BethAnn tapped a fingernail against the gold discs hanging from her ears.

"Seems to me—"

"We'll be happy to." Lori nudged him under the table, then realized she'd kicked the wrong leg. Her eyes went wide as an embarrassed laugh bubbled in her throat. Hopefully he hadn't noticed.

No sooner had she thought that than his lips twitched. He knocked her back with his foot. She coughed and covered her mouth as she said, "Rest assured we will make the most of our budget, BethAnn. I'll be sure you have the reports by Wednesday."

"Tuesday would be better," BethAnn reasoned, and her face suddenly brightened. "I have meetings with caterers all day on Wednesday."

"What caterers?" What breakfast she'd eaten turned to a ball of clay in her stomach. "The committee already agreed Jason Corwin would be—"

"Well that was all because of you, wasn't it?" BethAnn said in that breathy, flyaway voice of hers. "None of us know Jason as well as you do, and well, I've heard how temperamental these celebrity chefs can be. Honestly, I can't take a chance like that. Besides, I think it's best to spread the wealth, don't you?"

"Considering we only have two restaurants in town that could handle an event like this, no, I don't." Was this woman really so spiteful she'd put the entire festival at risk because Lori had stood up for herself? "This is a Butterfly Harbor event, BethAnn. We should be showcasing local talent and businesses, not bringing people in from the outside." Lori's throat went hot against the anger. Forget the effort the committee had gone to, Jason had spent the last few weeks tweaking and finalizing the menu. "Not to mention that Jason has a huge social media following that can only bring attention to the event. Have you even met Jason?"

"I haven't had the pleasure, no. I'm sure you understand I have to make this as easy on the committee as possible now, Lori."

"You don't think you owe him the respect of a discussion at least?" Lori shot back.

"There weren't any contracts signed. There's no legal reason why I can't change my mind." Her eyes sparked with challenge.

"There wasn't a contract because Jason was donating his time to the cause. You do know what this does to the event's budget, don't you?"

"It's all being handled."

"Does that mean you won't be using Calliope's produce?" Lori didn't have to ask; she already knew the answer and her anger grew at all the extra work her friend had gone to in order to provide enough food for the dinner.

"I'll know more after Wednesday, but I wanted to give you a heads-up. You'll spread the word, won't you?"

Lori bit her tongue, afraid that if she opened her mouth she might inadvertently bite BethAnn on the…

"Your order's ready, BethAnn." Paige stepped up behind the older woman and swung a handled paper bag in front of her.

"Oh, thanks, Paige. Mmmmm." BethAnn lifted the bag to her face and took a deep breath. "Cinnamon buns and waffles." She aimed a pointed, familiar sympathetic look at Lori's anemic plate. "Enjoy the rest of your breakfast."

"I swear I keep waiting for her to say 'and your little dog, too,'" Paige muttered after

BethAnn was gone. "Boy, Holly was not kidding about her, was she?"

"Did she seriously just fire Jason via surrogate?" Matt turned disbelieving eyes on Lori.

"Yes, she did." Lori's chest tightened at the thought of having to tell Jason he'd been passed over because BethAnn was irritated with her. "So much for town unity."

"You think Gil knows what she's trying to pull?" Paige asked.

"He won't hear it from me." Lori gathered up her belongings. "BethAnn's counting on me ratting her out and I won't give her the satisfaction. She thrives on conflict and she'd like nothing more than to cry on Gil's shoulder about how mean and uncooperative we all are." How mean and uncooperative Lori was. Deceptive ploys for selfish results. Geez Louise, it was like she'd been teleported back to high school.

"What are you going to do about it?" Paige asked.

"About BethAnn?" Lori blinked at Paige. "Nothing." She'd been down this road before; not with BethAnn, but with people like her who were all about show-woman-ship but lousy on follow-through. At some point Beth-

Ann would throw up a white flag and risk the success of the entire event because she'd been too vindictive to put the town first.

As much as Lori loved the idea of Beth-Ann falling publicly on her face, this festival was too important. To everyone and to the town. "Matt, I know we had plans to check out the houses—"

"Go talk to Jason," Matt said. "We can't get started on anything until we get that budget in place anyway. I'll head to the station and see what we're dealing with there. Text me when you want to meet." He scooted out of the booth.

Lori arched a semiteasing brow in his direction. "You'll answer this time?" She flicked a smile at him. A truce maybe? Given they now had a common foe in BethAnn Bottomley, it seemed prudent to add Matt to her army of supporters.

"Cute."

Lori's heart fluttered as the smile that stretched his full lips reached his eyes. She watched him push himself out of the booth and reach down to adjust something with his leg and head to the register.

"So." Paige held up a hand as she darted

over to the next table to fill coffee cups before returning to finish their conversation. "You and Matt are back on track?"

"Matt and I are friends." Lori might need to consider getting that tattooed across her forehead at this point. "There is no track."

"Oh. Really?" Paige didn't look convinced as she glanced over her shoulder in time to notice Matt look back at Lori. "Friends is a good place to start. Kind of a boring place to end up, though."

Lori stomped on the seedling of hope taking root in her chest. "Not everything is as simple as it sounds." That she was echoing Matt's earlier sentiments scored high on Lori's irony meter. She could, of course, tell Paige the truth about what had gone wrong with her and Matt, but the last thing she wanted was for her brother to find out Matt was still married. "And while I know you're still basking in the afterglow of your wedding, not all of us are destined for your happily-ever-after."

"Why not?" Paige set the coffeepot down on her table with a clunk as she stepped closer to block Lori's leaving.

"Because we aren't all—" Lori didn't know

how to finish that sentence other than to indicate Paige's form with her hand.

"What's this?" Paige's green eyes sharpened like glass as she mimicked Lori's gesture. "Female? Breathing? Human?"

"You know what I mean." Lori turned in the booth, gripped the edge of the table and waited for Paige to shift out of the way. Which she didn't.

"I know what I think you mean, to which I will say it's a load of nonsense. You and Matt are nuts about each other. Anyone who sees the two of you together can see it, feel it. For cripes' sake we don't need the griddle on in the kitchen. I can just slap a couple of burgers on the table between you and they'll be done in a hot minute."

"Please." Lori didn't know if she liked the idea that all over the diner she'd been transmitting feelings she was trying to get rid of.

"Fear isn't a good look on you, Lori." Paige reached around Lori to stack their empty plates. "I wasted a lot of time stuck in my own way. I let fear control me. I let fear control my child and because I did, I almost missed out on a really great man, not to mention an amazing life."

"I'm not you," Lori whispered, and for the second time that morning, felt disapproval radiating off people she considered friends.

"Of course you're not me. You're also not Holly or Abby or, thank goodness, BethAnn 'The Steamroller' Bottomley. You're Lori and guess what? You're a pretty amazing person who deserves everything the rest of us do, including love." She scooped up the silverware and dirty napkins. "Everyone seems to realize that except you. That reminds me, you are coming to the barbecue next weekend, right? Starts around two. And no excuses because they won't fly."

"Hey, Paige, I'm ready to order," one of the customers called out.

She waved in acknowledgment, balanced the plates on sturdy, practiced arms and started to leave, then turned back around. "Fair warning—you even think about not showing up, I'll sic Charlie and Simon on you and make you their new project." She pointed to her daughter, who was sitting in her usual seat at the counter, skimming through her e-reader.

"You wouldn't." Lori swallowed hard. The idea of being the target of Simon's and

Charlie's legendary adolescent scheming was enough to chill her blood.

"Oh, you try me. And in the meantime, if you need help taking BethAnn down a peg or two—"

"Or twenty?"

The tension and frustration on Paige's pretty faced eased. "Or twenty. Be sure to let me know. There's little I love more than helping my friends."

CHAPTER EIGHT

"HEY, LUKE, YOU HAVE a sec?" Matt rapped his knuckles on the doorway before he poked his head into the sheriff's office. When Luke Saxon didn't answer, and instead, sat staring blankly out the window from behind his desk, Matt knocked again. "Boss?"

"Hmmm?" Luke shifted in his chair and looked at Matt as if he couldn't remember who he was. "Yeah, sorry." He cleared his throat, pushed himself up in his chair and tugged at the uniform collar. "What's going on?"

"Well, first, I'm assuming I can pass Cash back to you now?"

"Woof."

The retriever didn't wait for an invitation and padded over to Luke's chair, pushed his head under Luke's hand for a quick pat, then retreated to his plush bed in the corner with a contented sigh.

"Yeah, that's fine. Thanks for watching him." Luke tapped restless fingers on his desk. "Anything else?"

Matt glanced into the office where Fletch and Ozzy had their heads together in front of one of the computer screens. He stepped inside and closed the door. "What's going on?"

"What do you mean?" Luke asked.

"I mean Holly's acting weird and now you are, too. Is everything okay with you two? Simon okay?"

"We're fine. Simon's great. He practically took over for the tour guide at the aquarium. Now he's got it in his head he wants to be an oceanographer. Or a marine biologist. Heaven help me, I see SCUBA lessons in our future."

Matt wondered if Luke was aware of the goofy grin that appeared on his face whenever he spoke of his recently adopted stepson. "Sounds like Simon." The geeky little kid, just shy of ten now, had been blessed with a quadruple dose of brainpower compared to the rest of them. At least it sounded as if Simon had moved past his desire to be a superhero and toward something more practical. "So if everything's okay…"

"Everything's great," Luke said quickly. A little too quickly. "I'm not supposed to talk about it. Yet."

"Uh-huh." Matt took a seat on the other side of the desk and stretched out his leg. The action reminded him of a day not so long ago when he'd come to the station to claim his stolen firearm; a trip that had resulted in him becoming a deputy. "At the risk of getting in touch with my feminine side, spill."

"Holly's pregnant."

Matt watched as the shock that spread over Luke's face transformed into a combination of panic, fear and eye-twinkling excitement. "That's great. Congratulations. Right?"

"Yeah." Luke leaned his elbows on his desk and scrubbed his hands over his face. "It's great. It's amazing and…terrifying. I mean, I love being Simon's dad. Next to marrying Holly, it's the best thing that's ever happened to me, but a baby." He threw Matt such an expression of helplessness that Matt couldn't not laugh. "I don't know anything about babies."

"You'll learn." Matt chuckled as he got control of himself. Was there anything that could terrify a full-grown man more than the idea of becoming a father? "I bet Holly knows enough for both of you. She's been through this before, remember?"

"Uh-huh." Luke nodded, took a deep breath. "Yeah, I need to remember that. It's just." He looked at Matt. "This is different, you know? This is unknown. With Simon, he was already grown. I didn't have any say in how he'd turn out."

"Well, there's the first thing you're wrong about," Matt countered. "You've had a huge impact on him. You gave him that added stability only a father can. The stability you and I would have done anything for at his age." The same stability he was determined to give Kyle. As Matt said the words, as he watched the light shift on Luke's face, he realized what this was about. "We've had this conversation before, Luke. You're not him."

"You mean my father? I know that."

"Do you?" Matt challenged. "Because I'm seeing the same panic I saw when you thought about adopting Simon. There's not this invisible switch that's going to get flipped. You're nothing like him. You never have been." The fact he was sitting in the sheriff's chair should have been proof enough.

"Speaking with authority, are you?"

Matt shrugged. "My father knocked a different lesson into me." One Matt couldn't shake no matter how hard he tried or how successful he was. "And yes, I've caught myself falling into his patterns, but I pulled myself out." Because if he didn't, he wouldn't have a life worth living. "DNA doesn't determine what kind of man, what kind of fathers we'll be. Only our actions do. I've been witness to enough family expansions to know that when they put that little baby boy—or girl—into your arms, you'll finally be able to set your personal history aside. It'll be all about them."

"A girl."

There it was again, that quirky grin, and in that moment, Matt had no doubt his friend was going to be just fine. "I take it I need to keep my mouth shut about this," he teased. "I can't go run out and buy you a box of pacifiers or diapers yet?"

"We're going to tell everyone at the barbecue next weekend. You're going to be there, right?"

"Even if I hadn't already hit up Calliope for a gift for Paige, I'd make it a point to attend."

"Hang on," Luke said when Matt got to his feet. "You came in here for something."

"Oh, right. I think I might have become the unofficial deputy representative of our beautification project last night."

"Okay," Luke said. "Is this bad news?"

"Only for me," Matt admitted. "This was your and Fletcher's idea. I was just the mouthpiece last night. And I might have brought Lori Bradley on board to help cochair."

"Ah. Lori. I get it."

"Get what?" As if he had to ask.

"Not to worry, Fletch and I are happy to back you up on whatever you need. Feel free to take the lead from here on. We trust you."

"You do?" Matt wasn't so sure this was a good thing. Part of him was hoping for a little pushback even as the rest of him wished it was only him and Lori working together.

"I'm all for my deputies finding stability in their personal lives. Fletch has been taken care of. Now you, then all I'll have to worry about is Ozzy."

"I'm not taken care of," Matt argued. And given how his breakfast with Lori had gone, he wasn't sure he ever would be. "She insists we're just friends."

"Huh. The definition of *friends* must have changed in recent days. You want to use this opportunity to improve the town to win over Lori, go for it. We'll be happy to assist."

"I don't need your and Fletcher's assistance." He just needed to get his feet out of his mouth and prove to Lori once and for all that the future he wanted didn't have anything to do with his soon-to-be ex-wife and everything to do with her. "Not yet anyway. But I did want to give you a heads-up in case I need to take some time off. Not only because of this project, but there's also Kyle."

"What's going on there?"

"I'm supposed to meet with Kyle's caseworker and the judge in the next couple of weeks. There's been some discussion about him getting an early release."

"From what you've told me, Kyle's turned things around. But it's not going to be easy, taking in a fifteen-year-old with his history."

"A history the two of us are all too familiar with." Rex Winters, Kyle's father, could have given both of their fathers a run for their money. "You think I can pull it off? This parental thing?" It was, after all, Luke's idea in the first place that he take on the role of parent.

"As a friend recently told me—" Luke sat back in his chair and clasped his hands behind his head "—only our actions determine the kind of fathers we'll make. And honestly? I don't think Kyle could find a better person more suited to be his guardian. You're an honorable man, Matt. Real honor isn't something that can be beaten out of you. No matter how hard the punch."

IT WASN'T OFTEN Lori purposely postponed doing a job that needed doing. She knew those invitations should go out tomorrow morning and there wasn't any doubt she'd get them done. But every time she approached the stack on her dining room table, it was as if a tornado siren blared in her head and sent her racing for safety. It wasn't the promise of paper cuts or sore fingers stopping her; only the idea that she'd let herself get bullied into doing work she'd have been happy to tend to if she'd only been asked instead of ordered. *Respect.*

Was that really so difficult?

Which was why, as the sun was setting on

the weekend, she'd changed into her grubby gardening clothes and threw herself into all the cleanup tasks in the greenhouse she'd been putting off for weeks.

Hair twisted high on her head, a stained tank top over her worn sports bra, the too-baggy-in-the-knees and a-little-too-tight-around-the-waist jeans constant evidence of her horticultural dedication, she tumbled into the familiar peace that being among her garden and plants brought her. Evenings like this, she could lose herself for hours, puttering and planting, trimming and organizing as she inhaled the soft mingling fragrances of herbs, flowers and mossy, thin-vined trees.

Which was why she didn't hear the doorbell ring. But she did hear the echo of a knock on her side gate before Matt's voice broke through the silence.

"Lori!"

"What the—" She snapped to attention, her filthy hands freezing in the potting soil. She pulled free and stepped outside. It was dark and she shivered in the chilled air. The solar lights she'd scattered about the yard guided him to her, and as he approached, still wearing his uniform, his arms filled with an oversize paper bag, she saw him smile as he took in the scene. "What are you doing here?"

"At some point you're going to get tired of asking me that. As if that's any way to greet a guest." He set the bag on her back porch and walked right past her, eyes twinkling with curiosity. "Do you know how long I've been waiting for an invitation to see this?" He jerked his chin toward the cedar-and-glass structure her grandfather had built the summer she and Fletch had come to live with him. "You weren't kidding. It's amazing. Makes Calliope's look like a shack. You want to show me around?"

"Why?" She flexed her hands, following behind him like a buzzing bee. "Matt, it isn't a great time—"

"Would it ever be a good time?" That he asked the question so casually had her snapping her mouth shut. "If the rest of your weekend went like mine, you needed some decompression time. Do you know this town is in the middle of a runaway dog epidemic? Seven, I repeat seven, canine companions made a run for it in the last twenty-four hours and I swear they planned it together."

"You're making that up."

"I think they've started a gang. The Bark-yard Boys." He grinned. "Ask me how long it took me to come up with that."

"Most of the day, I'm sure." She would not laugh. She would not...

"And then I thought to myself, who better to decompress with than you?"

She should get bonus points for not snorting in disbelief. "Yeah, sorry I didn't text you back." Her conversation with Jason about BethAnn's change of plans had gone better than expected. With Jason at least. He'd had plenty of experience with temperamental clients and took the news in stride. "I needed to stick close to Abby to stop her from sending a pitchfork-wielding mob after BethAnn."

"Didn't appreciate her fiancé being slighted, did she?"

"She's not the only one." Lori resisted the urge to scrub her filthy hands on her jeans. "Look, Matt, I'd love to show you around, but I'm really a mess right now." She swiped a hand over her forehead.

"You are?" He turned and looked at her, and to his credit, he wore the same inter-ested, appraising expression he had during one of their so-called "dates." "You look great. Friend to friend, of course," he added with more emphasis than she thought was necessary. "You look happy."

"Plants make me happy."

"Then show me what you've been up to. Then we can have dinner and get going on those invitations BethAnn was on your case about."

Lori's brow tightened as she frowned. "How do you know I haven't already..." She trailed off, unable to resist smiling at his skeptical eye roll. "Okay, so I've been putting it off."

"I don't blame you, but knowing you, you also planned on forgoing a good amount of sleep so you can get them done. Consider me your secret weapon. After I see inside. I'm going in." He gripped either side of the door frame and leaned inside the dimly lit greenhouse. "You coming?"

She watched him disappear into her sanctuary. "Do I have a choice?" Muttering to herself, she followed. *So be it.* She was a hot, sweaty, grimy mess, but this was his choice. He'd have to take her as she was. Because that's what friends did, she reminded herself even as she longed for a shower and a change of clothes. Why didn't it bother her more that he knew her well enough to understand her aversion to the invitations?

It should irritate her. Instead, she was reminded of why she'd almost fallen for him in the first place. Because Matt Knight, despite his serious lapse in judgment where his *marriage* was concerned, really was a good guy.

"Is there anything you can't grow?" Matt asked her when she joined him by the miniature roses she'd spliced in the hopes of crossbreeding. "This is amazing, Lori. Everything's so alive. And that's saying something because I've been known to kill cacti."

"That's probably because you just leave them on their own." She retrieved a round red-tinted Hedgehog cactus from one of the wide window ledges and brought it over. "Most people think you can just set them somewhere and ignore them, give them a drink now and then. But they like attention. They like interaction. And if not the sound of someone's voice, I've found music works. Just something that proves they're alive. Add a few hours of sunshine and they're good to go."

Matt didn't respond. It wasn't until she set

the plant in front of him that she lifted her chin and found him watching her.

"You could say the same about some people."

"I suppose." Her stomach flipped with familiar longing. She loved how he listened to her, as if what she said mattered to him. As if she mattered. But she'd let herself believe that before and it had all been a lie. "You can take this one home if you'd like. Give it a try. See if you can keep it alive."

Matt didn't look convinced. He reached a tentative hand toward the tiny pink flower that had bloomed at the top. "I'd hate to see anything happen to it."

"If you see it going sideways, you can bring it back to me," Lori said. "You can also take it to the station and put it on your desk. It would probably get a kick out of the conversations you all have there."

"Well, it wouldn't need much reminding its alive, that's for sure. Okay." He seemed to have convinced himself. "I'll give it a shot. So what's this you're working on?" He strode around the African violets and pansies to her potting table. "Looks interesting."

"It's a fairy garden," Lori explained. "For

Charlie. I thought Paige and Fletcher have probably gotten a ton of wedding and house-warming gifts. Charlie should have something of her own, something for the new house. And she's been asking me to teach her to garden."

She'd had fun going through her yard, choosing various hearty herbs, succulents, and sturdy-stemmed flowers to incorporate amidst the small stone path, tiny wire garden gate and the toadstool-shaped plaster miniature house she'd found in her odds and ends. A few accented details, some thistle in the background for height and, as soon as Lori made a stop at the Wings & Things Gift Shop in town, she'd add a redheaded little fairy to the scene.

"She'll love it." Matt inclined his head. "I like how it sparkles, these glass stones you added."

"They attract butterflies," Lori explained. "Actually, I was thinking about a few different crafty things we could add to the front yards. We can hand out instructions or even maybe have a workshop at the community center if kids want to come make some. We can do butterfly feeders, butterfly baths, even dangle crystals from fishing…"

Matt stepped closer. So close. Too close. She pressed her lips closed, ducked her head as his hand brushed up her bare arm and made her shiver.

"I think that sounds like a good idea. The personal touch." His voice caressed her, soothed her, even as his presence unsettled her. She could feel the warmth of his body against the cool night. But still she refused to look up, refused to see what she feared she'd find in those beautiful, vibrant brown eyes of his. "You're always thinking, aren't you?"

"Mmmm. Sure." She shrugged. "There's always something that needs doing. Always something that—" She didn't get to finish the thought. Didn't have the strength—or maybe the will—to move as his hand slid up to cup the side of her face.

Her heart pounded so hard in her chest she thought she heard thunder rumbling through the sky. Her skin tingled, her blood warming as if lightning had struck dead center of her chest. And then his lips were on hers. Gentle, tender, as if testing her resolve; testing her determination to keep him at arm's length when all she wanted to do was wrap her own arms around him and never let go.

"I like how you're always thinking," he whispered and pressed his forehead against hers. "Smart girls are hot."

Tears prickled the back of her eyes, tightened her throat. Why did he do this to her? Make her want the one thing she knew would only hurt her in the end? Why did he let her believe in something that could never be hers? "So are men in uniform," she said before she could stop herself. "But you know what?" With more strength than she thought she possessed, she lifted her dirt-caked hands and planted them flat on his chest. She pushed herself away. "Friends don't kiss friends like that."

"No." Matt caught one of her hands before she could pull free. "No, they don't. But maybe I'm on my way to earning another chance at being something other than friends."

She wanted to. Oh, how she wanted to, but trust was the one thing she had in very short supply. It was on the tip of her tongue to utter her surrender, to throw caution aside, to unlock that part of her that only a few weeks before could have been his if only he hadn't walked away from her. But she couldn't. Not now. Not yet…

"I should finish Charlie's present." She watched as disappointment flashed across his face. Replaced almost instantly with a sad, understanding smile.

"How about I watch?"

"Quietly?"

"If you want." He released her hand and walked around to claim the high stool in the corner. He perched there, leg stretched out, and settled in as she retrieved the last items for the fairy garden.

She wasn't in the right mind frame for conversation, but as silence dropped around her she regretted the request. Matt watching her was almost as unnerving as Matt kissing her. Almost. She needed to gather her thoughts, steel her resolve and stop dwelling on the fact that a kiss from Matt Knight had done everything she'd ever dreamed it would do.

But it also broke her heart.

"I'M GOING TO run upstairs and take a quick shower," Lori told Matt a little over an hour later when she led him inside her two-story cottage.

"Okay if I reheat dinner?" he asked her as she darted through the kitchen as if in a rush to get away from him.

"Um, sure. Yeah. What are we having?"

"Vegetarian lasagna, salad and…"

"Don't say it." Lori groaned even as her eyes brightened. "Jason's famous garlic bread?"

"Don't you know it. A little Abby bird might have told me it's your favorite."

"Yeah, well, that little Abby bird has a big beak. I'm going to gain five pounds just thinking about all that butter." She pointed upstairs. "I'll be back in a few minutes. Make yourself at home. There's beer in the fridge— wine, too. Or…whatever."

"Works for me. Oh, well, hello there." Matt looked down at the snow-white cat currently curling itself around his legs. "And what's your name?"

"Winchester. Winnie for short," Lori called from down the hall. "I have a slight obsession with this TV show about ghost-hunting brothers. Thought she was a he when he first found me, but the name had already taken."

Matt set dinner on the marble countertop and bent down to pet Winnie. The cat's purr was almost as loud as a car engine. "Are you starved for attention? Doesn't she pet you?"

Winnie flopped over and stretched full out, exposing her stomach even as she aimed a demanding look at him.

"You're easier than your master. Or do you run the house?" Matt did the cat's bidding and scrubbed his hand over the soft fur until Winnie had had enough. She righted herself, blinked odd sky-blue eyes at him, and then toodled down the hall, tail high. "Guess that answers that question."

He pulled the cardboard containers out of the bag and set them in the oven to warm, hunted through the cabinets for a serving bowl for the salad, plates, and whatnots. He forewent the beer and wine and settled for coffee, which he set to brewing in the pot by the sink. As he listened to the water rush through the pipes, he did as she requested and made himself at home, beginning with a quick scan of the project schedule and pre-liminary budget she'd printed out.

Thorough organized, and proof positive he was working with the right person, he set aside any qualms or uncertainties that they could effectively complete the project in their allotted time; provided they got as many volunteers as he anticipated.

He scribbled a few notes in the margins, added a few supplies and ideas she hadn't included, nothing that would tip the budget or schedule too far, and turned to more pleasant matters and went exploring.

It hadn't only been the greenhouse Matt was always curious about, but also Lori's home itself. It was one of a half dozen homes donned storybook cottages, that with their colorful paint, oversize shutters and unique rooflines made him think of fairy tales and dollhouses.

He'd assumed, given their exteriors that the homes were minuscule on the inside, but this was actually quite spacious, with its updated kitchen, short hallways and high ceilings. Crown molding accented crisp walls in shades of white, grays and blues. He'd bet the hardwood floors were original, dating back to the houses' construction in the early seventies. Once upon a time, these houses had been tourist attractions in their own right.

The corner shelving unit in the living room

displayed a multitude of picture frames filled with smiling faces, most of whom he didn't recognize. A middle-aged, rather stoic-looking couple standing stiffly side by side in a photograph Lori had all but angled out of sight. Her parents, he guessed as their conversation in the diner yesterday hit him full force. Even in the picture, he could see a lack of parental empathy or understanding.

As opposed to an oversize frame displaying an older man, balding, in jeans and a polo shirt in front of the greenhouse Matt had only just visited. Lori's beloved grandfather no doubt. And then there was Fletcher. Her older brother, his coworker and friend. There was no mistaking that charmer as Fletch beamed into the camera in preselfie days. He must have been maybe sixteen, seventeen then? And Lori—who was tucked possessively and warmly under her big brother's arm—would have been thirteen.

He found himself smiling at the thought of a teenage Lori, her round, friendly face open and shiny beneath long, sun-streaked hair. He'd suspected her weight issues went back a ways, and while she was heavy, there was beauty. Beauty that stole the breath from his chest. Beauty he was beginning to believe she didn't realize she possessed.

He saw the weight, but it hadn't taken him more than a few minutes after meeting her before her dress size didn't matter; how could it when her heart was so big? He'd never met anyone so giving, so caring or so scared. Was it odd they'd never talked about her weight before yesterday? Had he been wrong to avoid the topic? And if he did bring it up, what did he say? Why was it even an issue? Except he could see it was. For her at least.

If it was important, surely she would have, wouldn't she? She was amazing; everyone loved her, liked her. Respected her. And yet he'd watched her at breakfast, picking through that fruit salad with little to no interest; as if eating was something to be suffered through. As if she was ashamed.

The floorboards on the second floor creaked and he realized the water had stopped. He headed back to the kitchen, but detoured into the dining room, where, as expected, he found three boxes filled with invitations and envelopes. Three big boxes.

"What on earth?" Irritation shot through him. What was she thinking handling these all on her own? And what was with BethAnn that she'd just hoisted the job onto Lori's already overburdened shoulders?

"Sorry it took so long." Lori wicked her damp hair out of her eyes before she secured it with a clip on the top of her head. "I found mud in my hair, so, well... Ah. You found my project."

"I found BethAnn's project," Matt said, and hoped he didn't sound as snippy as he felt. "Let me guess. Stuffing the envelopes would damage her manicure?"

"You sound like Abby." Lori laughed but it sounded forced to Matt. "It'll be fine. I have time."

"We have time. After dinner," he added. "I told you I'd help and I will. Why did you tell her you'd do them?"

Lori frowned, as if she hadn't really considered the question. "Because it has to get done."

"And because you never say no to anyone," Matt countered.

Lori's eyebrow arched. "I've managed to stand up for myself in a few instances. Tell me why this is any of your business? I can juggle a lot of things at once, Matt. Don't worry. I won't go back on my word to help you."

"It never crossed my mind that you would. But that's not the point. BethAnn's a bully."

"True." She slapped the lid back on the box he'd been looking through. "But why am I going to make more of a problem out of this than it has to be? I keep telling myself she must be very unhappy to act the way she does. She's stuck."

"Stuck?"

"She's not going to change, Matt. And it's not fair of us to expect her to," Lori muttered. "Plus, I think it's pretty evident she's miserable. Honestly, it's just easier to go along with her than try to fight her. As was proven yesterday, remember?"

"That was petty. Firing Jason like that."

"That's BethAnn. And is this what we're going to talk about all night? BethAnn Bottomley?"

"I sure as heck hope not." Matt shuddered and brought a familiar smile to Lori's full lips. Lips he'd finally kissed less than an hour ago. Lips he wanted to kiss again—if she ever gave him another chance. He sniffed the air. "I think the coffee's ready."

"Excellent. I can use a pick-me-up. You okay eating in the kitchen?"

"Wherever you want," he said as he followed her, his own lips curving at the sight of her superhero sweats and matching tee. Who knew Simon had a kindred spirit in the assistant hotel manager? He could smell coconut and lime, no doubt her shampoo or soap and the scent invigorated him far more than a gallon of coffee ever would.

Friends, he reminded himself. They were just friends. For now.

But he'd made progress. She'd let him a little further into her life despite her reluctance.

As far as Matt was concerned, that made tonight one of the best nights of his life.

CHAPTER NINE

LORI HAD TO ADMIT, however reluctantly, that Matt had been right. Having someone help her with the invitations not only got them done in record time, but also gave her something to concentrate on other than her irritated resentment at both BethAnn and herself for having been coerced into taking on the task in the first place.

Having a friend bring her dinner was a nice bonus. Except the more time she spent with Matt—alone—the more she had to accept she might be underestimating her friendship abilities. Being around him, talking with him, reminded her of all the things she'd secretly longed for but had convinced herself she could never have... Until she did believe. Only to be disappointed, once again.

Winnie had settled herself into a ball in one of the empty boxes on the table, occasionally batting at a scrap of paper or Lori's or Matt's hands. Matt seemed to enjoy the cat's attention and took a few minutes here and there to play with her. At least until Winnie got bored and turned her fuzzy butt on the two of them and went to sleep.

Lori grabbed the last stack of filled envelopes and thanked her sore fingers that they were almost done. But that also meant the time for small talk was over and soon, he'd leave. And Lori would be stuck with the same unanswered questions swimming around in her head. Questions she was too uncertain to ask.

Why was she so scared? Asking about his marriage, about his pending divorce—what harm would it do? She'd already put a stop to whatever had been happening between them. Or had she? Her resolve had flown the way of the dodo given what had happened between them in the greenhouse. Her head was spinning, and yes, partially in that way she'd always fantasized about, but also because she honestly didn't know how or what to predict as far as Matt was concerned.

"Told you we'd make a good team." Matt's deep voice broke through the silence in the house and her tumultuous internal debate.

He swept his arm over the table to collect the trash before straightening the completed envelopes in their boxes. "What?" he asked when he caught her looking at him.

She glanced away and plucked another label off the sheet. She paid a little too much attention to making certain it was straight. "Nothing." She was such a coward! When was she going to stop being scared of everything?

"Whatever you're thinking, it isn't nothing, Lori."

"It's none of my business." Could she sound any more cryptic? Or pathetic? "Have you spoken or seen Kyle lately?" Geez, since when was a juvenile delinquent a safer subject than Matt's past romantic life?

"He's earned video chat privileges, actually." Matt didn't look convinced that the teen was her intended topic of conversation. "I talk to him at least once a week."

"How's he doing?" She'd have to have been living under a rock for most of her life not to know the troubled boy's disturbing history. Kyle's father had been one of the nastiest people ever to inhabit Butterfly Harbor. Not just mean, but cruel, callous and, by the time he was killed last year in an explosion that had nearly taken Luke Saxon, as well, downright dangerous.

For a while it seemed as if his son was going to follow in his footsteps. Kyle Winters had been racking up arrests faster than most kids collected video games. After his father's death, Luke and Matt had both stepped up where Kyle was concerned. First thing on their agenda was to ensure Kyle owned up to and paid for his mistakes, which meant a lengthy stay in a Juvenile Detention facility.

"I don't think anyone's going to recognize him when he comes home," Matt said. "Besides letting his hair grow out, the group therapy sessions he's been in have helped him focus on other things, instead of all the negative crap. He's managing the anger. He's getting good grades in school. Last time we talked he was reading *The Count of Monte Cristo*. At his age, I think I was still reading superhero comics."

"Nothing wrong with that," Lori said, thinking of her own comic collection in the guest room. "You're still planning on taking him once he's released then?"

"I am." He seemed to hesitate. "I'm trying to adopt him. Why? Do you think it's a mistake?"

"What? No, of course not." Had she sounded otherwise? "I think adoption is great. Gives him a greater sense of stability. Not that what I think matters. It's your decision."

Matt leaned back in his chair and pinned her with a look that had her squirming in her chair. "Would it make a difference, with us? If I did change my mind about him?"

"You mean if you didn't take him in?" Lori's stomach quivered. She was running out of envelopes and excuses not to delve too deeply into any one topic. "Hypothetically, if we were still seeing each other, yes, you changing your mind would make a big difference." She could tell by the way his entire body stiffened that she'd hit a nerve. "Because you'd disappoint me, Matt. Lying to me is one thing, but breaking your word to Kyle, not giving him the home you promised him would shatter any belief I had that you're a good man. Worse, it would break whatever trust he's built up. But again, what I think doesn't matter."

"What you think matters a lot. For the record, it's never occurred to me to change my mind about Kyle. I've been where he is. There was a long period of time where I didn't have anyone to guide me or give me any sense of home."

"It hurts, doesn't it?" Her voice dropped. Her heart pounded in her chest as she voiced that which she'd only kept to herself for weeks. "Finding out someone isn't who you thought they were?" Realizing he could take her question in a variety of ways, she scrambled to explain. "That's what happened with my parents, after our brother drowned. Instead of them coming together, they disappeared into their own grief and forgot they had two other kids who still needed them." Two other kids who had lost their baby brother. "A breach like that… We felt abandoned. It's not something that can be fixed overnight. If ever." Nor could trust be fully restored with a friendly dinner and a helping hand.

Or by a kiss in a greenhouse.

She took her fear by the throat and stifled it, forced herself to look up. Where she expected to find hostility, defensiveness, or even anger on his face, she found the same Matt who had taken her out to dinner, to the

movies, danced with her at Holly's wedding
and laughed with her on a prolonged out-of-
the-way walk home. The same Matt she'd
begun to believe might just want more than
what Lori had ever been offered before.

"I'm seeing that. Now."

He did seem to understand that what he'd
broken between them couldn't be healed with
a mere apology or explanation. Progress, she
supposed.

"I'm going down to see him in a little over
a week. Maybe you'd like to come with me?"

"Why?"

"Because it might do him some good to
see a friendly, familiar face. And because
you understand him a little better than most
people."

Lori considered the idea. "I don't know
him that well. I don't know that I ever really
talked to him a lot."

"He didn't talk to anyone a lot," Matt said.
"But if he's coming home, I'd like him to
have at least a couple of people comfortable
with him. Other people he can turn to."

"You want to build him a community."

"Until he can build his own, yes."

Lori knew what it was like to be on the

outside looking in. She also knew what it was like to have people prejudge based on appearance or, in Kyle's case, reputation. "If you think I can help him, sure." She nodded. "I'd be happy to come with you."

"I'll have them add you to the list of approved visitors then. Thanks. It'll also be nice not to have to make the drive alone."

"Be still my heart, what a romantic." She surprised herself by making the joke.

"I was wrong, by the way."

"Again?" Boy, she was on a roll tonight.

"I was wrong to think not telling you about Gina was tantamount to protecting you. If I'd said something from the start, you probably would have been fine about it."

"*Fine* might be an overstatement." Lori's attempt to add levity to the suddenly weighty conversation fell flat. "I don't think most women appreciate being told the man they've been dating is married."

"Yeah." The light in his eyes dimmed. "I really screwed up with you, didn't I?"

She could let him off the hook. She could try to convince him none of it mattered and that they could move on from here, but that felt like the coward's way out. Lori was so tired of being a coward. "It hurt. To think I didn't warrant you telling me something as important as that. I felt stupid, as if I should have known even though I couldn't possibly. Nobody likes being made a fool of."

Matt didn't immediately respond, as if he was focused on choosing his words with care. "This was never about hurting you, Lori. When Gina and I got married, we were kids. She was looking to escape her situation and I'll readily admit to wanting to play hero. It's what you do when you've spent your entire life being told what a failure you are. What a failure you'll always be."

"Matt." She reached across the table, touched his arm. His voice sounded raw, as if he was scraping down to the layer of his soul he'd kept buried for too long. "You don't have to do this. Truly, it's none of my—"

"I want to tell you." He looked down at her hand. "I want you to know. There was nothing heroic in marrying Gina. Not when I got everything I wanted—a career, a purpose, and she ended up trapped. Part of me loved her. I think. I always wanted better for her, but we spent more time apart than we ever did under the same roof. But I made a promise, to stay with her. To provide for her, which I was able to do while I was in the army. Then I came back and whatever hopes I had of building a life with her, well…" He shrugged. "It was clear she never anticipated being married to an amputee who wasn't anything like the boy she'd married. She'd had enough and she left."

Lori swallowed hard. From the time he'd told her about being married she'd never really thought about the circumstances, or the reasons.

"I didn't file for divorce right away because it felt like admitting defeat. It felt like I was surrendering to failure and for whatever reason, I couldn't do it. And then I moved here and I met you and…" He shook his head. "And everything changed."

Understanding eroded her anger. "Telling me the truth meant breaking the promise you made to her." One of the reasons she liked Matt so much was because he was honorable. How honorable was it of her to judge him for not walking away from something without giving it proper thought?

"Gina's my past. A past I want to move

beyond. I'm tired of living in limbo, of not going after what I really want."

"And what is that?" Her heart slammed against her ribs.

"I want you."

Lori's head spun. It was one thing to dream about hearing those words, but what should she do with them? For her, trust was as fragile as spun glass; once it was broken there was no way to gather up all the shards. But maybe, maybe, she could put it back together in a different form.

Did he really want her? Her, Lori, with all her excess baggage. As much as she loathed the self-doubt, there was a reason she couldn't shake it. She'd spent most of her life building up a shield of protection, resisting the temptation to step foot outside anything beyond her comfort zone. Because of him, she'd done just that. Because of him, she'd gotten burned.

Again.

"I don't know what to say." Because admitting how much she cared for him felt like tossing a match on a full gas can and there was no controlling the ensuing explosion.

His gaze dropped. "You're not throwing

me out of your house so I'll take that as a win for now. I'm going to earn back your trust, Lori. I'm willing to do whatever it takes to prove to you that I care about you."

He must, otherwise why would he still be pushing the issue?

"If you don't believe anything else I've said, please know losing your trust was the last thing I ever wanted to do. I hope one day you can forgive me."

The shield around her heart cracked; she could hear it, feel it and the pulsing in her chest took on a healthier, steadier rhythm. "Okay."

"Okay, one day you might forgive me, or okay, as in I'm forgiven?"

No matter what, he could always make her smile. "Okay as in I accept your apology." His explanation, nay confession all made sense in a weird kind of way, but she didn't want to get his hopes up. She didn't want to get her hopes up even though she could feel the happiness building inside of her. "I want to ask you to promise never to lie to me again, not even by omission, because I think I understand how personally you'd take an oath like that. No." She squeezed his arm, shook her head and silently urged him not to interrupt. "Not now. We aren't there yet. Let's…start over."

"How far back are we going? Because I'd love a shot at reintroducing myself—"

"We can pick up from where we are, and where we are—" she took a deep breath and as she released it, let go of the anger and hurt she'd built up in the last few days "—is needing to get this project underway. We only have three weekends before the festival." Maybe by then she'd have enough courage to let him in. She cleared her throat and pulled her hand free. "I saw where you made some notes on the budget. I'll make the changes and get it sent over to Gil's office in the morning."

Matt arched an amused brow. "Isn't that surreptitiously telling him what your conversation with BethAnn consisted of? I thought you weren't going to tattle?"

Lori shrugged. "This isn't tattling. It's keeping him informed on a major town project as well as letting him know how his new right hand is managing things."

"Sneaky." Matt grinned. "I like it."

Yeah, so did Lori.

He put the last of the envelopes in the box

and stacked it on top of the other completed ones. "So about that fairy garden for Charlie. I take it you're bringing that with you on Sunday? To the barbecue?"

"Uh-huh." Lori hesitated, and suddenly, she heard Paige's voice in the back of her head. It was time to start pushing through the fear. "Did you maybe want to go together?"

"Lori Bradley, are you asking me out?" His eyes glowed. "This is so sudden. I don't know what to say."

"Say yes, already." She wasn't about to admit—out loud at least—how much she enjoyed his teasing. "And that's if we survive Saturday," Lori added. "It's going to be a crazy day corralling all those helpful people."

"I'll make sure to go around and pick up the sign-up sheets this week. There's bound to be some talent on those pages."

"Sounds good." She found herself nodding even as she started mentally searching her closet.

"Even better." He leaned across the table, brushed his hand over the side of her face and pressed his lips against hers. "It sounds like a date."

"YOU KNOW HOW bad news always comes in threes?" Abby stood in her office doorway at the other end of the inn's lobby, her normally open, ebullient expression obscured by what Lori could only describe as storm clouds. "First Jason loses the catering job, then we had the contractors who were supposed to get the last of the guest cabins remodeled stop showing up. Now Alyssa just called." She pressed her finger into her temple and closed her eyes. "She fell during her morning jog."

"Oh no. I hope she's okay?" Lori stood up behind the registration desk as her boss and friend's stress level exploded.

"Other than a broken leg, she's fine, thank goodness. But she's going to need surgery, which means she'll be laid up for at least the next two months. All the way through the festival." She wandered over looking a bit shell-shocked. "What else could go wrong?"

Lori bit her lip.

"What?" Abby narrowed her eyes.

"Nothing." But Lori had answered too fast. "It's just, I was going to ask if I could cut back a few hours a week so I could get a jump start on the whole project with…" She shook her head. "Never mind. I'll find a way to make it work."

"No, let's talk about this." Abby rested her chin in her hand as Lori clicked open the inn's booking calendar and employee schedule. "That project's important and not just to you. To the entire town. Besides, I want you to kick butt on those houses just so I can watch BethAnn squirm."

"Not that you hold a grudge or anything."

"Nobody disses my husband-to-be," Abby mumbled as she walked around the back of the desk to look at the calendar. "Okay, so, the good news is Alyssa was working fewer than twenty hours a week and Paige is still willing to come in for housekeeping and fill in on her off time. I'm betting with the right bottle of wine, I can convince her to up those hours."

Lori nodded. "True. It's really only weekends I'm worried about. We're doing our first clean out and prep day on Saturday—"

"We already have that covered…"

They went back and forth for a while, deciding to expand the other part-time workers up a few hours a week to cover for Alyssa.

"You know what we need?" Abby tapped

her pencil on the edge of the desk. "We need another you. Someone with a flexible schedule but who is also reliable and proactive. I don't want to hold anyone's hand."

"Can we afford to hire someone?" Lori knew the inn's operating budget had been increased ever since the buyout, but enough for another employee?

"At this point I don't think we can afford not to. Plus, I'm more concerned about getting a construction crew I can count on. I've got those cabins scheduled for rent during the festival."

"One thing at a time." Lori leaned back in her chair. "If you're serious about hiring someone, I might have an idea."

"If you say BethAnn Bottomley I'm afraid I'll have to fire you."

"Please." Lori rolled her eyes. "I was thinking of Willa O'Neill."

"Oh." Abby's eyes went wide then nodded. "That's an interesting choice. Hmmm. Willa."

"I was talking to her the other night and her mother's doing better, but money's still an issue for them. I'd be happy to train her, get her up to speed. If you agree she'd be a good fit?"

"Is she up for it? She's awfully shy."

"Shy we can work with. There aren't many people I'd trust to share my job, but Willa's one of them." Besides, the young woman needed a serious confidence booster. She made Lori look like a social butterfly by comparison. Something to urge the younger woman out of her cocoon might be just what Willa needed.

"Well, that's enough for me to give her a shot," Abby said. "Solution found. Go for it."

"What? You mean you want me to hire her?" Now it was Lori's turn to be surprised.

"If I can't trust you with something like this, who can I trust? As long as your hours are covered by someone who knows what they're doing, I'm fine with it. Besides, we both used to babysit Willa. It's not like she doesn't already know us, which is half the battle with new employees."

Lori narrowed her gaze. Abby was known for having an agreeable nature, but when it came to the inn, she was a bit territorial. "That was awfully easy. What's going on?"

"Maybe I'm just preparing myself for the

inevitable." Abby shrugged. "You can't stay here forever, Lori. You're far too talented to spend your life working as an assistant manager and I'd rather be prepared than be blindsided."

"I'm not staying? Where am I going?" What else would she do? She'd had this job since she'd finished high school; held on to it through community college then through the online school where she'd earned her management degree.

"Wherever you want to." Abby inclined her head. "I don't think you realize how excited you seem to be about this whole landscaping idea. You seem, I don't know, happier. Unless it's something else putting that smile on your face. Or maybe someone?"

"Stop it," Lori warned as Abby backed out of the room and into the dining hall. "Matt doesn't have anything to do with the smile on my face!" Except Abby was right. Matt had everything to do with it.

CHAPTER TEN

IF THERE WAS one thing the residents of Butterfly Harbor knew how to do, it was come together for a common goal.

As Lori coasted down the hill on her bike toward Monarch Lane early Saturday morning, she caught sight of a stream of neighbors and friends heading north to their targeted cul-de-sac on Hollyhock Hill. Some carried toolboxes, others had tool belts cinched around their waists; others had coolers and water bottles. They were in for an unseasonably warm day, which Lori considered both a blessing and a curse. It was good news for paint, bad news for energy levels.

Off in the distance, she could see someone waving a monarch butterfly flag as if directing everyone closer. A rumbling truck deposited an industrial Dumpster before heading back out of town. It wasn't until Lori herself was nearly on top of him that she saw the flag-bearer was Matt.

"You're getting an early start." She hopped off her bike.

"Didn't have a choice really." Matt grinned. He was out of uniform today and wore cargo shorts and a plain white T-shirt. It wasn't the first time she'd seen his prosthesis, but she couldn't recall him ever being so public about it. What she wouldn't give for a bit of that self-confidence of his. She'd been determined to be comfortable and practical for the long day ahead and had dug out an old pair of denim shorts and an oversize, loose-fitting tank. It felt good for a change, not struggling with a long skirt and bike.

"Morning, Lori, Matt," Holly called out from somewhere in the crowd. Lori shielded her eyes against the still-peaking sun and saw her friend was handing out steaming foil packets while Simon and Luke poured coffee and tossed cans of sodas. "I thought they were just handling lunch."

"Luke and I talked about it the other day and thought the promise of breakfast might entice some more people. You ready?" He tugged his baseball cap farther over his eyes and let out a sharp whistle. "Come on in. We've got breakfast sandwiches to get you going. Claim a spot and let's get to this!"

Lori pulled her bike and wagon out of the way. As she scanned the crowd, she realized it would be easier to name the people who hadn't turned out. She spotted Abby helping her grandmother out of a car before she led her to the pop-up tent the Cocoon Club was setting up as a water station. Mrs. Hastings, Paige and Fletcher's neighbor, was being escorted by Charlie from the community center across the street.

Butterfly Harbor had turned out in spades and Lori felt her heart expand.

"Morning Matt, Lori."

The deep voice of Gil Hamilton had Lori spinning around in surprise. She took in the mayor's less than professional attire. Funny. She didn't think he even owned a pair of jeans. "Morning, Gil." Lori couldn't hide her smile. "Nice of you to come."

"Well, after seeing that ambitious list of yours, how could I not?" If he meant the statement to be anything less than complimentary, he failed miserably. "I'm going to go on record and apologize for ever doubting there was support for this project." He held his hand out to Matt. "I shouldn't have let BethAnn convince me this was ambition run amok. You're doing a good thing here."

"We're doing a good thing," Lori corrected. "In fact, if you'd like to get things going—"

"No." Gil took a step to the side to let the Willingham family pass. "No, I have no claim to this at all. You and Matt do what you need to. I'm just here to help where I can."

"Good to know," Matt said. As Gil moved into the throng of residents, Matt grinned at Lori. "Who says miracles don't happen?"

"I don't even know what to do with that." Lori laughed. "You ready to rally the troops? I'll get that list from Harvey—"

"I'm not doing the rallying," Matt said, and sent an entire cluster of butterflies to fluttering in her stomach. "You are."

"Me? No." She shook her head. "I hate public speaking. You know that. The town hall was bad enough."

"You know everything on that schedule of ours backward and forward." Matt reached out and took her hand. "Besides, I spend enough time telling people what to do. Time for you to jump out of that safe zone you occupy." He wrapped an arm around her shoulders, pulled her into him and pressed his lips into her hair. "You wanted to make a difference in this town. This is your chance."

She clung to him, one arm around his waist, and absorbed the confidence and encouragement. Something shifted inside of her, something she'd never experienced before. Something that made the first insecure twenty-six years of her life fade into the distance.

"Now go."

Lori stumbled as he gently pushed her forward. She froze, her feet feeling like cement in the crunchy, dead grass. She lifted her arms to cross them around herself, to pull herself in, but she glanced over her shoulder and found Matt watching her with a glimmer of pride in his eyes.

"I think I've had this nightmare before." She knew she'd had this nightmare before, but instead of laughter, catcalls and jeers, she heard encouraging cheers. People waved water bottles and hammers in the air like protest signs at a march. By the time she found the front of the crowd—where Holly had been handing out breakfast, most of the butterflies swirling inside her had calmed down.

She cleared her throat. If only her body would make up its mind between hot and cold. She was sweating and shivering all at once. The crowd fell silent; anticipation pressed in on her. "Good morning."

"Now we know you're louder than that, Lori!" a voice called from the back.

Laughter chimed as Lori caught sight of Oscar Bedemeyer wearing the most godawful pair of overalls over his stooped, ancient figure.

Lori cleared her throat. Her ears rang. The blood pounded in her head. Only when she saw Matt circle around to stand behind Holly did she begin to relax.

"Good morning, everyone." She almost didn't recognize herself. Where she expected criticism and suspicion in the faces around her, she saw excitement and joy, along with a number of sleepy eyes drooping even under the weight of the cups of caffeine in their hands. "I don't think there are words to tell you how happy I am to see this turnout. It's truly more than Matt and I expected, so thank you." The self-doubt and nerves faded under the job that needed doing. "Our goal for the day is to get these five houses on Hollyhock Hill repainted, the new windows installed and all the old landscaping ripped out. We want a blank canvas. We also want all of these homes looking their best. Matt, Ozzy and Fletcher were out here the last couple of days to power wash the houses. So what we're looking to start with is the fun task of gutter cleaning."

From then, everything seemed to flow into a rhythm. The crowd divided themselves into teams, each under the guidance of captains that included Ozzy, Fletcher, Harvey Mills, Holly and Matt. It occurred to her at the last minute that Gil would have made a good captain, but further thought had her considering his working as part of a team was a better idea.

Within minutes, ladders were propped up on the sides of houses while hammers were pulled out to start prying old windows off the facades.

Lori pulled back, getting out of the way as the town got to work with little to no hand-holding, parents guiding their kids both in helping and staying out of the way. Simon and Charlie stood on either side of her, Simon in his new Waterman tee and Charlie in a sagging pair of purple shorts and a butterfly shirt.

"What are you going to do, Aunt Lori?" Charlie turned her freckle-kissed face up and squinted.

"First things first." She crooked her finger at the little girl and drew her over to her bike where she dug around in the attached wagon. "This is for you." She pulled out a visor she'd decorated with butterflies and plopped it on Charlie's head, reveling in the awed *oooooh*. "You wearing sunscreen?"

"Uh-huh." Charlie tugged the visor over her eyes. "Mom put on two coats. I am slathered. Thank you for this."

"Simon! Your turn." The blue baseball cap she'd found at Wings & Things reminded her of the hats Matt wore. "Sunscreen?"

Simon rolled his eyes behind thick-rimmed glasses. "Yes."

"Simon!" his mother called. "Front and center, young man! You're on weed-pulling duty!"

"It's like I get permission to destroy stuff."

Simon's eyes glittered as an evil grin spread over his face. "Now that is cool."

"Can I be your helper today?" Charlie asked with a bit more trepidation than Lori was used to. "If you need one?"

"If I need one?" Lori shot her an overrelieved expression. "Charlie, I can't tell you how happy I am to have you offer. You know what I need?" She retrieved her tablet computer and clicked open the list of tasks that needed to be accomplished by the end of the day. "You can be the official checker-offer. How does that sound?" She handed her a stylus pen.

"What do I do?"

"I've listed each address along with all the things we need to do at that particular house. As you see them being done, you just make a check mark. Like this." She marked off the gutter cleaning for the first house. "See? You can do that, right? When everything has a check mark, we're done for the day."

"Until next weekend, right?"

"Right." And the next.

It didn't take long for people to settle into their respective tasks. Rakes and shovels clanked, wheelbarrows squeaked, orders were shouted, but all the noise melded into a comforting confirmation that all their plans were coming together.

Only a few issues arose, including an exploding water hose, more than a couple of falls, and an overeager gutter cleaner who deposited a huge pile of gunk on Ozzy's head, which resulted in a water fight that left the workers on one house soaked and laughing.

Lori took out her house plans and, as the yards cleared, she could see a much-clearer vision for the plants and landscaping material she hoped to use. Luke and Fletcher were already elbow-deep in the ground, examining and replacing the watering systems. She kept an eye on Charlie while she wandered around the houses, returned to the pop-up tent where their older residents were doing their bit by handing out water bottles and granola bars.

It wasn't until she heard the sharp honk of a horn that she looked at her watch.

"Finally!" Simon groaned as he mock stumbled toward the oversize van from the Flutterby Inn. Abby and Jason hopped out, flung open the back doors and started unloading paper boxed lunches for everyone.

Lori glanced to Matt, who, from his perch

on the top of a ladder, let out another whistle and called break time. Soon after, her team of workers were scattered around the yards, digging into the sandwich lunches that included macaroni salad and fresh-baked chocolate chip cookies.

"Well?" Matt headed her way. "How are we doing so far?"

"Better than expected. Look for yourself." She took his hand and led him to the road entrance. "Two houses are already painted. The windows look great."

"They were worth the two-hour drive for pickup," Matt agreed.

"I'm thinking maybe we should add window boxes if we have time." The ideas were coming fast and furious now. "Depending on what our budget's looking like."

"You could also make up extras for people, in case they want them for their own yards and windows."

"Oh, that's an idea." She made a mental note to check out wholesale sites for the boxes.

"You two need to eat something," Abby said as she and Jason approached with extra boxes. "Lori, this is amazing so far. We can't wait to jump in."

"You're going to help?"

"Don't sound so surprised." Jason handed her a lunch. Lori couldn't help but be reminded of the surly, withdrawn man who had arrived in Butterfly Harbor earlier this year. He'd had a definite bad boy vibe about him, with a grimace-hiding beard and tired, grieving eyes. At least until Abby had gotten a hold of him. Or maybe it was finally finding a place where he belonged, a town far removed from his native New York. "Matilda's been wanting to take over the lunch shift for a while, so we're yours for the rest of the afternoon."

"You know what we could do?" Lori turned to Matt. "We could get a jump start on the next group of houses."

"Gutters and power washing?" Matt nodded. "Good idea. Jason, you good heading that up?"

"Point me where you need me."

"And give him lessons with the power washer, please," Abby added as the two men headed down the street. "He's about as good with power tools as I am with a stove."

Lori gulped.

"I'm kidding." Abby shouldered her and winked. "Kind of. Come on. Let's eat and you can fill me in on the progress."

"With the houses, right?" Lori peered into the box and her stomach growled.

"Yeah, sure." Abby grinned. "With the houses."

"NEXT WEEK WILL be when the magic happens." As the sun began to set on what had been a full day of work, Matt leaned against Jason's van and tried to take the weight off his leg. He winced against the pain arcing up his thigh, but it was a good ache. An ache of accomplishment.

"It's looking pretty magical to me already," Jason said. "And, um, sorry about…" He circled his finger at Matt's still-soaked shirt.

"I needed cooling off anyway." Matt waved as people headed off toward downtown, hopefully to stop at the diner for dinner before they went home and collapsed. "Nothing better than a bunch of sweaty, tired people, right?"

"Next Saturday it starts all over."

"We've got a jump start at least. Should go

faster." Matt had spent enough time around people to know the first round was always the most enthusiastic. They needed to keep people motivated, to remind them over the next few days that only when everything was done could they claim mission accomplished.

"You ready to head home?" Jason asked Abby as she trudged forward with Holly and a sleepy-looking Simon.

"Yep." Abby took a deep breath. "Boy and howdy, that was a full day. I never knew Lori was such a taskmaster."

"Me either." Matt couldn't help but beam with pride. He'd been hoping she'd come out of her shell at some point, but today she'd exceeded his expectations. "Speaking of, it's looking like it'll take a crowbar to get her out of here."

"Simon, go get Charlie, please." Holly tapped her son on the shoulder. "Next week you guys get Paige." She pressed her hands against her lower spine and leaned back. "I'm less exhausted working at the diner."

"You didn't overdo it, did you?" Matt asked before he remembered he was the only one who knew she was pregnant. "Um, I mean, none of you did, right?" He turned overly attentive eyes on Abby and Jason.

"No." Abby frowned and fortunately missed Holly's shocked glare in Matt's direction. "If anything us girls whipped your butts. I see the pressure washer worked well."

"And on that note—" Jason swung an arm around his fiancée's shoulders and steered her to the passenger seat. "We will see you all tomorrow at the barbecue. Fair warning, I'm doing the ribs."

"I'm thinking you'll have to fight Fletcher for that privilege," Matt called. "Sorry," he murmured as the van drove away and he was left alone with Holly. "Forgot you haven't told anyone yet."

"No, *I* haven't." Holly brushed a hand down his arm. "But I appreciate your concern. I waited tables ten hours a day, six days a week while I was pregnant with that one." She pointed a thumb at Simon, who had collapsed on the ground while Charlie stood listening to Lori and Calliope discuss something, probably something about plants. "This felt like a vacation. You're doing a good thing with Lori, Matt. I'm glad to see you two are working things out."

"Me, too." All day he'd had difficulty focusing on the work, but then he'd hear Lori laugh, or catch a glimpse of her walking by or bringing people water. Whatever trepidation she'd had at the town meeting, whatever doubts she'd been clinging to, near as he could tell, she'd banished all of them. Maybe it was time he should tell her about the hearing, about the role she was expected to play if the judge needed to speak with her.

Then again, after the day they'd had, he was probably too tired to put a coherent thought together.

As Holly wrangled Simon and Charlie for the walk home, Matt found himself once again turning his attention to Lori. She was blooming before his eyes. And he'd never, he decided as he walked to her, seen a more welcome sight. "I think it's time we called it a day."

Lori and Calliope turned at his declaration. Streetlamps buzzed to life and cast the circle of homes in a rich, warm light. In varying hues of creams and whites, with window frames and doors painted in alternate reds, blues and a rich walnut brown, they barely resembled the run-down structures that just this morning appeared to be straining to remain upright. The interiors would wait, but for now, this long-neglected section of Butterfly Harbor was on the verge of a rebirth.

"We'll be needing your truck this week," Calliope told him after she called for her sister. Stella came racing around the corner. "Beginning Wednesday I think. I should be able to have the proper plants organized by then."

"Gives me time to get the ground cover and mulch from Harvey," Lori agreed as she made notes on her tablet. She sighed, dropped her head back and took a deep breath. "I can't believe we pulled it off."

"I can," Matt announced. "Calliope? Can I give you and Stella a ride home?"

"Thank you, but we'd rather walk," Calliope said to a groaning Stella. "Unless you'd rather not stop for ice cream on the way?"

Stella perked up immediately and, after bidding Matt and Lori goodbye, hurried off ahead of her sister.

"I think I'm too tired to eat ice cream," Lori said, but the smile she gave him was one of relief. "Everyone did great today, but

I don't know that I could have done this without you."

"Of course you could have." He held out his hand and for the first time, she didn't hesitate before slipping her fingers through his. "I already put your bike and wagon in the back of my truck. I'll drive you home."

"My hero." Lori leaned her head on his shoulder. "I think I'm feeling optimistic enough to not even worry about whatever shoe might be about to drop."

"I don't even want to think about it," Matt said. "But you know what I do want to think about?"

"Mmmm. What?" She smothered a yawn behind her hand.

"Our date. Tomorrow. I was thinking maybe I'd pick you up a little early. Maybe we could go for a walk on the beach before we head over to Paige and Fletcher's?"

Her hand tightened around his. "Sure. I can make that work."

"Good. One o'clock then?"

She turned her face to his, blinked exhausted, happy eyes at him and nodded. "One o'clock."

CHAPTER ELEVEN

LORI COULDN'T REMEMBER the last time she'd slept in so late. Maybe it was that yesterday had drained nearly every drop of energy out of her, but in the best way possible. Seeing all her friends and neighbors working together for a common goal, hearing the laughter in between grunts of exertion and yelps of accomplishment had done more to elevate her mood than a year's worth of sunshine.

And today she got to celebrate with a date with Matt.

She stretched her arms over her head, let out an excited squeal before she could stop herself.

Caution, she reminded herself. She had to be more careful this time, but she just had such a good feeling about things. The past was cleared up; they were on the same track now, working together. Things were going well enough for her to move beyond dipping her toe in the romantic pool to maybe putting her whole foot in.

She rolled over, hugged her pillow and snuggled in against the thin beam of sunlight peeking through almost-closed curtains. She had the morning to herself, which gave her enough time to call the Flutterby and check in with Willa, who was working out even better than either she or Abby hoped. She planned to spend the rest of her morning in the garden and greenhouse and filling her soul with all the good things life had to offer her.

There was nothing sending clouds her way.

The second the thought passed through her mind, she wanted to kick herself. What was she doing, daring the universe to throw obstacles in her path? She wasn't normally a superstitious person, but given how much she was enjoying a drama-free few days—it helped that BethAnn had been out of town since Wednesday—she really needed to be ready for the next bump in the road. Which, given Lori's luck, would land squarely on her head.

As if reading her mind, a gentle thud hit the bed. Lori looked up as Winnie made her morning stroll up her legs and settled on her hip, barely tolerant blue eyes blinking as her "feed me now" motor revved. "Hey, baby." Lori reached out and scratched the cat between her ears and swore Winnie smiled at her. "You hungry?"

Lori's own stomach growled, but as she blinked the last of the sleep out of her eyes, the only thing on her mind right now was coffee. She stretched, dislodged Winnie and kicked herself up out of bed.

It wasn't until she was properly caffeinated, had fed the cat, showered, and fixed herself some scrambled eggs and mushrooms that she took the time to acknowledge the fluttering in her stomach was a combination of anxiety and excitement. She'd felt this way before, weeks ago, when she and Matt had first started unofficially seeing each other.

The idea of a Sunday get-together with friends wasn't new to her; she'd attended plenty of events and gatherings over the years, but she couldn't help but feel a little giddy at the prospect of arriving with someone. For once, she wouldn't have to sit on the periphery and watch her friends, and her brother, with their significant others. For once, she could be part of a…

"Not a couple," Lori said in a tone that reminded her of her mother, a thought that was enough to stifle—or maybe suffocate—the hope fluttering in Lori's chest. Her mother couldn't open her mouth other than to criticize, which was only one reason why neither she nor Fletcher had much contact with their parents. They hadn't even made time to come out for Fletcher and Paige's wedding— after Paige had spent days convincing her husband-to-be that he needed to invite them. Surely a wedding would be the perfect opportunity to heal the fractured family. He'd given in and Lori's heart had broken for all of them when they'd received the curt "we're unable to attend" reply.

"Thank goodness we had you, Grandpa." Lori missed him so much sometimes she ached. It had been nearly four years since Axel Bradley had died, and yet everywhere she looked, even though she'd redecorated the house and removed the forty-plus years of his personal touches in exchange for her own, she could still imagine Axel walking down the stairs in the morning or hear him tap his fingers three times on the door frame into the kitchen before he entered.

The familiar restlessness jangled Lori's nerves and she found herself getting to her feet and popping two slices of bread into the toaster. As the transfixing aroma of toasting sourdough wafted through the air, she pulled open the back door and, after grabbing her garden scissors, she dived into the morning-kissed flower garden bordering the house and fence line. A few minutes later, her arms filled with daisies, snapdragons, lavender and big, billowing zinnias, she returned and filled a vase, arranging and settling them into a glossy, late summer bouquet to take to Paige.

She bent over, pressed her nose up close and let the calming scent and softness erase the looming sadness that threatened to descend. A sadness she pushed away with the focused image of Matt Knight and the promise of a nice, summer day ahead spent with friends.

She glanced at the clock as the toast popped up. Ten thirty. Still plenty of time. After a thicker than necessary drizzle of

Calliope's honey, Lori took a bite and headed out to the greenhouse.

KEEPING BOTH EYES on the clock at the sheriff's station, Matt scrubbed at the residual paint spatters dotting the backs of his hands. Other than a sore back and leg, they were one of the few aftereffects of a more than successful first round of neighborhood beautification.

He'd been tempted to walk Lori into her house to make sure she didn't fall asleep on the porch, but suspected that would only lead to other temptations neither of them were ready for. He settled for waiting until her bedroom light clicked on and he could see her standing at her window. She'd lifted her hand, pressed fingers against the glass, her face illuminated by the dim glow of the bedside lamp.

"I think we are in the clear," Ozzy said with almost as much hesitation as Matt felt. Nothing like tempting fate to intervene and ruin what was left of a beautiful late summer day. After yesterday, everyone was looking forward to the relaxed, friendly atmosphere of Fletch and Abby's backyard.

But first, Matt was looking forward to some quality, non-project-related time with Lori.

"I'm going to flip the switch to forward the calls." Ozzy ducked his head and went tap-tap-tapping on his keyboard.

"Go for it." Matt couldn't remember ever willing a more uneventful day at the sheriff's station since he'd taken the job. For once, the universe seemed to be on his side and provided him and Ozzy with a nice, calm Sunday morning with nothing more than a runaway poodle, a rebellious burglar alarm and a noise complaint from Cora Dumbrowski, who was, ironically, as deaf as a post. By the time Matt got back from her house and logged in his four-sentence report, it was almost twelve thirty.

"There's not a weekend that goes by that I don't thank Luke for getting a hold of that computer program." Matt collected his cell phone, grabbed his jacket and powered down his desktop. When Ozzy wasn't looking, he bent down and whispered a goodbye to the cactus Lori had talked him into fostering. "See you at Fletch and Abby's later, right?"

"Yep. You, uh, bringing a date?" Ozzy asked a little too innocently.

"Maybe." Matt grinned. "Why? Am I wearing a sign?"

"No. But every time the phone rang this morning you looked as if you wanted to strangle it. And not because you're looking forward to Fletch's inaugural grillfest." Even from across the room Matt heard Ozzy's stomach growl. "I ran an extra mile this morning so I could enjoy Jason's famous ribs."

"Pork is a great motivator," Matt agreed. Things were looking up for all of them. Now if he could only speed up time and get through Kyle's hearing without having to bring Lori into the situation, he could call them perfect. "You okay to lock up?"

"Go on already. You're driving me nuts. Say hi to Lori for me."

"You can say hi yourself later." Before his fellow deputy changed his mind—or found something Matt had forgotten to take care of, he was on his way to his car. He had just enough time to get home, shower and change. Maybe.

He'd just parked in his driveway and was making his way up the brick path to his front door when his phone rang. Key in hand, he pulled out his phone, half expecting to hear Ozzy on the other end prank calling him with a fake emergency. Which is why he didn't pay any attention to the caller ID when he answered. "You'd better not be playing me, buddy."

There wasn't a response. He pushed inside the front door and frowned when silence greeted him on the other end. "Hello?"

He heard a catch of breath, a humming of sorts. Matt clicked on the hall light even as a prickle of unease crept under his collar.

"Matt."

Matt's blood went cold at the familiar, ghostly voice. "Hack? Is that you?" For an instant he was back in Iraq, lying on the side of the road, ears ringing against the barrage of explosions and the death rattle screams of his friends and fellow soldiers. He leaned his free hand against the wall for balance. "Hacksaw?"

"Yeah, it's me. I'm sorry to call out of the blue." Hack's voice trailed off and Matt wished he could reach out and grab hold of her.

"Where are you? Are you okay?" Of course

Hack wasn't okay. Hack hadn't been okay for a very long time.

"I'm, um, in this little town near you. Durante, I think? I—there was an accident. I'm at the sheriff's station. My car's totaled and, God, Matt, I'm sorry. I don't have anyone else to call."

"You did the right thing." Matt headed back to his car. "You stay where you are, okay? I'm coming to get you. Hack?" He stopped long enough to force himself to breathe. "You sober?"

"Eighteen months, six days, and...seven hours."

"Good. Good, okay." One less thing to worry about.

"I'm sorry, Matt."

"You never have to apologize to me, Hack. For anything." He slid into his car and started the engine. "Hang tough. I'm on my way."

THE TICK-TICK-TICKING of the wall clock in the kitchen may as well have been a brass band with the way it echoed in Lori's head.

She'd forced herself to wait until noon before she'd gotten changed, before she'd spent over twenty minutes staring into a closet filled with clothes that weren't going to magically change size, or suddenly help her lose thirty or forty pounds. Her hair wouldn't cooperate, but she was patient. No need to be so picky. She just needed to be comfortable, which she would be in the peach-and-white-striped maxi dress she pulled on over a white tee.

By twelve fifty, she set her purse by the door.

At twelve fifty-five, she wiped off the counters, refilled the cat's food bowl and sat down at the table to wait.

The knots in her stomach had knots. Knots of anticipation. Knots of fear. Knots of excitement. But those she managed to untie, at least for a little while. Until the clock continued to tick.

And no knock sounded on the door.

One ten. One twenty. One…thirty.

Lori pressed her glossed lips together. He was a deputy. Chances were he got caught up at work and couldn't call. Or maybe she'd gotten the time wrong?

Doubt crept in, stealthy, its sharp talons digging into her heart as it did its best to grab hold and override reason. She was overreacting. Matt was probably just running late. Except Matt was never late. One of those military hangover issues he joked about. If he wasn't fifteen minutes early, he was running behind.

She picked up her cell and checked it. Nothing since the last time she'd looked. No text. No voice mail. No missed call. Her fingers trembled as she dialed his number and waited as it went to voice mail.

"Hey, Matt. It's, um, Lori." Her stomach churned as she struggled to find words that wouldn't make her sound pathetic. "Just checking in. Hope everything's okay with you and I'll, well, I guess I'll see you at Paige and Fletcher's."

She clicked off, then, before she thought better of it, she called the station. The message requested she key in a code to forward her call to one of their on-call deputies. She didn't enter it.

Lori went into the living room, looked out the bay window into the street where she saw the same neighbors' cars she'd seen all morning. No sign of Matt's truck. No sign of Matt.

Nausea churned in her stomach.

She'd been stood up.

Memories of another day that stretched to another evening, another night threatened to wash over her, but she shook her head, refusing to let what had devastated her then overwhelm her now. She was being ridiculous. Life happens. Plans change and, well, maybe the prospects of spending an afternoon with her hadn't been as appealing as it had been last night.

Still, she deserved a phone call at least. Didn't she?

She squished her toes in the blister-inducing shoes she'd been saving for a special occasion. An occasion where she hadn't planned to walk much, but it looked as if she was going to be walking after all. Sitting home, waiting for the bell to ring, putting her life on hold all because of some guy—she'd done that in high school and it had ended in disaster.

She wasn't going to do it again.

Lori hurried upstairs, changed her shoes, redid her hair so it was up off her neck and readjusted her plans as she retrieved her bike from the side yard. She hooked the smaller wagon to the back as she did when she didn't feel like walking and stashed her bag along with Charlie's gift and Paige's flowers inside.

A few minutes later she was peddling down the street, and cursing herself for once again, letting hope guide her to disappointment.

MATT HAD TO circle the block twice to find a parking space near the sheriff's station in Durante. It wasn't until he high-stepped it down the street past a real estate office, coffee shop and fitness club and pushed through the double glass doors, that he began to breathe again. But only barely. His mind felt cloudy, stuffed, as if he'd been caught in a spinning sandstorm back in Iraq.

"Matt." Sheriff Sean Brodie headed down the dingy gray hall toward him, not surprisingly out of uniform as it was his normal day off. Tall, but still a good three inches shorter than Matt, Brodie was one of those cops who would have looked right at home at the O.K. Corral slinging his six-shooter with Wyatt Earp and Doc Holliday.

The neighboring town's sheriff was someone Matt considered an "unknown quantity." He hadn't put Brodie firmly in either the friend or enemy column as he didn't personally have any real beef with the man. That said, Matt knew plenty who did. Sean Brodie had grown up in Butterfly Harbor, palled around with Gil Hamilton, which hadn't earned him many points. The fact he'd been angling for Luke Saxon's job not so long ago didn't work in his favor. Still, near as Matt could tell, Brodie was a straight shooter who got the job done.

"You made pretty good time," Brodie said as he waved him back.

"Might have pushed a few speed limits along the way." Matt returned the offered handshake. He kept his voice even and friendly in case things with Hack weren't as cut and dried as she'd been led to believe. "How's Hack, er, Kendall?" After all these years, he still had trouble remembering to use the former grunt's real name.

"Doing okay, all things considered. Looked exhausted so I put her in one of the cells. Door's open," he added with a quick lift of his hand when Matt jumped to conclusions. "No need to lock her up. Accident wasn't her fault, but it sure looks like it took the wind out of her sails."

Hack's sails had been ripped apart years ago, but that wasn't his story to tell. "Good to know."

"Didn't realize until she hung up she's a friend of yours."

"We served together. Iraq," Matt clarified in case Brodie wasn't aware of his service. "She's had a rough go of things for a while." Until he'd heard her voice, part of him had wondered if she was dead. "She said her car's a loss?"

"Totaled, unfortunately. A couple of kids out for a joyride plowed through a red light and jackknifed her. It's a miracle she wasn't hurt. Kids' parents are going to take care of things, but she couldn't give me a number for a mobile."

"She hates those things," Matt said. Again, not his story to tell. "You can call me. Can I see her?"

"Yeah, of course. I had one of my deputies clean out her car. Wasn't much in it other than a duffel and some odds and ends. From the paperwork inside she hasn't had it very long."

"She's moved around a lot." Matt walked beside Brodie toward the holding cells. As homey and small as Butterfly Harbor's station was, nestled in the comforting roots of ancient redwoods and cypress trees, the Durante station was as sharp as glass. Angles, stained linoleum polished to a blinding glare, and walls that echoed.

"She must be a good friend if you came right out."

"One of the best I've ever had." He caught a glimpse of the sign to the cells and stopped. "She's not in a great frame of mind as you probably saw, so if you're thinking—"

"Not thinking anything of the kind." Brodie surprised Matt by not looking offended. "Just confirming she'll have someone looking after her. She looks…lost."

"*Lost* is as apt a word as any," Matt agreed. "Anything she needs to take care of before I get her out of here?"

"She's good to go. But before you leave, I heard about the project you're heading up over in the Harbor."

"You did?" Matt asked.

"Met Gil for drinks last night. He was boasting about what a great job everyone did, especially you and your partner, Lori."

"He did?" Was he hearing things? "I have to admit I was surprised to see him turn up to help. This wasn't a project he was eager to get behind."

"Man's got a lot on his plate," Brodie said. "Sometimes he loses perspective."

"Then he needs to find it again. After those break-ins, those homes became a liability. They attract problems. Monarch Lane was in a similar situation not so long ago, but once Luke started pushing to have windows replaced, facades repainted, there was a significant drop in vagrancies and vandalism." It also helped that people had started caring again. "I wouldn't be surprised if his reaction had more to do with who's pointing out the problems than his being asked to help fund the solutions."

"Gil doesn't tend to see things from a law enforcement perspective," Brodie agreed. "You know he thinks most of what has gone wrong with the Harbor is his family's fault. His father's fault. He takes everything that happens there, especially things that go wrong, personally."

Matt gave that some thought. Something he hadn't considered and it also explained a lot about Gil's behavior. "Savior complex then?"

"I don't think that's it." Brodie shook his

head. "It's the show he puts on, but honestly? I'm with you. He needs to find a more tactful way to do things." Brodie shrugged. "Not that it's any of my business. Personally, you're on the right track. You start bringing people back, you start selling those homes— it can only be good for surrounding areas, too. You need any extra hands, you put out the call. We've got your back."

"Neighbors helping neighbors, huh?" Now that was something he hadn't considered until now. "Consider the call made. We plan to start up at eight sharp next Saturday." He shook his hand again and, after Brodie strode back down the hall, Matt took a deep breath. He pushed open the door. "Hack?"

"Yeah." He heard the distinctive sniff of tears and steeled himself to ignore them. "I'm here."

The last thing Kendall "Hacksaw" Davidson would ever want from him—from anyone—was sympathy. But that's exactly what struck him when he walked down to her cell. There she sat, on the metal cot, a wadded-up blanket by her side. Her white tee was spattered with blood. A trio of butterfly bandages almost covered an ugly gash across her left cheek. Her long black hair hung limply around her shoulders, but it was her eyes—and the lack of life in them—that hit him straight in the gut.

"Thanks for coming." Her voice was so soft, almost imperceptible. Had he not been looking at her, had he not seen shadows of the woman he'd served with behind the haunted, ghostly expression, he never would have believed this was the woman who had served beside him with more courage and spirit than most of the men.

"We made a promise." He stopped just outside the cell, forced himself to keep as casual a stance as possible. Hack had been as skittish as a colt for a while now. He'd learned not to push, not to come in too hard. "You call, I'm there. No questions. And vice versa, remember?"

"As if you'd ever deign to call me." A slight smile curved her thin lips. She leaned against the brick wall, rested her booted foot on the edge of the bed. All she needed to complete the picture was a tarnished harmonica and a tin tray of food. "You don't need me, Matt. You don't need anyone."

If she only knew how wrong she was. "I always need my friends."

It should hurt to look at her, to be reminded that they had been part of an amazing group of dedicated soldiers who could fight and celebrate in equal measure. Men and women who had put everything—their lives, their very souls—into serving their country. Seeing her now, it was all he could do to keep the ghostly screams of their friends at bay. "You ready to go?"

"You can just drop me at the bus station." She shoved to her feet, picked up the duffel the sheriff had found in her car and slung it over her shoulder.

"No can do," Matt said. "Besides, sheriff could have done that. You're coming home with me."

"You don't want to do that," she said with something akin to fear in her eyes. "Matt, honestly, I just wanted to see you again, for a few minutes. To know you're okay. That you're doing well. You look…" She sagged against the bars. "You look really good. You look happy."

"I am happy." He shrugged. "Got myself a great job, good friends. I found a house that's too big for me. And I met this amazing woman…" His stomach dropped to his toes. "Oh no." He looked at his watch. It was after two. "Oh man, I did not do this. I did not forget her."

"What's wrong?"

"I need to get back. I need to call…" He swore as he patted his pocket. "My phone's in the car. Let's go."

"What's her name?" Kendall called as she hurried after him.

"Lori." Even as he said her name he couldn't breathe. How could he have forgotten? "Lori Bradley. I work with her brother."

"Sounds cozy. Just how many cops are in this town of yours?"

"Enough to keep even you out of trouble." Matt fell into the familiar banter as easily as slipping into a pool. They could beat around the bush with small talk for endless hours, and for now, he was grateful for it.

"Matt, I meant it when I said just leave me at the station—"

"I'm not leaving you anywhere," Matt said in a tone that had Kendall snapping her mouth shut like a cuttlefish. He tried not to run back to the truck even though it was all he wanted to do. "Your first instinct was to call me and I swore, if and when I heard from you again, I'd be there. Get over it. You're coming to Butterfly Harbor with me."

CHAPTER TWELVE

"AUNT LORI, IS THIS really for me?"

If Lori needed a remedy for her wounded pride, all she had to do was look into Charlie's bright green eyes to be healed.

"It is." Lori handed the oversize pot to the little girl even as her cell buzzed for the fifth time in the last half hour. Irritated, and feeling more than a little petulant, she ignored it. "You told me you wanted to start learning about plants, so consider this your starter kit." From the back of the wagon, she retrieved the blue-and-green tool caddy, loaded up with all the items a beginning gardener would need. Charlie wobbled her way to the barren area in the back of the yard and set it in the dirt.

"Thank you, thank you!" Charlie squealed as Lori handed her the new tools. She plucked them out, one at a time, and set them on the ground around her to examine.

Lori glanced around, caught Paige's curious expression as her sister-in-law approached.

"I thought you were coming with Matt."

"So did I." She looked away before Paige could read her expression. "Change of plans."

"This is amazing! Mom, look what Aunt Lori gave me!" Charlie called. "It has colored rocks like the books say you need to attract butterflies!"

"That's really lovely of you, Lori." Paige slipped her arm around Lori's waist and hugged her. "You're so good to my little girl."

"Your little girl deserves it." Seeing Charlie's excitement was all the thanks she needed. Truth was, most kids made her nervous. They always had, even when she'd been one. They were unpredictable, and at times, unkind. She never knew what was going to come out of their mouths and she always felt as if she was bracing herself for a fight. But spending as much time as she had with Charlie and Simon recently, she was beginning to develop an affinity for children. Well, some children at least.

Being around whispering kids and judgmental teens had helped Lori develop both a thick skin and a quick tongue. Matt had thought her sense of humor bordered on insulting, but for Lori, it was an all too important defense mechanism. One she would be more than happy to surrender.

"Was I supposed to bring something for dinner?" Lori asked as she saw Holly and Luke stride through the back gate with an oversize picnic basket in Luke's hand. What else was there to bring? The tables were piled with salads, side dishes, slow cookers and every kind of hot dog ever made.

"Absolutely not," Paige assured her. "You brought yourself and that's all that was required. Besides, I'm kind of hoping to pick your brain over the next few weeks about how to pretty this place up." She reached up and tightened her ponytail. "You did superb things with the front yard, but I'm afraid I'm at a loss of what to do with all this."

Lori had the exact opposite problem. She looked around the expansive property and could imagine explosions of color interspersed with paving stones, dusty moss eking around the edges as clusters of violets, thistles and lavender entwined to fill the bare space.

"I can come up with some ideas for you. Who are you going to hire to do the planting?"

"You."

"What? Me? But… I'm not a landscaper. And you want a professional."

"I want you to do it. We can talk about pricing later, and I'll be keeping an eye on what you do with those homes on Hollyhock Hill. I just know I want it to be butterfly friendly so that one will stay occupied." She pointed to Charlie, who had plucked the tiny fairy out of her spot and was hiding her in the sprigs of rosemary.

"Hi, Paige. Hey, Lori!" Simon raced past them as he pushed his thick glasses higher up his nose. "Mom and Dad brought lots of stuff. Blackberry pie, too."

"Oh, yum." Paige let out a moan that Lori completely understood. "We're going to have a full house, so I'm off to find a couple more tables. Fletch left some in the garage back there. Keep an eye on them for me?" She pointed to the terrible two kneeling in the dirt.

"Happy to." And Lori was surprised to find she meant it.

"YOU'RE DOING THIS to punish me, aren't you?" Kendall sagged in the passenger seat of Matt's truck and pouted harder than eight-year-old Charlie after losing at poker.

"Yeah, that's right." Matt unhooked his belt and shoved open his door. "I'm bringing you to my friends' housewarming to punish you."

Kendall looked out at the Tudor cottage with the stained glass monarch butterfly window over the front door. "I'll just wait here."

"And the second I disappear you'll hotwire this thing and take off to who knows where." He leaned back in, gripped the steering wheel and glared at her. "You have a head injury, you're exhausted and I'd bet half my year's salary you haven't eaten anything other than convenience store food in weeks. I'm not letting you out of my sight until I'm sure you can stand on your own two feet for more than thirty seconds at a time."

"You've gotten bossy," Kendall grumbled, but she pushed open her door and dropped to the ground. She picked up her bag and dug around inside and pulled out a black T-shirt. "You weren't this bossy in the desert."

"No, but you were. You're going to change out here in the open?"

Kendall blinked, as if his words didn't make sense. "Would you prefer I join the party in a shirt covered in blood? I don't think that's the atmosphere they're going for."

"Fine." He closed his door and took his time circling around the back of his truck. What he wouldn't give for that shower and a change of clothes, but the only thing he was thinking about right now was finding Lori. "There's going to be alcohol."

Kendall shrugged as she tugged her shirt over the sagging waistband of her pants. She'd always been thin, but since he'd seen her last, she'd turned skeletal. "Figured. It'll be fine. Stop worrying about me so much. I'm just along for the ride. Give me a chair and some potato salad and all is good with the world."

"You could do with a vat of the stuff." As if anything could ever make Kendall's world good again. Matt could hear the muted music and celebrators in full revelry well before they reached the back gate. "I know how hard this is for you," Matt said when he gripped the gate latch. "Being around people."

"Good. Then you know you'll owe me down the line. Let's go, Superstar. The sooner we get this over with the better."

Never before had Matt been quite so grateful for a large crowd. It wasn't yesterday on Hollyhock Hill packed, but just about everyone he was on a first name basis with was in attendance, including the former sheriff; Mrs. Hastings, Fletcher and Paige's across-the-street neighbor; along with Willa O'Neill and her mother and siblings.

"It's like walking into a Stepford community," Kendall muttered under her breath. "I've only seen scenes like this on those cheesy TV movies."

Matt grinned. He could see where she'd say that. With the lush lawn and a NASA inspired grill currently entertaining most of the men in attendance, this was indeed the very personification of suburban perfection.

"Matt. About time you got here!" Fletcher broke ranks and pushed through his friends. His welcoming expression shifted to one of suspicion when he caught sight of Kendall. "You, ah, brought a friend, I see."

"Hope you don't mind," Matt said even as he scanned the yard for Lori. He swore he could hear her, but he had yet to set eyes on her. "Hacksaw Davidson. Sorry, Kendall." He cringed. "Old habits. We served together over in Iraq."

Fletcher's hostility faded, but not completely. He offered his hand. "Fletcher Bradley. Welcome."

"Thanks. Appreciate the invite." She shoved her hands in her pockets and rocked back on her heels after returning the greeting. "Matt here rode to my rescue, which is why he's late. Car accident." She jerked her head in a way that accentuated the cut on her face. "Superstar's always reliable in a crisis. You're Lori's brother, right?"

Fletcher's eyebrows almost disappeared under the too-long hair. "Yes, I am. You know about Lori?"

"Only what I've spent the last hour or so hearing. I'm looking forward to meeting her, but I think that'll have to wait until Superstar here apologizes for standing her up."

"Standing her…up." Fletcher's face went blank as he looked at Matt. "Tell me you didn't."

"I wish I could." At first he thought Fletcher was having a laugh, but there was nothing remotely humorous in Lori's brother's expression. "Suffice it to say I screwed up again. Where is she?"

Fletcher took a long drink of beer, longer than Matt thought necessary, as he almost withered under Fletch's stare. "She's over there." He indicated the back part of the yard. "Charlie and Simon talked her into a game of water cannons. Ozzy's backup. Feel free to make yourself a target."

Matt frowned. He'd never seen Fletcher in quite this mood before. "Fletch—"

"Don't apologize to me," Fletcher snapped. "And be ready to drop to both knees where Lori's concerned." He moved in, and for an instant, Matt wondered if he was about to get punched. "Remember what I told you the other night? She's got wounds that never really healed. Lucky you, you just reopened one of the biggest she has. Fix it. Or walk away. Kendall? Or do you prefer Hack?"

"Either's fine." Kendall shrugged.

"What can I get you to drink, Kendall?" Fletcher asked.

Matt purposely didn't look at her, knowing if he did she'd take it as a lack of faith in her still-fragile sobriety.

"Don't suppose you have any lemonade?"

"It just so happens we do. Paige!" Fletch bellowed as he stepped back for Kendall to join the party. "One lemonade please. And a quick checkup if you don't mind."

"A quick…what?" Kendall spun a full circle, panicked eyes landing on Matt as Fletcher grabbed Kendall's arm and guided her to one of the picnic tables.

"Paige is a nurse," Matt explained as his friend was pushed onto a bench and pinned with a look that would have made any big brother proud. "Relax. She won't hurt you. Much."

Matt circled the party, stopping when needed to say hello or grab something to drink. He tried to ignore his growling stomach as the aroma of smoking meat and roasting onions and peppers permeated the air.

"Ah-ha!" Charlie jumped out from around the corner of the house, water cannon aimed high, wide eyes alight with excitement. "Ooops." Her hand flicked off the trigger at the last second. "Sorry, Deputy Matt."

"No problem." He dropped a hand on her head. "Where's your aunt?"

"Aunt Lori!" Charlie yelled as she dived

out of sight again, then screamed as Simon let out a cackle of comic book villain proportions. "No fair! Awww, man! I'm soaked again!"

Matt poked his head around the corner and found Ozzy had pinned Lori in the corner of the fence line. Both were drenched from head to toe. Lori's lashes were spiked, water dripped off her hair, off her nose, and the laughter erupting from her was almost enough to make him forget what he'd done.

Almost. He knew the instant she spotted him. Her arms went lax and she dropped her water cannon. "Matt." She drew her free hand across her mouth and sputtered as Ozzy took aim. "I'm out."

"Double darn." Ozzy backed off, hoisted his cannon over his shoulder and headed toward Matt. "Whatever you did, I'm glad I'm not you. Charlie, Simon, we need to find another fourth."

"I bet my dad will do it!" Simon yelled. "Dad!"

Suddenly Matt and Lori were alone. "I'm sorry." How many times was he going to have to say those words to her?

She stared at him. The only reason he

knew she was still alive was that he could see her breathing. And that her hand clenched into a fist.

"I—something came up and I—I should have called. I tried to once I—"

"Once you remembered?" She pushed her damp hair off her face. "Nice." She started toward him, but he soon realized she didn't have any intention of stopping.

He reached out and caught her arm. "Lori, please."

"I really, really don't want to get into this with you here," she said in too calm a voice.

"A friend called, someone I promised to help. Someone I had to help. She—"

"She?" Lori wrenched her arm free. "She. Of course it's a she." He'd never seen her so angry before. So hurt. "Why wouldn't history repeat itself?"

"I don't understand." Matt glanced over his shoulder to where Fletcher stood watching them with what Matt could only define as a dead-man stare. "What history? I didn't do this on purpose, Lori. I...okay, I got tunnel vision and forgot. What else should I have done?"

"Nothing. Nothing, Matt. This is my issue,

not yours. I don't have the…" She looked at him as if he could find the words for her. "I can't keep doing this." Was she talking to herself or to him? "I can't keep getting my hopes up only to be disappointed. It's a roller coaster." She looked at him, resignation on her face. "And I hate roller coasters."

"Meaning what? We're back to being friends? No discussion?"

"Meaning I don't like what this is turning me into. I'm starting to sound like a jealous needy shrew."

"There's nothing to be jealous of." Not that he didn't like the idea she cared enough to be jealous. "Hack, I mean Kendall, she's a friend, Lori. That's all she's ever been. I couldn't say no when she called. I made a promise."

"I have no doubt. That's what you do best. It's who you are. But how do you think I feel knowing you forgot all about me when she did call?" The hostility faded from her face. "It's okay, Matt. Really. It's best we take this as another sign we really aren't meant to be anything more than friends."

"I refuse to believe that." But he could feel her slipping away from him; she was closing that door he'd worked so hard to reopen. "Please, let's talk this out."

"Talk about what? How I stood at my living room window, counting the minutes like a pathetic teenager waiting on her prom date? I called the station. I called your cell…"

"I had it on vibrate. I didn't hear it."

"Wow. Okay. I guess that changes everything." She turned her face away, but not before he saw tears spring into her eyes. "I should be grateful this time around didn't come with a public humiliation follow-up."

"What are you talking about?" Public humiliation follow-up? What was he missing here? "I got here as fast as I could so I could explain, so I could apologize."

"I appreciate that. You're a really good guy, Matt, but it's time for me to admit I'm not relationship material."

Was he really getting the "it's not you, it's me" spiel? "Look, this doesn't warrant this big an overreaction. Let's just go somewhere and—"

She jerked as if he'd slapped her. In the next seconds her eyes cleared, the color in her cheeks drained and she pulled herself together. "You know what? You're right. I am overreacting. Which is further evidence we need to put a stop to this before it goes too far. Apology accepted, Matt. No hard feelings. Now if you'll excuse me, I'd like to get something to drink and enjoy the rest of the party." She shoved the water cannon into his hands and walked away.

How could Lori feel as if the rug had been pulled out from under her when she'd been the one doing the pulling?

It had been three days since she'd stomped on the brakes with Matt. For the second time. In those three days she'd thrown herself into the landscaping project and found completely useless aspects of her job to train Willa on. Three days with not one text or phone call from Matt.

"What did you expect?" Gathering her purse and sweater from behind the registration desk at the Flutterby, Lori once again told herself she'd done the right thing. Except she'd done it for the wrong reason. She'd broken things off with Matt not because he'd hurt her by not calling. But because she'd gotten scared, because her feelings were getting too real, and in her experience, real only led to heartache.

Except her heart still ached anyway. She dropped her things on the desk and sat back down, rubbed a shaking hand against her chest. She missed him. More than she expected. More than she should.

More than she wanted to.

The tension between her and Matt hadn't gone unnoticed by their friends. Without even knowing the situation, Fletcher had taken her side, which from what Lori had heard, meant they weren't getting along at work. Holly and Abby had both ambushed her at her house last night with a gallon of Rocky Road and three very large spoons to quietly demand she talk to them. She'd sent them and the ice cream away after insisting she was fine.

She wasn't fine. She was bordering on pathetic and it was beginning to tick her off. What relationships didn't have their issues? Who cut a man off the way she had while he was trying to apologize, while he was admitting to being in the wrong? Wasn't that some kind of relationship felony? She rested her head in her hands and took slow, deep breaths. What on earth was the matter with her?

Matt was a good guy who'd made a mistake. A mistake she hadn't let him completely explain. How was he to know everything he'd done that day was the stuff her teenage nightmares had been made of. She hadn't told him anything; she'd never talked about it, not even with Fletcher, who, along with Abby, had witnessed the fallout firsthand. What had she done?

Tears prickled the backs of her eyes. Why couldn't she just let herself trust? Just a little?

The front door popped open. A cool breeze washed in along with the thin, dark-haired woman she recognized from the barbecue. She wore all black, from her tight ponytail to the loose black tee, sagging cargo pants all the way to the sturdy work boots on her feet. She was down to one bandage on her cheek, hadn't made any effort to cover the scarring on the other side of her neck. The shadows under her eyes were even more pronounced than Lori remembered. Matt's *friend*. Kendall something?

"Welcome to the Flutterby Inn." Lori

winced as her voice cracked. Way to show confidence. "You're, ah…"

"Kendall Davidson. We weren't properly introduced the other day." She approached with her hand out. "You and I need to talk."

Lori straightened to her full height, not realizing it was a subconscious intimidation tactic until Kendall inched her chin up and arched a brow. "Do we? About what?"

"About you dumping the best guy on the planet." She released Lori's hand, jerked a finger toward the coffee urn on the side table. "That fresh?"

"Yes." Lori blinked. She supposed there was something refreshing about a woman who said exactly what was on her mind. "Help yourself."

"Great. Thanks." She filled a cup to the brim, didn't bother with cream or sugar and sipped. The sigh that escaped her lips had Lori smiling against her will. "Shall we sit?" She pointed to the pair of teal-and-gold upholstered wingback chairs by the bay window. "One thing I've noticed about your town. Every view is spectacular. But that might be the best." She pointed to the crashing waves rollicking against the rocks at the base of the cliff. "Postcard material for sure."

"It's why we put it on the brochures." Lori walked around the desk and sat on the chair across from her. The way Kendall settled into the cushions, crossed her legs and peered at Lori over the edge of her cup made Lori wonder if she'd taken an odd combination of etiquette and self-defense classes. "I didn't dump Matt."

"Given the way he's been sulking around his house the last couple of days, I beg to differ. Do you know who I am?"

"The friend of the best guy on the planet?" Matt was sulking? Over her?

Kendall smirked and shifted her gaze to the window, to the ocean, and for an instant, Lori suspected she drifted to someplace else. "We served together. In Iraq. Three tours. We bonded instantly. Can't explain it. There's just something…steady about him, you know?"

Lori nodded. She did know. Although where Matt didn't seem particularly haunted by his military service, Kendall looked as if she'd brought back a planeload of ghosts.

"He ever tell you how he lost his leg?"

"An IED explosion." Lori folded her hands

in her lap. "I didn't ask for details. I wasn't sure how to." She didn't think he wanted to talk about it.

"You could have." Kendall smirked. "Knowing Matt he would have shrugged it off with a joke. The attack took out our entire convoy. Except him and me." She drank more coffee as her eyes took on that distant haze. "Eight of our friends, gone." She snapped her fingers. "Like that."

Lori didn't have any frame of reference other than horror, sympathy and admiration for what soldiers went through. Any words she might have uttered seemed completely useless.

"Our caravan was hit by mortar fire. Flipped our vehicle. I was caught inside. Could feel the flames licking my face." She brushed fingers against her scarred cheek. "My clothes caught fire. Figured that was it. Next thing I knew Matt was dragging me out. He got us to cover, but not before an insurgent shot him seven times. Three bullets went in his leg. Nearly severed it then and there. Next thing I know, we're being evac'ed to different hospitals, him stateside and me to a military base in Germany. Third-degree burns over eighty percent of my torso. Needless to say I no longer wear bikinis. You can laugh," Kendall said. "It was meant to be funny."

Lori wasn't sure she could.

"Matt came to get me in Durante because he'd made a promise," Kendall said. "I bet you know him well enough by now there's very little he takes more seriously than that."

None of this was news to Lori. It only confirmed what she already suspected about him. "Why are you telling me all this?"

"Because you need to hear it. And because Matt would never tell you anything that might change your opinion of him."

"Nothing you've told me would do that." How would illustrating his obvious heroism do anything than make her care about him more?

"Good. Then you can begin to see why my calling him the other morning caused him to short-circuit." She waggled her fingers near her temple. "Hearing my voice, I know he went back there. To that day. I know he did because I did. I didn't have, don't have, anyone else to call and, well…honestly? I was more scared after that stupid car accident than I care to admit. He didn't forget about you on purpose, Lori. He didn't not show up because he didn't feel like it or because he didn't want to see you. He did want to see you. I know this because he practically burned out his truck trying to get back to you to explain. But never once did he make me feel as if it was my fault or as if I'd cost him anything. Even though I clearly did."

"The accident wasn't your fault. You said yourself you didn't have anyone else—"

"Yet here I am, explaining things to you and hoping you'll give him another chance. I'm not his responsibility, Lori. But that doesn't mean he doesn't think I am. I'm... broken. I think in some weird way he's convinced himself he can put me back together." She looked back at the ocean. "He can't. No one can."

Lori didn't like the vacant expression on Kendall's face. She appeared a little too peaceful, a little too calm.

"He likes you, Lori. A lot. He told me about his divorce, which if you ask me was a long time coming. I also let him know what an idiot he was for not telling you about Gina from the get-go."

Feeling the need to explain, Lori blurted, "It wasn't the being married that hurt so much as the—"

"The secret. He didn't trust you, which only makes you trust him less, right? Wow." She let out a laugh. "If my head docs could only hear me now. It's like I listened to them or something. Everyone has their thing that keeps them from being happy. We are our own worst enemies. Matt will bend himself into a pretzel to help people, even if it means damaging his own relationships. He needs help with that. He needs the right person. But that person has to believe that in the end, she's what matters to him. Whatever your history is, Lori, whatever it is that you're letting come between you, get it out in the open. We both know you aren't ticked at him because he didn't call you. That's just stupid."

Having reached the same conclusion, Lori couldn't argue. "Are you always this blunt?"

"Only when it matters. Only when I see someone throwing away something potentially life changing simply because they're scared. And for the record, if I thought for one second you weren't worthy of him, I wouldn't have hauled my butt over here. I'd much rather be sulking in that rainforest of a backyard of his." She smiled as Lori sat up straighter. "Yeah, he said you'd have that reaction. I think he was planning on using that as a temptation device to get you back. Some girls like diamonds. Matt's girl likes plants."

"I get what you're saying," Lori said. "I do. But…"

"Holy hamburgers and French fries." Abby shoved through the glass doors of the dining room, cell phone in one hand, a crumpled piece of paper in the other. "Lori, can you believe that freaking contractor is trying to back out…oh. Hi. Kendall, right?" Abby's brow furrowed. "I'm sorry to interrupt. Thought it was a slow day."

"It is," Lori said. "Kendall and I were just talking."

"About Matt," Kendall added, and ignored Lori's horrified look of warning like an expert. "I'm thinking we need to lock these two in a closet together or something. Get them to talk it out."

Abby kicked out a hip and planted a tense fist on her waist. "Holly and I attempted to convey that same message only with ice cream. You doing better?"

"Time will tell."

"What's up with the contractors now?" Lori asked in an effort to change the conversation.

"He's reevaluated his estimate after he's done almost half the work. Says he can't proceed with the project unless I give him another five thousand on the spot."

"That's a rip-off," Kendall muttered.

"Right?" Lori nodded. "Even if money was an issue, that's tantamount to extortion. Don't do it."

"Ya think?" Abby held up the wadded paper like a torch. "I knew the guy was too good to be true, but corporate liked his bid."

"If it wasn't for corporate, the inn would have closed and you know it. The jerk's bid was thirty percent below everyone else," Lori explained to Kendall. "Now we know why. He's holding the guest cabins hostage."

"What's left to do?" Kendall asked as she finished her coffee.

"Oh, only half the flooring, the baseboard and trim, new sinks in the bathrooms—"

"Show me." Kendall stood.

Lori and Abby stared at her. "Show you what?" Lori asked.

"The cabins. What's left to do."

"Because…?" Abby hedged.

"Because I have some construction experience and I'm bored out of my mind."

"What kind of experience?" Abby asked.

"Enough to finish the job. Not enough to be licensed. I've been doing handyman jobs on and off since I was discharged, but my dad was a carpenter. Uncles were electricians. I had a saw in my hands before I could hold a fork." She pushed to her feet, wiped her hands on her pants. "And, I oversaw construction on our base in Iraq part-time. Can't hurt to have me look, right?"

"No, it couldn't," Lori said before Abby could answer. "Is that where *Hacksaw* comes from?"

Kendall nodded. "It was either Hacksaw or MacGyver. I took the one that wasn't trademarked."

"What's your rate?" Abby asked. "This guy's already blown through three-quarters of the budget."

"I'm negotiable. But I can tell you it'll be less than five K."

"I can take her down—" Lori offered but Abby waved her off.

"I've got it. I need to get some fresh air anyway. Besides, you're off for the rest of the day. Be somewhere else. Plant something." Abby gave her a similar look to the tolerant one Kendall had perfected. "Talk to someone." The two women headed out of the inn, chattering like old friends.

Leaving Lori alone with the one—or two—things she didn't want to deal with: her thoughts and her feelings for Matt.

"ARE YOU GOING to leave me anything to play with?" Matt lounged against the door to the garage as Kendall sorted through his toolbox and workbench. When she wrenched open the metal cabinet where he stored his power tools, he surrendered. "What's going on?"

"Got a job." Kendall bent down, peered through the shelves and dug out his drill, handsaw and sander. "Over at that big yellow inn on the cliffs."

"The Flutterby?" Matt asked.

"Yeah. I stopped by to talk to Lori and met Abby. Turns out her contractor flaked on her, demanded additional payment to finish the contract and what he did finish was crap." She pulled out an old duffel bag. "Can I use this?"

"Take whatever you need. What's she paying you?"

"Room and board to start. She's says there's an apartment over the diner that's empty. I'd only have to pay utilities. It's small, but it has everything I need. Besides—" she looked over at him before she continued stuffing tools into the bag "—you don't need me cramping your style. Especially once Kyle moves in."

Matt cringed. He'd been wondering if Kendall staying with him was going to be an issue with Kyle's caseworker. Then again, he hadn't gotten around to calling Chris with the news that Lori wasn't part of the equation any longer. He'd really made a mess of things. "You're welcome to stay as long as you want. As long as you need."

"Uh-huh. Thanks. Truth is, I hadn't planned to stay more than a couple of days but—" she stood up, planted her hands on her hips and smiled at him "—this town isn't so bad."

"High praise indeed, given your upbringing."

"You know what they say. You can take the girl off the farm—"

"You ever get farm sick, you can get your fix up at Calliope Jones's place." He turned and walked back to the yard that had been the focus of his attention for most of his day off. When he'd bought the property he'd had grand ideas of a big backyard kitchen, maybe a spa, a nice seating area where he could enjoy the stars when the walls closed in.

Instead, he had a couple of wooden deck chairs, a table and ankle-high grass he only cut when he had to.

"You heading over there tonight?" Matt asked.

Kendall strode out of the garage with the duffel over one shoulder, a big red toolbox in her other hand. "Maybe. Depends." She dropped both by the back gate. "Might want to borrow your truck at some point."

"You know where the keys are. If you wait until tomorrow, I can leave it with you when I go to work."

Kendall shrugged. "Nice night, huh? Is it always like this?" She arched her back and tilted her chin to the sky.

An odd charge sparked the air, as if something was going on he didn't understand. Why should today be any different? There was a lot he didn't understand lately.

"Pretty close. You want pizza for dinner? I can call and order—"

The doorbell rang.

"That was fast," Kendall deadpanned.

"Even by Zane's standards. Be right back."

"Uh-huh." She walked over and dropped into one of the chairs.

Matt checked his cell as he went to the front door. No messages from work or from friends. Nothing to indicate why someone might have stopped by unexpectedly. He pulled open the door as he slipped his phone back in his pocket.

"Lori." There was no stopping the smile that spread across his face. She looked pretty, standing there under the twilight glow, her hair tied up in that messy knot that made his fingers anxious to explore. Her T-shirt was the color of a ripe avocado and drifted snugly over her curves.

Every ounce of tension knotted in his body eased. Just seeing her, being around her, made him feel better. Made him happy.

And reminded him how completely stupid he'd been.

"Hi." Her smile was quick, then she ducked her head, tucked a stray strand of hair behind her ear. "I, um… I was thinking maybe we could talk. Over dinner?" She hefted a paper bag. "Ursula's fried chicken."

"And double mashed potatoes?"

"Yeah. Oh, hey, Kendall." She stepped to the side as Kendall swept out of the house with the tools.

"Lori. Nice to see you again. I'm going to make myself scarce."

"But I brought enough for three!" Lori called.

"No thanks. I'll eat at the diner. I'll have the truck back to you by morning, Matt." She hiked into the cab and revved the engine.

"She's different," Lori stated. "I like her."

"So do I," Matt agreed. "Come on in. I made iced tea. You want some?"

"Please."

Matt couldn't remember ever having a more polite conversation in his life. He took the bag from her hands and led her through the great room into the kitchen.

"This is nice. Big. It suits you." Lori set

her bag on the floor by the glass door. "And I can see what Kendall was talking about." She pointed to the backyard. "What's going on with this?"

"I got inspired," Matt confessed. After seeing all her plans for the cul-de-sacs and the detail she'd gone into, he looked at his own property now with more than a bit of shame. "Gotta get it cleaned out first, as I learned this weekend." He poured two glasses, so many questions poised behind his lips, but he kept them to himself. She'd come to him. Best to let her take the lead. "Outside?"

"Sure." She accepted the glass as he opened the door for her. "You've got your work cut out for you." But nowhere in her eyes did he see disapproval as she took in the wannabe jungle. What he did see warmed him from the inside.

"Might be looking for some advice down the road. If you know anyone."

She smiled as they sat, her glass cupped between hands he noticed were trembling. "I guess you're wondering why I'm here. Especially after the other day at Paige's."

Matt sat back. "I know why I hope you're here." That somehow he was going to be given another chance. But before he let that happen, he had to tell her the truth.

"Kendall came to see me today at the inn. She wanted to explain a few things."

Matt nodded. "She mentioned she'd seen you." He'd been dying to ask what they'd talked about but he knew from experience Kendall was as close-lipped as a Cold War spy.

"I know there's nothing going on with the two of you. Romantically."

"Never has been." Matt sipped his tea and wished he'd added more sugar. Sweet tea this was not.

"I didn't think there was. She's a lot like you. Tough. Straightforward. Honorable."

Yeah. Really honorable. He'd been surreptitiously using Lori to solidify his custody case. "I sense we're building to something here, Lori. You don't have to play with me. Whatever it is—"

"Yeah, building up to it. There's this thing…" She waved her hand, as if compelling herself to confess. "I've never talked about it before. A couple of people know, like Fletch and Abby and maybe Holly, but I've never…" She took a deep breath. "Whooo.

Okay." She fanned her face. "This was a lot easier when I was rehearsing it on the walk over."

Dread pooled heavy in his gut. "You're not sick, are you?" He sat forward and gripped her hand.

"Sick?" She looked surprised. "No, no, it's nothing like that. Well, that's not true, I've got some things…but that's not why I'm, oh man." She pressed her lips into a hard line. "I'm just going to dive into this. It's completely humiliating. Even after all these years. Back when I was in high school, I don't know if you can believe this or not, but I was a little on the shy side."

"You don't say?"

"Don't tease me," Lori said with a laugh. "Not now. I was also, well… Heavy. Heavier than I am now, proportion wise. Once I grew taller some of this distributed a bit better."

His eyes and temper sharpened. "I hope this has something to do with the story."

"It has everything to do with it. Fletcher and I moved here to live with our grandfather when we were teens. After our brother drowned, things got difficult for my parents. They, well, they lost interest in just about everything but their own grief. And they blamed Fletch for Caleb's death."

Matt absorbed the reality of that statement. "He was just a kid, wasn't he?"

"Hmmm. Almost thirteen." Lori nodded. "I was eleven. Anyway, cut to a few years later and Fletch is doing great in high school while I struggled. I didn't have a lot of friends. Abby was a couple of years ahead of me and was getting ready to graduate. We hadn't really connected yet. As you can imagine, there was a boy. I had a huge crush on him. He was in a band. He was super smart. He also played football."

"That is the trifecta for teenage crushes, I believe."

"For the purpose of this conversation, let's call him Dick."

Matt covered his laugh with a cough.

Lori didn't seem to notice. "I made such a fool of myself over him. It was hardly a secret, which is kind of where this story takes a turn." She rolled the icy glass of tea across her forehead. "He was a senior. I was a sophomore. At that age, all we want is to be accepted, especially by the people we really like. The people we wish we could be. One day Dick and his girlfriend had this huge blowup, right there in the hall where everyone, myself included, could see. After which, he came right over and asked me out. Boom. Just like that. Dream come true." She cleared her throat.

Anger circled inside him like a typhoon. "I'm really not liking where this is headed,"

"That's because you're a decent guy." Lori shook her head. "The details don't matter, only that I spent the next couple of weeks living every unpopular girl's dream. He took me to the movies, out for burgers. He bought me little gifts. There were car rides. We hung out with his friends…we held hands." Her breath caught in her chest as she blinked angry tears free. "He gave me my first real kiss. I hate that he gave me my first kiss."

She wasn't the only one. He wanted to reach out and take her hand, wanted to hold her. To kiss her and make her forget about this stupid boy who had clearly hurt her.

"I spent all my money on new clothes. Fletcher even drove me to the city so I could shop at one of those expensive stores that have larger sizes. Bless his heart, Fletch sat in the store while I tried on dress after dress.

What eighteen-year-old boy wants to wait while his sister tries on clothes?

"And then it happened. Dick asked me to the school dance. I was so excited. Some girls didn't even get asked at all and here I was, going with one of the most popular boys in school. I even managed to lose some weight before the big day. Not a lot, but enough so that I was proud of myself. I had my hair done and my makeup. I was so nervous I made Grandpa and Fletch leave. I didn't want a big fuss when he picked me up, so they went out and I waited. By the living room window. For over two hours."

Her words were like a brick to the face. She'd waited. Just as she'd waited for Matt on Sunday.

"He finally texted, said he had car trouble and for me to meet him at the high school. He'd be waiting for me inside. So I got on my bike, fancy billowing dress and all, and I went." She blew out a long breath. "He and his friends were already there. And so was his girlfriend, who was standing there with her phone, videotaping me as I climbed off my bike, got rearranged and raced to the door. I was a fright by that point of course. It had started raining—"

"Stop." Matt set his glass down and moved to the edge of his chair. "Please don't tell me any more because if you do I'm going to find whoever did this to you and break their face."

"Always everyone's white knight." Lori smiled at him, a sad, regretful expression that broke his heart. She lifted a hand to his face. "Where were you that night?"

Where was he? Married to a girl he didn't love. Trying to get out from under his abusive father's fist. Dreaming of a life that would be anything other than the one he'd been living.

In her own way, Lori had been dealing with the same thing.

"Long story short, turns out I was an experiment. The subject for their AP psychology term papers. They'd never broken up. It was all a setup. Everything I told him about myself, everything I confessed, he'd recorded. And then the two of them turned in a paper entitled: 'The Weight Effect on Self-Esteem and Social Anxiety.' He'd lied to me, from the start. He'd used me, used my faults, my flaws, my dreams, not only to promote his own scholarly agenda, but because he and his girlfriend, they thought it would be funny to humiliate me in front of the entire school. Because who cares when the fat girl is made fun of. They didn't get that chance by the way."

"Because Fletcher hid the body?"

"No." Her laugh actually sounded genuine. "Because the psychology teacher was horrified. All the teachers were. But it was Mrs. Hastings who brought down the hammer." Lori smiled through the drying tears. "She expelled them. Then she and the other faculty members wrote letters to all the colleges Dick and his girlfriend had applied to explaining exactly what they'd done. Scholarships were rescinded. Admissions, too. In another year, my junior year, both families moved out of town. I've told myself I was lucky. None of it made it onto the internet so, yay. I guess I won." She sniffed. "And in answer to your question about Fletcher? He didn't kill Dick. But Dick's prized classic automobile somehow found its way to the bottom of Milkweed Lake."

"I've always liked your brother." None of this eased the angry ache inside of him. "I am so sorry you had to go through that."

"I didn't tell you all this so you'd feel sorry for me." Lori shook her head in defiance. "That is the absolute last thing I want. If anything, the entire event helped make me who I am, and aside from a few character quirks, I think I'm doing pretty well. I just needed you to understand why I find it so hard to trust that anyone, especially a good man like you, would have any interest in me. All my life I've never believed I was worth anything. My parents barely spoke to me unless it was to criticize. They thought of me as a failure because the only thing that ever gave me any comfort was whatever I could find in the kitchen. But that night of the dance, I gave in and let myself believe I was special. That I was worth someone's attention. Someone's love. So when you didn't even call to say you'd be late?" She pulled her hand back, but he caught it, entwined his fingers with hers. "It brought all that up again. And I was afraid all of this, between us, was nothing more than some big joke at my expense. And then you showed up with Kendall and—" she shrugged "—my heart broke."

Guilt choked him. As bad as he thought things had gone, they were even worse. "I'm so, so sorry." He needed to tell her the truth about Kyle, about how he needed her to testify that he was part of his life, but doing so meant admitting he'd been lying to her again.

"Please stop saying that. It wasn't your fault, Matt. It isn't your fault. It's me. I'm like Kendall. Something's broken. In here." She pressed her glass against her chest. "Part of me wants to believe so badly that what's between us is real, but the other part... I'm so tired of being hurt. Of being rejected. Of being lied to and used. I don't know if I have it in me to trust you, to trust anyone the way I need to in order to have something genuine and lasting."

"You do," Matt said. "And if you don't yet, we'll just find a way to build it up again. I I—" No. He couldn't say it. Not now. She wouldn't believe him, not after she'd told him all this. "I care about you, Lori. More than I ever thought I could care about anyone. You're beautiful and kind and generous and you still try to help people even when they're nasty and negative. You're more worthy of love than anyone I've ever met. Certainly more worthy than I am." He leaned forward and pressed his forehead against hers, silently

willing her to accept his words as fact, even
as he silenced the voice inside of him urging
him to admit the truth—that he needed her
help with Kyle. But even he knew what he'd
done was no less cruel than what had been
done to her in the past. He had been using
her, despite caring for her. Somehow he had
to find a way to fix it. To fix everything. "I
wish you could believe in yourself as much
as I believe in you."

"I do, too." She blinked and a tear trickled
down her cheek. He caught it with his thumb.
"I'm trying, Matt. I really am trying, but this
might take more than you're able to give and
I don't want you to—"

He kissed her. Because he knew what she
was going to say. That she was afraid he was
wasting his life on her. Wasting his heart. He
wasn't. He knew that with absolute certainty.
Because he'd already spent thirty-two years
wasting his life.

A life that hadn't started until the day he'd
met her.

She sobbed. Her fingers stroked the side
of his face as he moved his mouth over her
trembling lips, until he was certain she'd

stopped dwelling on all the things that could and might go wrong.

"We're going to take this a day at a time," he whispered against her mouth. "I'm going to find a way, every day, to prove to you that you're worth every minute of my attention. And someday soon, you're going to be confident enough in who you are to fight for yourself in every way possible." He smiled at her gasp of shock. "I have faith in you, Lori. Now you just need faith in yourself."

CHAPTER THIRTEEN

IT WAS ODD, Lori thought as the freeway bumped under the cab of Matt's truck on the way to visit Kyle, how easily their lives had fallen into a pattern. Who would have guessed that splaying her heart open the way she had would settle her? It was as if the barriers between them had disappeared; she didn't worry about saying the wrong thing so much now. She didn't brace herself for the worst.

It helped they were both busier than ever. Thanks to advance planning, the second Saturday, despite having a lower turnout of volunteers, had resulted in a more streamlined effort. Lori had acquired her own gardening army and by midafternoon, all the flora had been situated in its new home with economical redwood bark as a ground cover both to retain moisture and give a finishing touch. The tiny pops of color amidst drought-resistant plants and a good thatching of milkweed that now lined each house below the window line, promised a winged insect paradise once the blooms erupted.

By the end of the day, the second section of houses were finished, which allowed Matt and his team to start on the third while a group broke off to unroll the new sod along the side area of the street. They were well on their way to being ahead of schedule, and while Lori loved watching the transformation, she was ready to be done. Which was probably why she'd headed over to the second cul-de-sac the last couple of days after work and got a jump start on the planting.

"Have you heard anything from BethAnn lately?"

"Hmmmm?" Lori looked across the truck's cab at Matt as the morning sun shone against his silky hair. They'd gotten an early start, but that meant hitting rush hour traffic. "Now that you mention it, I haven't." Last she'd heard BethAnn had narrowed down the catering choices to two companies, both of whom Lori suspected were far out of budgeting price range. "Why, have you?"

"Something Gil said on Saturday got me to thinking. Calm before the storm?"

"No way of knowing," Lori said. "Something tells me we'll know something when we know." And then, knowing BethAnn, they were all going to suffer for it. "Tell me about Kyle. What's going on with his case?"

Matt checked his mirrors before he shifted to the next lane. "Next hearing is scheduled for a week from Monday. Hopefully that's when the judge will let him out and approve the adoption."

One thing she had learned of late, discussing Kyle's case wasn't on the top of Matt's list of preferred topics. She'd lost track of how many times he'd changed the subject or given her a one-word response, the subject is closed, answer.

"You get his room finished?"

"Yeah." He scrubbed a hand down the side of his neck and winced. "I really hope I'm not jinxing anything."

"I'm sure you're not." Lori had trouble understanding why he was worried. Matt was a stable influence with a good job, a good support system, most of whom were in law enforcement. "It isn't as if there's a lineup of people willing to take him on. It'll be fine."

He reached out to hold her hand, something he'd been doing a lot of late. Something she'd gotten used to far, far too easily. "I'm glad you're coming with me. I bet he's tired of seeing just my face all the time."

"I hope he doesn't mind. I could end up being a third wheel here."

Matt shook his head. "The two of you got along great on that video call. I don't know that I've ever heard him laugh like that."

"Then I don't have to feel guilty about usurping all your conference time?" After the initial uncomfortable introductions, she'd told Kyle about a new series of books she'd started only to find out he'd just finished the first one. Lori glanced into the backseat and the small box containing the rest of them. It wasn't buying his affection. Not exactly. But books had always been an escape for her, a way to dream beyond herself. That seemed like something Kyle might need as time had no doubt crept to a standstill.

"You don't have anything to feel guilty about. You'll be a good influence on him, Lori. You've already been a good influence on me." He took the turnoff as Lori's stomach tightened. "Hey. Why are you so nervous?" He squeezed her hand.

"Because it's like meeting your parents only in reverse."

"You've known each other for years. By sight anyway. So in a way he already knows you. Relax. It'll be fine."

Except she didn't quite believe him. There was a hesitancy in his voice, a tension that had been growing over the past few days. Maybe it was something with work or maybe there was something going on with Kyle's case he hadn't told her about. Whatever it was, she was determined not to push. He'd tell her when he was ready.

Progress, she told herself, as she'd moved past the "this is none of my business" disclaimer. By the time they'd parked at the facility and were headed inside, the nerves were back. They'd all but robbed her of speech as they had their belongings searched and were escorted to the visitor's area. She couldn't sit still on the metal chair and must have rearranged the box of books for Kyle a dozen times before Matt took a hold of both her hands.

"Now you're making me nervous."

"I know. Sorry." Her cheeks flushed.

"Stop apologizing or I'm going to kiss you."

Something inside her loosened. There was the funny, teasing man she'd come to rely on. "That would embarrass Kyle more than it would me. Speaking of Kyle." She saw the teen step into sight on the other side of the glass. She tugged her hands free, stuck them in her lap. "Okay, here we go."

Matt scooted his chair closer to her then got to his feet and held out his hand. "Kyle. How are you doing?"

"Okay." Kyle offered a timid smile and in that moment, Lori relaxed. She'd been imagining the dangerous, troubled boy she'd seen around town, the boy who had been struggling to survive. Matt was right. He looked different. He was taller than she remembered. Not nearly as scrawny, but that probably came with decent nutrition rather than rampant parental neglect. She'd gotten an inkling of the change in him on the video call, but seeing him now, his onetime bleached blond hair replaced by a soft brown. Eyes that she remembered as angry crinkled at the corners when he smiled. He had dimples. Who knew? "Hi, Lori."

"Hey. I hope you don't mind me tagging along."

"No, it's cool." Kyle took a seat, eyed the box with childish curiosity. "Is this for me?"

"It is." Lori pushed it a little closer.

Matt turned his head, chuckling under his breath.

"I thought maybe after our last conversation you'd like them," Lori explained.

Kyle popped open the lid, set it aside and stared into the box. He sagged in his chair.

"If you've already found them—" Uncertainty swept over her in a cool wave.

"No, I didn't." Kyle blinked. "You really brought them for me?"

"Well, yeah." Lori frowned, glanced at Matt.

"Thank you." He lifted one of the hardcover books free, ran gentle fingers over the cover. "No one's ever bought me a book before. I've stolen a few—" His eyes went wide. "Sorry. Never mind."

"No one should ever have to steal a book." Lori kicked Matt under the table. "You know Holly from the diner?"

"Yeah. She let me eat there for free sometimes."

"Holly's good people," Matt said.

"She's the best," Lori agreed. "I remember talking to her about her son, Simon, one time and she told me the one thing she wouldn't ever deny him was a book. Toys or games or whatever else she could argue with him on, but never ever a book."

"That's cool. She and the sheriff got married, didn't they?" Kyle asked.

"They did," Lori confirmed.

"They're about to have a baby, too," Matt added. "Well, in a few months."

"I feel like I've been gone forever." Kyle cracked open the book and brought it to his face. Matt grimaced, but Lori's grin only widened.

"I love how books smell," she said.

Kyle nodded. "Thank you. I'll give them back when I'm done."

"You will not." Lori sat back in her chair as the tension drained from her body. "Those are yours, Kyle. Whatever you want to do with them is fine."

"So…" He looked around the almost-empty visitor's room. "If I wanted to leave them here in the library for other kids, that would be okay?"

Lori nodded and made a mental note to have a new set waiting for him when he came home. She felt Matt's hand on her shoulder and reached up to take his hand. "That would be more than okay."

And with that, whatever worries or concerns she had about getting along with Kyle Winters, vanished.

"MATT. GOOD. I was hoping to catch you here today." Kyle's caseworker joined him at the visitor's counter, looking as harried and stressed as always. Tall, lanky and wearing a suit Matt suspected he might have found at a thrift store, Chris Walters looked as if he'd put his first foot out of college only days before. "I believe we're all set for the hearing."

"You've heard from the judge?" Matt looked down the hall where Lori had stopped at the ladies' room.

"Not directly, no, but I did get confirmation she received my amended report about your situation. I mailed you a copy. She should be notifying us in the next few days if she wants Lori to testify on your behalf."

It was all Matt could do not to clamp a hand over the caseworker's mouth in case Lori heard him. "I brought her with me today. She and Kyle hit it off over video chat so I thought they should connect in per—"

"She's here?" Chris's face lit up. "That's great. I was going to ask you for her contact information so I could interview her—"

"Interview who for what?"

Matt closed his eyes. There were many things he loved about Lori Bradley, but her bat-like hearing was not one of them. "We were just talking about one of Chris's other cases," he lied. Try as he might, he hadn't been able to find a way to tell her about the role she might play in Kyle's custody case. He certainly didn't want to do so with an audience. "Lori, this is Chris Walters. He's Kyle's caseworker."

"Oh, hello." Lori extended her hand and Chris, looking more than a bit shell-shocked, accepted. "It's good to meet you. Do you see any problem with him being released to Matt's custody?"

"Ah, there might be some things that need ironing out." Chris made it sound more like a question than a statement of fact. "We'll know more after the hearing of course, but I think we're good for now. Will you be there?"

"Me?" Lori blinked. "No. There's a big event dinner in town that day. I'm not sure I can get away. But Matt will be there for sure." She rubbed a hand up his arm. "He's looking forward to getting Kyle home and settled."

"So you two are…" Chris hedged. "Dating?"

Matt's disgust with himself had peaked. "Yes, dating. That's what we're doing." He slipped his arm around her waist and pulled her close. "Nice, stable, dating life."

Chris didn't look convinced.

"And I thought I was the one with anxiety issues." Lori laughed while Matt was certain he was turning green. "We're still getting used to things. Is something wrong?"

"Nope, nothing's wrong. Right, Chris?"

"Remains to be seen. Matt, do you mind if I have a word?"

"Yeah, of course." He dug into his pocket for his keys. "How about I meet you at the truck?"

"Sure. Nice to meet you, Chris. No offense, but it would be great not to see you again."

"I get that a lot," Chris said with a strained smile. One that vanished the second Lori walked out the front doors. "What's going on, Matt?"

"What's going on with what?"

"You suck at lying." In that instant, Chris went from overworked government servant to defiant, irritated crusader. "You told me you and Lori were serious. That she was a part of your life."

"She is. Now," Matt admitted.

"Meaning when you told me about her the first time she wasn't?"

Matt hadn't squirmed this much since his basic training days. "Things were complicated back then."

"Back then was only a few weeks ago. I sent in information to the judge based on our conversation, Matt. Based on you telling me you had a stable female influence in your life who could be of benefit to Kyle. What's going to happen when the judge questions her?"

"You said that might not happen." At this

point, he was putting all his money on that scenario.

"I also said this judge is completely unpredictable. She's the judge you don't want in this situation, Matt. She takes each case individually. She will examine every single detail, every single statement, and will not just pass him through." Chris pointed to the door. "If she even gets a whiff of dishonesty it's game over. That woman, Lori, might be the only person who can ensure you get Kyle, and from what I just saw, she has no clue what's expected of her."

"I'll handle it," Matt said. "I'll tell her."

"Yeah, well, you'd better. And you'd better hope she doesn't think what I'm thinking right now. That the only reason you're dating her is because she looks good on paper."

"Careful." Anger surged. "That's not a smart thing to say about the woman I love."

"If you loved her you wouldn't be playing her."

The accusation struck Matt's sense of honor dead center.

"Get your act together, Matt. Fix this. You

make sure she's ready to testify that you're a fit guardian, otherwise you can kiss your hopes of being Kyle's father goodbye."

CHAPTER FOURTEEN

"You good to handle things from here, Willa?" Lori had waited until the last expected arrivals for the day had checked in to the Flutterby before getting ready to head out. She had a huge To Do list, beginning with Willa and Nina's front yard. Jasper was taking his mom and little sister out to an early dinner so Lori, Charlie and Paige could whip the landscaping into shape. But before she headed over she wanted to stop by the sheriff's station with a couple of gifts.

"I'm good." Willa nodded. The deer in the headlights expression had faded in recent days as the young woman became more familiar with the job. She was a quick study, rarely had to be told anything twice and, thankfully, found ways to keep herself busy during the downtime. "I'll stick close to the phone, though. Something tells me the Hemmingbergs are going to need some extra attention."

Lori didn't want to add fuel to the fire, but she agreed. The civil lawyer and his wife, both longtime friends of BethAnn Bottomely, had traveled from Los Angeles to attend the festival. It was clear, given their initial reaction to the town, that they weren't overly impressed.

That BethAnn was due to meet them for dinner at Flutterby Dreams anytime had Lori all the more anxious for escape. She'd managed to go nearly two weeks without having to deal with the monstrous community organizer, but she still had ears. The woman had been running roughshod over everyone she came in contact with. Word from Harvey's Hardware was she was one short circuit away from a complete meltdown.

"You have my cell if you need anything. And Abby should be back from Calliope's soon."

"Thanks. I'm sure everything will be—"

The front door opened and in swept Beth-Ann looking as if a tornado had deposited her on their porch. It wasn't that BethAnn didn't appear presentable. But with the wrinkled ivory shirt, askew collar, and hair that looked as if it had been styled by a swarm of bees, she certainly didn't look like herself.

"We really need to get a back door to this place," Lori muttered, and earned a grin from Willa as she faced their visitor. "Good evening, BethAnn. Here for dinner with your guests?"

"I made reservations," BethAnn announced. "I assume you got them."

"Yes, ma'am," Willa said. "You're just a few minutes early, but if you'd like to take a seat, we have complimentary wine and—"

"I'd like to be seated now." She stopped to stand directly in front of Lori, knocked her chin up and stared up and into her eyes. "Do you not make allowances for special customers?"

Special customers? BethAnn hadn't even been bothered to meet with Jason to discuss his catering services and here she stood at Jason's pride and joy demanding special treatment?

"I can go check—" Willa took a step back, but Lori held up her hand.

"No, you won't, Willa." Lori was so tired of this woman's attitude. "Dining room hours begin at six, BethAnn. Which is why we don't accept any reservations beginning before six fifteen. As Willa said, you're welcome to relax here in the lobby while you wait for your companions."

"I don't want wine and cheese. I don't want anything other than to be seated at my table—"

"And you will be. When it's ready." Lori's patience stretched thinner than a spider's web.

"I am a paying customer." She pushed a trembling hand through her hair. "I expect to be treated with respect."

"You're not the only one," Lori said. She caught movement out of the corner of her eye and saw BethAnn's guests heading down the stairs. "Listen to me, BethAnn." Lori lowered her voice and did her best to control her temper. "Unless you'd like to cause a scene in front of what I'm assuming are very influential friends, I suggest you get yourself under control. You don't get to come in here and start ordering everyone about. This isn't your committee. This is a place of business. And as such, we have the right to refuse service to anyone. Now grab yourself a glass and chill out."

"You're impertinent and out of line." Beth-Ann crossed her arms over her chest. "I demand to speak with your superior."

"Lori doesn't have many superiors." Abby closed the front door behind her. "But if you mean her boss, that would be me."

"Excellent." BethAnn spun around. Even without seeing BethAnn's face, Lori knew when she realized who Abby was. Her spine couldn't have gone any stiffer if it had been made of steel. "You're engaged to that chef I fired. Clearly you're not the person to handle this. Who do you report to?"

Any sympathy Lori might have felt for the clearly overstressed BethAnn turned to smoke.

"BethAnn is our newest expert on how to win friends and influence people." It was a poor attempt to lighten the mood. Clearly BethAnn didn't want to lighten anything. She'd come in here looking for a fight. Too bad Lori had stored enough self-confidence to happily give her one.

"Just a minute, please." Abby's eyes went as brittle as glass as she leaned over. "Willa, I'm sure our guests would enjoy the view from the lookout. Why don't you show them the way?"

"Certainly." Willa hurried around the counter. "Mr. and Mrs. Hemmingberg, if you'd come with me, please?" She retrieved two flutes of sparkling wine from the side table and carried them outside.

"We'll let you know as soon as your table is ready," Abby said to the couple. "The weather today is as perfect as it gets, so please, enjoy."

"Is everything all right, BethAnn?" The older, silver-haired gentleman wearing a suit that cost more than a luxury vehicle peered down his hawk-like nose while his snooty-looking wife clung to his arm like a bug to flypaper.

"Fine, just fine." BethAnn nodded but her voice shook. If looks could kill, Lori would be six feet under by now. "Festival doings, you know. Busy busy. I shouldn't be more than a few minutes."

"If you're interested, there's some lovely history about this part of Butterfly Harbor I can tell you about," Willa said as she escorted the Hemmingbergs outside.

When the door closed behind them, Lori

almost leaped back at the ferocity in Abby's eyes. "For the record, you didn't fire Jason, you left that task to one of my best friends. You may direct any complaints you have about me and my staff to Spencer Marshall at the corporate office. I can get the number for you. Last but not least, if you plan to patronize this establishment, you will do so politely. If you cannot do that, feel free to take your friends to another eatery. I'm certain Holly can find you three stools at the diner."

BethAnn glared at each of them before hefting her bag higher on her shoulder, stomped over to the table and poured herself a very full glass of red.

Abby tracked her all the way to the chair by the window, waiting until BethAnn was seated, then shifted her attention to Lori. "Go on. Get out of here. I'll keep an eye on Cruella while Willa plays tour guide."

"You sure?" Lori wasn't entirely convinced leaving Abby alone with BethAnn and sharp instruments was a good idea.

"I'm more than sure. Besides, you're running out of time if you're going to get Willa's front yard finished before she gets home."

"Oh, right." Lori hurried for her things,

then picked up the box lid she'd used to transport the small plants she planned to deliver. "Just so you know, I had her covered."

"I know you did." Abby nodded but Lori could still feel the waves of anger rolling off her. "But if anyone's going to earn complaints around here, it better be me." She smiled and winked. "I'm bulletproof where this job is concerned."

Lori laughed. "See you Saturday for the final batch of houses?"

"Would not miss it for the world."

WHILE OZZY, JASPER and Luke argued about whether to rearrange desk assignments in the sheriff's station—Matt and Fletcher couldn't care less—Matt found himself rereading the letter from Judge Jeannette Harris for the tenth time.

His fingers tightened to the point of crushing the official letterhead. As optimistic as the judge sounded in her communiqué, one thing was made perfectly clear: she was expecting Lori to testify at the hearing on Monday afternoon.

"Everything okay?" Fletcher stopped behind him on his way back from the coffee station. "That about Kyle?"

"Yeah. Final hearing notification." His stomach no longer did the jitterbug at the thought of having to tell Lori that he'd used their relationship to gain favor with the court. He couldn't avoid it—he'd have to have a serious talk with her. The sooner the better.

"Hope our letters of recommendation helped."

"They did, thanks." That his fellow deputies and more than a few of his neighbors had been willing to provide character references for him meant the world, but he could read between the lines in the judge's letter. The most important reference hadn't been provided: Lori. Which was why she wanted to hear from Matt's girlfriend herself.

"You're doing a really good thing with him." Fletcher slapped a hand on his shoulder as Matt folded the letter and stuck it in his jacket pocket. "You're going to make a big difference in his life."

"I hope so." Part of Matt wished he could talk his situation out with someone, but it certainly couldn't be Fletcher. He'd already gotten the evil eye when he'd finally arrived at the party the other day. And that was just because he hadn't shown up for a date due to an emergency he couldn't have avoided.

To say Lori's story about what had happened to her in high school hadn't had an impact would be lying. He'd never felt so angry on someone's behalf in his life. To think someone—a group of someones—would have treated her with such callous contempt made him wish he could go back in time and stop it from ever happening.

But if he did that, she might not be the Lori he'd fallen in love with. There was one thing Matt knew for certain: whatever happened in one's life, however bad or good, it shaped the person they would become. No wonder Lori had such compassion for others, but the result could just as easily have been the opposite. She could have let it destroy her.

Instead, Matt had to worry what he would end up doing?

The door to the sheriff's office popped open and there she was, arms filled with a selection of tiny plants, her round face alight with the promise of a beautiful day, and a smile made just for him.

"Afternoon, everyone." She set the narrow

lipped box on the counter. "Hope it's okay, I just stopped by to check on Matt and his cactus."

Fletcher choked on his coffee and sprayed Matt. "Nice." Matt glared at him as he swiped a hand across the back of his neck.

"Sorry." Fletcher laughed and returned to his desk.

"It's still alive," Luke said as he left the desk debate. "What do you have there?"

"Well, I got to thinking you could use a little cheering up around this place. It's a little dreary." Lori beamed at him. "And I need to clean out my greenhouse. Seems the perfect place to bring them."

"That's really nice of you, Lori. Thanks." Luke picked one up that had a tiny bright pink flower on the top. "This little guy will be perfect on my desk. Guys, come and claim yours."

"I'm set," Matt held up his hands in mock surrender. "I know when not to press my luck." That his plant was still thriving—and green—was a major source of pride for him.

"Me, too?" Jasper hobbled over.

"Of course. Just say the word. I can bring more."

"While I'm partial to dreary," her brother said as he claimed the largest of the plants, "I could use something to talk to that won't talk back. Thanks, sis."

"Sure. Will I see you all on Saturday? Only one day of work left."

"We'll be there," Luke assured her. "Ozzy, Fletcher and I are going over after our shift today to finish laying in that new PVC pipe. We'll finish taping off the windows on the last houses, too, so we can jump right in on painting."

"Excellent. Matt, I know we had dinner plans, but I told Abby and Holly I'd sit in on their last meeting with Calliope about the town barbecue. I hope that's okay?"

"No problem." As anxious as he was to discuss her testimony in court, he wasn't in any rush to admit his betrayal. Another day or two wouldn't make much of a difference. "Rain check."

"For sure."

"I'll track Kendall down, see what she's been up to lately," Matt said. If there was anyone to whom he could safely unburden himself to, it was his former combat buddy.

"She's been going gangbusters on the cabins," Lori told him. "Stop by and pick up dinner for the two of you at Jason's. I'll let him know you're coming."

"I will not turn down free food," Matt said.

"Oh, you'll pay for it." Lori grinned and it was then he realized she was flirting with him. Openly. In front of her brother. "But later and in private. Bye, guys."

When the door closed behind her, all eyes landed on Matt.

"What?" Matt's entire face went hot. "She probably just meant she'd cook me dinner or something."

"Uh-huh." Jasper elbowed Ozzy. "I'm going with 'or something' for sure."

"Careful, kid, that's my sister you're talking about." Fletcher angled his new plant friend this way and that before casting a side-eyed look at Matt. "You be careful, too."

"I always am," Matt promised, but for the first time, he was afraid he'd made a promise he couldn't keep.

CHAPTER FIFTEEN

WHILE THE SUBSEQUENT Saturdays hadn't resulted in as enthusiastic a turnout of volunteers as the first weekend, they ended the
project on an up note and well before sun-
down. While Lori set the last row of herbs
in place closest to the curving brick border,
Charlie came in behind her with a watering
can that was larger than she was, and gave
the plants a good, settling-in dousing.

Lori sat back on her heels and swiped
her hand across her sweaty forehead. She'd
turned into a planting machine, buzzing
through the prearranged blooms like a bee
on amphetamines. She'd barely stopped to eat
lunch. The closer she got to being done, the
faster she wanted to go. As she looked behind
her and admired the newly painted buildings,
new windows and bark-encased plantings,
she knew she hadn't been the only one. The
last bit of sod was being laid as gently and

meticulously as the first had been only a few weeks before.

And there, at the entrance of the cul-de-sac, Kendall was hammering into place a custom wooden carved sign noting its name: Marigold Way. It went perfectly with the other two she'd made for Hollyhock Hill and Pansy Place.

"That's it. We're done." Her chest expanded as tears exploded in her eyes. All the hard work, all the planning and worrying and details, they had all paid off. Butterfly Harbor was expanding its wings. It was ready for its new life.

"Not quite," Matt called behind her. "We need to christen one more thing."

Lori squealed as a jet of cold water hit her in the back. She turned on her knees, wielding her trowel in front of her face as Matt hit her full on with the hose.

Charlie laughed and turned the watering can over Lori's head. Simon and Paige joined in as cheers and laughter rang through the cul-de-sac.

"Enough!" Lori sputtered, and tried to catch her breath. The happiness bursting inside of her was too much to contain. She reached over and snagged Charlie's arms, pulled her in front of her as Matt's assault continued. Simon leaped forward to get in on the fun, and soon, everyone had jumped into the fray. "Okay, that is enough!" Lori called when reason took hold and she thought about how much water they were wasting. "Unless you want to deliver the water bill to the mayor personally."

"Oh, the mayor can make an exception for special occasions." Gil Hamilton strode into the cul-de-sac, a wan smile on his face as he turned an admiring eye to their hard work. "You all did great." He walked over to Matt, standing among his fellow deputies, and held out his hand. "I should never doubt you, should I?"

"We just do what we say we're going to," Luke said. "Excuse me. I think Simon needs his off switch hit." He dashed off and ran over to grab his stepson around the waist and haul him over his shoulder.

Lori shoved herself to her feet and squished across to join them. "Sorry," she said when she whipped her hair back and splashed the mayor. "Unexpected shower."

"I apologize for not making it out here

today," Gil said. "We had some things I needed to deal with for the festival."

"What things?" Lori asked. "I thought BethAnn was handling everything."

"So did I." Gil cringed. "I haven't been able to get in touch with her for a couple of days. And, well, honestly? I can't make any sense of her reporting system for the committees. I'm not entirely sure what's going on with what. I don't suppose she's kept you in the loop, Lori?"

Lori couldn't help but snort. "Last time I saw BethAnn she almost got her butt tossed out of the Flutterby. She was looking a little frazzled."

"Great." Gil took a deep breath. "Guess I'll need to reach out to everyone myself and see where things stand."

"I have an updated agenda for the cook-off and food market," Holly said as she and Paige came over from where they'd been collecting empty water bottles. "Calliope, Abby and I have everything handled including a list of food vendors and booths we'll be setting up at the inn and in Skipper Park."

"One less thing to worry about then. Good. Thanks." Gil nodded and shoved his hands in his pockets. "I'm beginning to suspect I made a mistake letting her take over so much. She was just so excited to be back here, and plus, well, she's not easy to say no to."

"No, she is not," Lori agreed.

"I'm going to take a walk over to her place, see if I can talk to her in person," Gil said. "I hope everything's okay and I'm just over-reacting."

"I'm sure it's fine," Matt said. "We're just going to finish cleaning up here and call it a done deal."

Lori almost jumped as Matt slipped his arms around her from behind and rested his chin on her shoulder. Instantly warmer, she leaned into him, clutched her hands around his.

Holly let out one of her blistering two-fingered whistles and brought everyone to a screeching halt. "Everyone who was here the last three Saturdays gets a free dinner and a slice of pie on the house tonight. Now let's get this place back in order and go eat!"

Lori's stomach rumbled at the mention of food. That granola bar she'd eaten four hours ago had long since been burned off. "I want a cheeseburger, onion rings and one of Holly's famous mocha shakes," she said over her shoulder.

"We could do that." Matt's voice dropped an octave into that sultry, Southern drawl that made her shiver. "Or you could come back to my place and I'll fix you my famous pasta primavera."

Lori's heart flipped in her chest and she turned in his arms. "Okay, that sounds good, too." She linked her hands behind his neck. "I don't think I'll ever be able to thank you enough for helping with all this." She loved how his hair felt beneath her fingers. Loved how when he smiled at her she felt like the most powerful woman on earth. If all he ever did was look at her like that once a day for the rest of her life, she'd be a very happy woman.

"There's no thanks necessary. I'm the one who kinda pushed you in to it."

"Calliope pushed me into it." Lori pointed an accusing finger at her friend who, along with Stella, was walking through the muddy puddles barefoot. "I can't remember a time I've been happier." She lay her forehead against his chest, afraid if she looked into his eyes, he'd see too much. "Whatever comes next, I'm ready for it."

"Are you?" Matt crooked a finger under her chin and tilted her head up. "Because there is something I need to talk to you about. Something I've been putting off for a while."

Lori almost couldn't breathe. "Something we can talk about over dinner?" Was it possible... Dare she think that maybe... No. She had to put a mental clamp on those thoughts. Things were moving fast enough. She couldn't let herself start daydreaming about proposals or weddings or love.

Except she already was. Because she did love him.

And she had. For a very long time.

"I'd like to go home and change before, if that's okay?" She plucked her soaked shirt out from her sticky skin. "Some maniac hose-blasted me and I'm all drippy."

"Yeah, that maniac loves you all drippy." He kissed the tip of her nose as she pulled away. "Come by when you're ready. I'll be waiting."

"Okay." She backed up, not wanting to take her eyes off him, but she finally did, feeling an odd desire to do a dance of joy. Tonight, she told herself, tonight was the night every-thing would change. Tonight she'd finally feel safe enough, trust enough, to admit her feel-ings. Out loud.

Tonight, she'd tell Matt she loved him.

"YOU FIGURE OUT how you're going to tell her?" Much like a nagging conscience, Ken-dall appeared at the most inconvenient time as a voice of reason.

"I'm getting there." Guilt niggled at him, eating away at his soul as he considered how best to approach the subject. "It'll be fine."

"I hope so," Kendall said with a shake of her head as she gathered up her tools and loaded them into the back of Matt's truck. "But positive thinking doesn't always pay off. Just a word of warning, that's not a woman expecting to have her world blown up tonight. She's happy, Matt. And she's head over heels for you. But then, that's probably not helping, is it?"

"No, it's not." Maybe he was worried over nothing. Maybe she'd believe he'd pursued a relationship with her because he'd wanted to, wanted her; and not because he needed the promise of added life stability to ensure his getting custody of Kyle.

Or maybe he was just kidding himself. He knew her history; he knew how fragile her trust in anyone was, but especially in someone with whom she'd become romantically involved. He could just roll the die and hope the judge didn't ask anything on the stand that would reveal his duplicity, but the idea of her getting blindsided in public was one that pulled that gamble completely off the table.

He owed her the truth. He owed himself that. This secret that was lodged between them was growing larger every day. Soon, he wouldn't be able to see around it anymore. He'd only see that he'd lied to her. Again. And the fallout would be far, far worse.

"You want me on standby for backup?" Kendall asked.

"You mean do I want you to hold my hand while I admit to deceiving her? Yeah, no. I think I'll let you off the hook on that one."

"Much appreciated." She shoved her hands in her pockets. "You know where I am when this goes boots up."

When not if? The confidence she had in

him was overwhelming. "Just keep a good thought, yeah?"

"Always do." But they both knew where Kendall was concerned, good thoughts were as useless as an unloaded gun.

AFTER A 6:00 A.M. wakeup call and a full day of gardening behind her, Lori should be pining for a long hot shower and curling up on the sofa with a book. Instead she got a second wind and, after she finally got home, showered and changed, she decided to walk to Matt's house. She probably should have taken more care choosing what to wear, but she didn't want to look as if she were expecting some big life-changing question or something. So she forwent her trademark maxi dress and chose a pair of crop jeans and loose tee the color of summer strawberries and dotted with tiny golden sparkles.

Water bottle in hand and bag slung over her shoulder, she dashed out of the house and, after she stopped to take a calming breath, headed out on the half-mile walk.

When she was ready to ring the bell, the nerves had returned. She needed to calm down. She needed to stop pinning all her hopes of a future on the next few hours. Whatever he had on his mind, she'd happily work through with him. Together. Her heart did its own little skip. *Together* had such a wonderful ring to it.

"Slow down," she mumbled. "You're still a ways from happily-ever-after." That thought alone was enough to sober her up. There was a lot they needed to talk about, beginning with expectations and what Matt's hopes for the future were. Now wasn't the time to hold back and it certainly wasn't the time to lie. He needed to know the baggage she'd be bringing with her, and then, once he opened that and sorted through it, she could begin to relax.

Before she scared herself into running away, she hit the doorbell.

When he opened the door, she realized the truth: she was done for.

"Hi." He gave her that smile that made her toes dance. He cleaned up so well and he'd dressed up. Well, dressed up for Matt. Jeans were a staple for him, but the button-down cobalt shirt he wore made his eyes sparkle like stars in a midnight sky.

"Hi. Sorry I took so long. It was such a nice night, I walked."

"I was just finishing getting everything prepped. Come on in." He reached for her hand and escorted her over the threshold. "You know where things are so make yourself at home. I bought a bottle of wine just in case."

"Wine sounds great." She followed him into the kitchen and noticed the root beer bottle next to filled bowls and a cutting board. "You aren't drinking?"

"No." Matt retrieved the wine and popped it open to pour her a glass. "As we've reached that all-cards-on-the-table stage of our relationship, I should probably tell you there are times I need to get it all out of the house."

"Alcohol?" She swirled the white zin in the glass and took a seat on the stool on the other side of the counter. "Is it a problem for you?"

"It could be." He shrugged. "You've told me about your parents, who sound like lovely people, by the way."

Lori rolled her eyes. "Don't they just?"

"Suffice it to say Luke's father and mine may have been separated at birth. He was a drinker long before I came into the world. Good news, bad news, everything was a reason to imbibe and most times, it had a Jekyll and Hyde effect. I never knew when the monster was going to appear. Could have been worse, I suppose. My mom could have lived through it longer than she did. She died before I could ever witness him abusing her."

It was a miracle Matt had turned out the way he did. "Made for a rough childhood then."

"Made me anxious to get out of the house." He made efficient work of a couple of carrots, then reached for the peppers. "Military saved my life. Gave me a reason and an honorable example of how to live my life. That's where I learned how important my word is. When you get rid of everything else, a man's word is all that matters."

Lori sipped her wine. "So you're afraid you're going to start to drink the way he did."

"I'm pretty sure I won't, but I've come close. It was a crutch while I tried to wean myself off the pain meds. Then Gina left, which was a pretty dark hole to climb out of. I caught it before it got too bad, but it's as close as I ever want to get. So when I see the edge creeping up on me, I get it out of the house."

"I can take it or leave it," Lori said. "If that makes a difference."

"The last thing I ever feel like doing around you is drinking." The smile that had faded over the past few minutes reappeared. "It is something I had to think a lot about when it came to taking in Kyle. He learned at an earlier age than me how destructive addiction can be."

"I would think it's better for him to be looked after by someone who recognizes the signs and can make a preemptive strike. If you're looking for a way to spin it to the judge," she added.

"Yeah, the judge." Matt sighed. "I need to talk to you about that—"

"Before you do." She took an extra-large drink of wine. "There's something you should be aware of. About me. I mean, if things between us are…you know, moving forward." Oh, wow, here she went again. She'd already had one confessional nightmare scenario. She really didn't want to have another. "Remember the other evening when I told you about, well, you know, that thing in high school."

"Uh-huh." His knuckles whitened as he

snapped his knife a little harder against the cutting board.

"Well, you asked me if I was sick."

She watched the color drain from his face as his chin popped up. "You said you weren't."

"Not sick, technically, but I have had some health issues for most of my life. Partly tied to my weight. My endocrine system is out of whack. Between my thyroid and something called PCOS…"

"I've heard of that." He set the knife down, leaned his hands on the counter and looked at her. "It causes infertility, doesn't it?"

"It can. And it might. With me." She flinched, but instead of shrinking away and changing the subject, she pressed on. He needed to know, whatever direction they might be headed. "I haven't looked into it that much because I never really gave it a lot of thought, other than assume I'd never be in a position to have to worry about it."

"About what?"

She gulped. She was in too deep to stop now. "About having kids." She took another drink of wine and, after hearing what he'd said earlier, wondered if she was using it as a crutch. She set the glass aside, but instead of folding her hands like she'd planned, he leaned over and grabbed hold of them. "There's no guarantee I can have them. Naturally, I mean. There could be issues. And even if I could, there's a risk of complications. I just thought you should know. In case that, you know, changes anything." Why didn't she just throw herself on the ground and profess her undying love for the man? She was inching back toward pathetic.

There were times silence was a good thing. This wasn't one of them. It felt as if half her life ticked by before he finally responded.

"Do you have any aversion to adopting?"

Her muscles went weak. "No. In fact, I thought maybe down the line at some point I might look into that. For myself." She looked for any indication he was leading her on. "It doesn't matter to you?"

"Of course it matters but not in the way you're probably thinking. It doesn't change how I feel about you. I've always been a whatever-happens-happens kind of guy. Given my genetic makeup, I wouldn't have a problem not passing that on to some innocent kid. Oh man." He stood up. "Oh man, I just got why Luke's so freaked out over Holly being pregnant. It wasn't just about his dad."

"Luke's freaked out?" Lori gripped his hands harder. "He looked about ready to pop ten champagne corks when they announced it at the party."

"Holly talked him off the ledge. He's getting used to it now. But he might need another therapy session. Or a round of poker. Come here." He tugged her hand and she slid off the stool as he drew her around the counter and into his arms. "Stop worrying that you're getting ahead of yourself by talking about kids."

"How did you—" She gasped as he pressed his lips against hers. All too light. All too brief.

"Because in the last few weeks, I've gotten to know you pretty well. Also, I'd be lying if I said I haven't imagined a bunch of little rug rats running around my house or yours. Or ours. However we might come by them is fine with me. Which is my way of saying I love you no matter what the future might hold for us." He kissed her again, and this time, Lori reached up and grabbed the back of his neck with both hands and returned the kiss.

"You love me?" She whispered against his mouth. "You really do?"

"I really do. By any chance, is there something you'd like to say to me? Not that there's any rush or—"

"I think I loved you the first time I saw you." How long she'd been waiting to say those words—to anyone, but especially to Matt. Everything she'd ever wanted—all the things she'd tried not to let herself believe might be possible, suddenly all of them were within her grasp. And all because of Matt. "You're the kindest, strongest, most honorable man I've ever met. I'm so glad my heart chose you."

The timer on the stove beeped. They turned as the steam billowing out of the boiling water arced toward the smoke detector. "Turn it off before you pull an Abby," Lori demanded, and shoved him toward the stove. And then she stood there, watching him. Loving him.

And thanked whatever forces had brought her to him.

"So this thing you wanted to talk to me about." Lori carried her plate to the sink while Matt cleared the table. "Was it something we still need to discuss?"

Matt crushed the sponge in his hand and squeezed his eyes shut. She had a memory like a steel trap. Of course she'd remember he'd had her over specifically because he needed to tell her the truth. "It can wait."

"You sure?" That she was making such a lighthearted joke out of it only added to the weight of his guilt. "It can't be more uncomfortable than telling someone you might not be able to have children."

Oh, but it could. Which was why he was looking for a way—any way—to find a means around it. "It has to do with Kyle," Matt managed.

"Okay. How about over coffee?" she urged as she pulled out the filter and popped open the can. "That reminds me, I stopped by the bookstore the other day and picked up some comics for him. There's this new series…"

Matt turned and saw her continue to talk, but the words didn't reach his ears. Maybe he was wrong. Maybe, given the conclusions they'd both come to this evening, this was the perfect time to come clean.

"You're not listening to me, are you?" She tossed a dish towel onto the counter and planted her hands on her hips.

"Sorry." He shook his head and added a forced smile he suspected might distract her. "It's like you're speaking a different language."

"Just wait until Kyle and I gang up on you." She walked over and took the plates out of his hands. "Stop worrying so much, Matt. Things will work out fine where Kyle's concerned."

If only he could be so certain. "Do you know something I don't?"

"Certainly I do. Is that my cell phone or yours?" She jerked her head toward the living room.

"Mine." While grateful for the reprieve, he sighed. "I should probably get it. It could be work." After Ozzy, he was the station's first call tonight.

"Go on. I've got this. Then we can have coffee. And talk."

"Yeah, okay." Grateful for the reprieve, he bolted for his phone, which turned out

to be a telemarketer who for once got a response other than "don't call this number
again." As he listened to the spiel on carpet
cleaning—he didn't have any carpets—he
tried to come up with the appropriate words
to explain...

The noise in the kitchen faded. Dishes no
longer banged. The water didn't rush. He
didn't hear the clatter of silverware or draw-
ers opening and closing. "Lori?"

He hung up on the telemarketer, tossed
his phone on the coffee table and headed
back. She was sitting at the table, his uniform jacket under her arm.

The letter from the judge was clutched in
her hand. "This fell out of your pocket."

Matt swore and thought about diving for
it, but he could tell it was already too late.
"Lori—"

"Let me guess. This is what you wanted
to talk to me about."

Every ounce of blood drained from his
face. "Let me explain." The second the words
left his mouth, he knew what he'd done. And
how it sounded. "Lori, please, it's not what
you think."

"What do I think?" she asked in a voice

devoid of any emotion. "What could I possibly think, given my name is referred to in this letter by a judge I've never even heard of?"

"You're thinking…" His mind raced so fast his head spun. "You're thinking that I only started dating you again because I needed your testimony in court." As bad as it had sounded in his head, it sounded even worse out loud. "As a character witness."

"Mmmmm." She pressed her lips together so tightly they disappeared. She winced, but when she lifted her gaze to his, he didn't see any hint of tears. No pain. He didn't see anything. It was as if the Lori he'd spent the last couple of hours with had disappeared and left a stranger in her place. "You are definitely perceptive. Must be those police skills of yours." She set the letter on the table and smoothed out the wrinkles. "I have skills, too, for instance—"

"Lori—"

"For instance." The words shot out of her mouth like bullets. "You've had this letter awhile. You've read it quite a few times. Almost as if you've been trying to figure out what to do about it."

"I—yes." The worst thing he could do was compound his secret with lies. With *more* lies. "I should have discussed it with you before. I was hoping Chris was wrong and that we wouldn't need you to testify, and then when I got this, I realized I had to tell you—"

"Chris. The caseworker. Okay, now I'm getting a clearer picture." Her cheeks went from pale to fire hot in the blink of an eye. "That puts my meeting him at the detention center in an entirely different context, doesn't it? All those questions about us, whether we were dating. If I planned to come to court with you. It all makes so much more sense now."

"I know how bad this looks, Lori, and I swear, when he told me my gaining custody of Kyle could hinge on whether I was in a stable relationship, that didn't have anything to do with me asking you out again."

"So aside from being gullible and naive, now you think I'm stupid, too."

"I do not!" How had things gone this wrong that she actually believed that? "You know what I think of you. You know how I feel."

"I know how you've said you feel, and now I know why, don't I? Because you needed a mother figure for Kyle. Because you need me to win your case. Tell me, Matt, did you choose me because you figured I'd be an easy mark or because I look good on paper?"

This could not be happening. This could not be exceeding every nightmarish scenario he'd imagined when it came to this conversation. He felt like he was on a runaway train and the brakes had just blown out. No matter what he said, he couldn't stop it. No matter what he said, he couldn't erase the betrayal he saw shining in her eyes. "May I start at the beginning?"

"Can't see what damage that could do at this point."

"I made a promise, Lori. To Kyle. Months ago. I promised to give him a place when he got out, to give him a home and someone he could rely on. And then the judge assigned to the case retired and this new judge turns out to be a stickler on placement. Chris insisted if he could give her assurances that I was in a stable relationship that it could only work in my favor. None of that changes how I feel about you, Lori. I love you."

A part of him died when she flinched at his admission.

"When?" she asked.

"When what?"

"When did you have this conversation with Chris the caseworker? You and I went weeks without speaking. You'd cut yourself off, didn't answer my texts or calls. For all intents and purposes we were done. Because you needed to figure things out about your *marriage*. So. How. Long?"

Matt didn't want to say, not when he knew the truth could very well be the final nail in their relationship coffin. "I spoke to Chris a few hours before the town council meeting."

"And there it is." Tears filled her eyes. "A couple of hours later you started talking to me again. All of a sudden, you want to pick up where we left off, make me a part of your life. Was the plan to make me fall in love with you so I wouldn't care when I found out you'd been lying to me the entire time? Did you think I was that pathetic?"

"Stop using that word," he snapped. "And no, that wasn't part of the plan." He swallowed the bile rising in his throat. "Because there was no plan. I wanted to be with you,

Lori. I wanted to be a part of your life. That you could end up helping me with Kyle was just a…bonus."

"You used me."

"No," he said again.

"Sure you did. This is all about getting what you need, what you want, about keeping the promise you made to Kyle. Now, if I don't testify, it'll be my fault if you don't win. Thanks for that."

He scrubbed a hand down his face. "You're wrong about so many things."

"What am I wrong about?" She slammed her hands on the table and shot to her feet. "What did I get wrong? All this time, this hasn't been about being with me. It hasn't been about my feelings or what I want. It's been about a promise you made and we both know Matt Knight does whatever he has to in order to keep a promise. Unless, it seems, that promise has been made to me."

Something in her tone broke through the haze in his mind. "You told me if I changed my mind about taking Kyle in you'd lose all respect for me. Do you remember saying that?"

"Of course I do. That's not what this is about."

"Yes, it is. What would you have had me do? When we first started seeing each other, you would have shut me down immediately if I'd told you. And yes, I needed someone in my life to prove I'm capable of maintaining a relationship. I needed stability and I'm sorry to tell you, Lori, but you're a stabilizing influence. Even if the only reason I did start seeing you again was to get Kyle, it doesn't change the fact that I fell in love with you."

"And I'm supposed to believe that why? Because I'm lonely and desperate for someone to love me? Because I let myself believe you wanted a future with me and Kyle was the bonus?"

"You're supposed to believe it because it's the truth."

"As if I can believe anything that comes out of your mouth." She tossed the letter aside and grabbed her bag. "I'm not weak anymore, Matt. I'm not so insecure that I'm willing to be with someone who didn't see me as anything more than a convenience who never even rated the truth."

"No, you're not weak. You never were." Matt caught her arm as she tried to stalk past him. "What you are is scared. What you've found is a bump in the road you'd rather get stuck on than try to work over. You know what I just realized? Once you read that letter, it didn't matter what I said, you weren't going to believe me. Did it occur to you you're looking for an excuse to destroy this? That maybe you've set your standards so high no one will ever be able to meet them? I've told you everything there is to say. But don't you dare walk out of this house believing I don't love you. If I didn't, I wouldn't have spent the last few days torturing myself over how best to approach you about this."

She didn't look at him. She didn't move. She barely breathed. She stood there, in his kitchen, his hand locked around her arm. Frozen.

"You have a choice to make, Lori. You can stay here with me, talk this out, find a way to forgive me or at least try to understand why I did what I did. Or you can run away." He released her and took a long breath. "Your choice."

She stood there, swaying, her jaw clenching as she stared straight ahead. Five seconds. Ten. Twenty. Thirty… Matt's hopes soared.

And then she walked out the front door.

CHAPTER SIXTEEN

IF THERE WAS one thing Lori refused to do it was wallow. Once upon a time she might have. Years, months, maybe even weeks ago she would have crawled into bed, pulled the covers over her head and burrowed into humiliated hibernation for days. And with more than a fair share of junk food. As if anyone ever wallowed with a bowlful of kale.

Things were different now. She was different. She was stronger. So after a few hours of fitful sleep, she got up and got dressed and left the house, sans cell phone because it had been buzzing half the night, and made her way to Calliope's farm. Her solace. Her refuge.

Okay, it was her wallowing place.

She took the long way, bypassing Monarch Lane and anyone she might know who might be awake before eight on a Sunday. The last thing she wanted to do was talk things out with anyone. Mainly because there was always the chance they'd take Matt's side.

It hadn't escaped her reasoning that Matt wouldn't be the man she'd fallen in love with if he hadn't done everything in his power to fight for Kyle. She just happened to be an unwitting weapon in his invisible arsenal. But if he expected her to believe he'd ended up falling in love with her as a result?

She wanted to believe it. But there was just enough self-doubt remaining that she couldn't.

"I've got a cache of bridges for sale if anyone buys that." She kicked a teasel weed like she was going for a goal, then another and another. Her stiff and sore calf muscles protested, but at least she was burning some extra calories and cleaning the sidewalk. By the time she reached the bottom of the hill, she'd worked off most of the mad.

What mad was left, however, shifted to irritation when she found Gil Hamilton in deep discussion with Calliope outside the farm's gate. She did not have the energy or wherewithal to deal with the good mayor this morning.

"So you are alive," Calliope said as she caught sight of Lori.

"That's the rumor," Lori said.

"We've been trying to get in touch with you since last night." Gil looked more frantic than she'd seen in months, maybe years. His eyes were puffy, his hair tousled and his clothes were wrinkled, as if he'd rolled out of bed fully dressed. "Didn't you get our messages?"

"I had my phone off," Lori said. "I didn't want to talk to anyone." Tears burned the back of her throat as Calliope turned those all-seeing eyes on her and let out a soft tsking in the back of her throat. "Don't go touchy-feely on me, Calliope, not this morning." She shook her head. "Not today."

"Wouldn't dream of it. BethAnn's gone missing."

Lori blinked. "Excuse me?" She looked at her friend, then to Gil, back to Calliope. "What do you mean *missing*?"

"She's not answering her phone. There's no sign of her in her house. Her mail is oozing out of that rooster mailbox of hers and the kid who delivers her paper says he hasn't seen her in days. She's gone."

"Please. BethAnn wouldn't just up and disappear." Just what she needed. Drama Queen BethAnn interfering with her quiet day.

"Have you seen her lately? She's been frazzled," Gil said. "I told you yesterday, she's been acting flat-out strange. I even checked with those friends of hers up at the Flutterby, and they haven't seen her since they had dinner the other night."

"That's when I last saw her," Lori said as the first niggling doubt struck. "I have to agree, she didn't look good."

"She's lost," Calliope said. "All that she's taken on since she's come back—it's too much. For anyone, let alone someone as fragile as BethAnn."

"*Fragile* is not the word I'd use to describe her," Lori said.

"Appearances can be deceiving," Calliope said. "Have you contacted the sheriff?" she asked Gil.

"It's been a busy weekend. Luke's got a holding cell full of drunk teens, Fletch is dealing with a break-in at the hardware store and Ozzy's over in Durante helping Brodie with their new computer system. He says he'll send someone to search her house as soon as they can catch a break, but so far no one's been able to find her."

"What about Matt?" Calliope asked.

"Maybe she left a note or a clue," Lori said before Gil could answer.

"What kind of note?" Gil demanded. "You're not thinking she did something—"

"Good heavens, no." Lori waved off that assumption immediately. "The scandal alone would stop her from doing anything self-destructive. What about her committee members?"

"They all quit," Calliope said, and earned a frustrated look from the mayor. "Well, she asked. They quit last week. Couldn't work with her anymore after she up and canceled all the arrangements that had already been made."

She'd canceled *everything*? "So everyone she was relying on to do the work she's been overseeing walked out on her, which means she was stuck doing it all herself." Because things weren't complicated enough. "None of which she's capable of doing."

"What do you mean she's not capable?" Gil asked. "She's a former congressman's wife. She's arranged tons of events…"

"She had a staff," Lori said. "You know she fired Jason as the caterer, right?"

"Well, yeah, but she said he was too expensive—"

"She fired him because she was mad at me for choosing Matt over her. Jason was donating his time. We had everything arranged, all the plans in place. She decided to start over."

"Great." Gil pressed his fingers into his eyes. "Which leaves us where with the dinner tomorrow night? We've got three hundred people rolling in to town expecting a one-of-a-kind outdoor experience. Where are we with that?"

"There's only one person who can answer that question," Lori said. "I'm going to head over to her house. I heard her tell one of the committee members she keeps a spare key in the stone turtle behind the gardenia."

"Isn't that breaking and entering?" Gil demanded. Lori had started back the way she'd come.

"It'll be entering. Call the sheriff on me if you want. But at least you know where I'll be."

SHE PICKED UP speed and made a right onto Bergamot Road, one of the more affluent streets in Butterfly Harbor. Old-fashioned

Victorian chic was what Lori's grandfather had called it. The homes displayed a touch of elegance with beautiful wraparound porches and lush front yards.

As the mail and papers were a sure sign something was wrong, Lori gathered all of it up and set it in the corner of the front porch, after which she retrieved the key from under the turtle behind what used to be a thriving gardenia. She heard the rumble of a car as it pulled to a stop outside BethAnn's home.

"You really want to start the day with me arresting you for trespassing?" Matt said as he climbed out of his truck.

"More than anything," Lori snapped back. "I have a key." She shoved it in the lock.

"So the mayor said. Come on, Lori, let me go in first." He was wearing his uniform and, much to her guilty pleasure, looked as exhausted as she was beginning to feel. He had dark circles under his eyes and whatever light might have shone in his eyes at one time had gone dark.

"She's not some knife-wielding psycho waiting for her next victim," Lori told him. "Besides, if she gives me any trouble I'll just sit on her." She pushed her shoulder against the door and shoved. "BethAnn!" Her voice echoed up the steep staircase and throughout the house that smelled stale and dank, as if it hadn't been aired out in weeks. "Come on, BethAnn, where are you?" She started toward the stairs, then caught movement toward the back of the house.

"No." Matt's hand locked around her arm in the same way it had last night. She stared down at his hand, then up at him. "I mean it, Lori. You might be the queen of everything, but this is my bailiwick. Behind me or go outside. Now." He put his arm out and pushed her behind him. "Mrs. Bottomley?" He kept his hand on the butt of his sidearm and moved toward what Lori now saw was the kitchen.

She stayed far enough behind him that she didn't have to touch him, but she could smell his aftershave, a spicy scent that made her determined head spin.

He stopped short, dropped his hand and his shoulders sagged.

"What?" Lori shot forward, grabbed hold of him as she peered around him. "Is she okay?"

"That depends on your definition of okay."

He walked over to the round wooden table and picked up the empty bottle of Scotch. And then another. He bent down for bachelor number three. "I'll put on the coffee."

Lori stood in the doorway, a hand to her throat as she took in the shocking, disheveled sight of BethAnn Bottomley. She was wearing what looked like ratty sweats and a too-big sweatshirt that was frayed along the cuffs. Her hair was matted and ratted. Her mascara had left long dark streaks down her cheeks. "Oh, BethAnn." Lori knelt on the floor beside her and took hold of one of her hands. The stench of alcohol made Lori's eyes burn. "What happened to put you in this state?" She lifted a hand to the older woman's hair only to pull back at the last minute.

"All my fault." BethAnn hiccuped and jerked in her chair. "Festival ruined. No food. No tables. Everything. Dinner. Just went… poof." She snapped her fingers in the air. "No one. Work with me."

"Why didn't you ask for help?" Lori asked as the aroma of brewing coffee permeated the room. "Open the back door, please, Matt. She needs some fresh air."

"She needs a cold shower."

"Help now, judge later. BethAnn. Oh, okay. I think we're moving now." She scrambled to her feet as BethAnn shoved up and dived out of the room. She slammed a door behind her, but nothing could stop the distinctive sound of retching from eking through the walls.

"Ah, the sound of my childhood. Brings back such fond memories." Matt searched the cupboards for a clean mug.

"I take it you left your compassion in your other jacket?"

"I save my compassion for people who deserve it. That woman has been nothing but nasty to you from the second she returned to town."

"So?" Lori shrugged. "I'm supposed to let her sink into this darkness because she's a—mean lady?" She altered her language at the last second. "People are complicated, Matt. They aren't always predictable."

"No, they aren't, are they?" He pinned her with a stare that had her squirming in her maxi dress. "It's amazing how easily you'll look past her faults but feel free to sit in judgment of others. I need to call Luke and let him know you found her."

"We found her, but yes. He can call off

the hunt. Bye." She wasn't about to admit he had a point.

Matt rolled his eyes. "Like I'm in the clear yet. I'm not leaving until you do. Who knows what she'll pull on you when she sobers up."

"Again, that would cause a scandal and even in death, BethAnn wouldn't tolerate that. Go. Report in. I'll take care of her."

She heard the water running in the bathroom and left Matt to check on BethAnn. She tried the door, found it unlocked and pushed in.

"What are you doing here, Lori?" BethAnn was leaning over the sink, a washcloth over her face, sounding slightly more sober than she had a few moments ago.

"People were worried about you. Gil called out the troops." Lori took the cloth from her and rinsed it out, then handed it back. "You should have talked to someone, BethAnn. You could have come to me."

"I did." BethAnn let out a very unladylike snort. "In a way. I couldn't stand the idea of you lording my failure over me. Like I need Little Miss Perfect rubbing my nose in what a disaster I've made of things."

She wasn't that bad, was she? She'd never

meant to make BethAnn or anyone else feel less than. "I think that's the first time anyone's ever called me little."

That earned her a small smile.

"I'm not perfect, BethAnn. No one is. We all make…mistakes." A tiny bubble of irritated anger named Matt popped in her chest. "What matters is that we try to fix what we break. Tell me what's going on with the dinner."

"No one would take the job after they heard who I fired. Who you fired," she corrected, and leaned over, groaning. "I called in every favor I had, even some from New York and they all said the same thing. Not to mention what they would have charged would put me on the streets. I missed sending in the deposit for the tables and chairs, and then the linens and tents… Everything you and the committee arranged, it's all gone, Lori. There's no dinner to be had and it's all my fault."

It was the first real sign of emotion Lori had ever seen from her. Everything before had felt forced, put on. As if she wasn't sure how she should act around people. But now?

There wasn't any denying BethAnn was fully cognizant of just how much she'd messed up.

"I suppose all that's true." Lori held out her hand. "Come on. Let's have some coffee."

"That's all you have to say?" BethAnn must have been in shock because she took Lori's hand without hesitation. "I just ruined what was supposed to be a premier Butterfly Harbor event and you don't have anything else? No I told you sos or I deserve it commentary?"

"I might have a few things to say, but you need to be clearheaded to hear them. Coffee. Now." She led her back into the kitchen, sat her down and put a full mug of coffee in front of her.

"I take cream and sugar," BethAnn grumbled.

"Tough. Drink." Lori pulled out her cell phone and set it on the table in front of her. She heard Matt talking outside and tried not to think about the way her stomach flipped just thinking about him. "I think we can agree," she said to BethAnn, "that you made things far more difficult on yourself than you needed to. You don't have to be the star of every show, BethAnn. You have to let people help you so things like this don't happen."

"The only reason I took on the dinner chairmanship was because I thought you were on the committee," BethAnn confessed. She rubbed her index finger against her temple. "I knew I could get anything done I needed to because you're so reliable."

"And then I went to work with Matt and left you—"

"Hanging out there on my own. I don't do well on my own," BethAnn confessed. "As you can probably see. I miss my Edgar. So, so much."

"I'm sorry he died," Lori said.

"One minute he was fine and the next, he dropped to the ground and was gone. No warning. Just gone. Fifty-seven years old and his life just ended. Mine did, too. It's just taking longer."

"Grief is difficult for everyone," Lori told her. "I assumed that's why you came back here, because it was your home."

"Except all my friends are gone now. They all left and the rest of you…"

"You have made it a challenge to like you. You try too hard, BethAnn." And Lori should know. She'd been trying too hard for most of her life.

"And now the entire town is going to suffer because of my ineptitude and selfishness."

"It might," Lori agreed, "but feeling sorry for yourself isn't going to fix anything. If you're willing to be part of a team instead of taking charge, there might be a way to salvage the welcome dinner. With a few tweaks, of course."

"What kind of tweaks?" The familiar suspicion that crept into her eyes actually had Lori grinning.

"Tweaks you're going to accept because otherwise I'm not going to save your butt." She picked up her phone, dialed Jason's cell and held up a finger when BethAnn started to question her. "Hey, Jason. You know that plan B we talked about a few weeks ago? Yeah, it's a go. Rally the troops. We have a festival to save."

MONDAY MORNING DAWNED OVERCAST, cold and under the threat of rain, all of which described Matt's sour mood.

Watching Lori work miracles with Beth-Ann Bottomley yesterday had only solidified Matt's feelings for her. Although it didn't come close to making anything better between them. She couldn't write anyone off, could she? Not even when someone had gone out of their way to make her life miserable. Not that Lori was ever miserable.

Matt was, though.

And so far, the only person Lori had written off was him.

He considered putting on his dress uniform, but given that in a few hours he'd pretty much be admitting to fabricating his relationship with Lori with the intent of deceiving the court, he was afraid it might burst into flames. Instead, he dragged out the only suit he owned—navy blue—and spent an embarrassing amount of time tying the blue-striped tie. When the joint in his prosthesis froze up, he found himself stumbling back on his bed where he lay, staring up at the ceiling for far longer than was necessary.

It had been three years since he'd first been fitted. Three years since he'd walked out of the rehabilitation center determined to live each day to the fullest. How could he not, given so many of his friends hadn't been given the chance? Yet here he lay, stewing in the toxic sludge of guilt and grief he'd suppressed for far too long. It was as if Lori had been the stone keeping everything from rolling down the hill. Now, with her gone, the avalanche had begun.

He picked up his phone, held it up as he scanned through his list of contacts. He stared at the name he was looking for, felt his heart pounding an unsteady rhythm in his chest. He dialed, brought the phone to his ear. Waited. "Hey, Doctor Mason." He cleared his throat. "It's Matt Knight. I'm sure you don't remember—"

"Matt! Yes, of course I remember you. You're a hard man to forget."

Matt closed his eyes. If only that was the truth. "I'm sorry I haven't returned your calls. I was… I was wondering if the offer of a new prosthesis was still on the table? I don't expect any favors and I'm not sure what my schedule has in store for the foreseeable future, but if there's a list—"

"You're already on the list," Doctor Mason said. "I just keep bumping people over you. Figured I'd hear from you at some point. You give me a call when you have a couple of days and we'll get you in to the VA, okay?"

"Yeah." Matt croaked. He pinched the bridge of his nose and nodded. "Yeah, that sounds good. Thanks, Doc. I'll see you soon."

He hung up and took a shaky breath. One step forward. Not a big one by most people's standards, but by Matt's? He'd just leaped the Grand Canyon.

"HEY, GREAT. I caught you before you headed out." Kendall walked up the path to his house and looked at her watch. "Aren't you early? It's barely noon."

"I need to talk to Chris about Lori." Matt tugged at the knot of his tie and wondered if this was what it felt like to be strangled. "We need to adjust our strategy now that she's not testifying."

"What do you mean she isn't testifying?" Kendall planted a hand on his chest when he tried to pass. "You told her the truth about everything, didn't you?"

"She found out the truth." Matt busied himself with his keys. "That letter I got from the judge? She found it in my jacket. Things…didn't go well."

Kendall's expression remained neutral. "She thinks you lied to her."

"I did lie to her."

Kendall blew a raspberry. "Please. Not about anything that matters. You're crazy about her. She'll come around and see that."

He shook his head. "Not soon enough. She's got trust issues, Kendall. Big ones and I blew a new hole in them. I need to come clean with the judge and hope she'll understand."

"So you're what? Going to surrender and pretend she doesn't exist? You going to moon over her from a distance?"

"I don't moon. And, well, maybe I'll have to make some changes. Durante's sometimes looking for new deputies. Seeing as the chances I'll get Kyle anyway are slim to none without her support, a new start might be in order."

"Over my dead body will you move away." Kendall followed on his heels to his truck. "I just made a commitment that's going to keep me in Butterfly Harbor for longer than I'd planned. You think I'm staying here without my best friend?"

"I think you'll make plenty of friends whether you want to or not," Matt said, but as he opened his door, he realized what she'd said. "What kind of commitment?"

"Well, seems Abby got to bragging to the mayor about what a great job I'm doing on those cabins of hers. For twenty percent below what that fool contractor was hired to do by the way. Word got around to Mr. Mayor, who asked if I'd be up to doing a refurbishment of the lighthouse. There's a keeper's house I can stay in. As much as I like the apartment over the diner, it's too… there's a lot of people around here." She blinked away that haunted look. "Might have to have some help here and there, but it's something I can tackle."

"That's great, Kendall." Matt went against every one of Kendall's issues and pulled her into a hard hug. "For once that mayor of ours is showing some sense. You'll do a phenomenal job."

"Not without you, I won't." She gripped the open car window and nearly fell forward as he closed it behind him. "You can't surrender, Matt. You can't just walk away and not fight for her. That's not you."

"You're right. That's not me." He stuck the key in the ignition and started his truck. "The only problem is, without her, I'm not sure who I am. Step back, Ken. I don't want you to get hurt, too."

"PICNIC TABLES TOWARD the north end of Monarch Lane," Lori yelled into a passing truck loaded with backyard furniture. She waved them on, started down the lineup of cars to direct people where to go.

"Can you believe people are willing to do this?" Paige had a stack of aluminum serving trays piled high in her arms as she headed from the inn to the diner. "I'd wager every patio set and picnic table in Butterfly Harbor is making an appearance."

"Including yours," Lori told her. "Fletcher dropped them off a while ago. How're the dinner plans coming along?"

"Jason's shut down the restaurant for today, and Abby's giving out vouchers for meals to inn guests for the diner. I've got a couple more runs to make to and from Calliope's. We're going to do watermelon kegs on each of the tables. I've got Luke and Ozzy working on those."

"If we can do extra watermelon without alcohol on either side, that'll be good."

"Yeah, that should work. Family-style farm-to-table meals was a brilliant idea, Lori."

"Well, Jason and I came up with it as an emergency backup plan in case things with BethAnn didn't work out."

"Guess we can add psychic to your list of talents. Hey, where's Matt?" She stumbled forward a little as Charlie barreled into her.

"He has court today." Lori had been doing her best to ignore the guilt for most of the morning. All this time Matt had been trying to appease everyone, live up to the promises he'd made—to everyone. He was being exactly who she'd always believed him to be. The exceptional man she'd fallen in love with.

"What's going on?" Paige asked as she passed the foil trays to Charlie and sent her scooting toward the diner.

"You need to leave those at the other end of Monarch Lane," Lori called to the compact car with a round patio table tied to its roof. "Go up and around, then make a left on Bleeding Heart Way. Fletcher and Jasper will direct you from there." She turned back to Paige. "What's going on where?"

"With Matt. You two have been insepara-
ble for a while now. You hit a bump?"

"You could say that." It was what Matt had
said to her and the more she thought about it,
the more she had to wonder if he was right.
Had she been looking for an excuse to break
things off? Was she looking for the easy way
out?

"You aren't going to court with him I take
it?"

"I'm busy. BethAnn!" She called to the
older woman, who was helping set up tents
along the ocean wall line where they'd be
serving drinks and water to dinner attendees.
"We've still got three pop-ups coming in so
make sure we have room for them."

BethAnn gave her a thumbs-up.

"Did you transplant her personality yesterday?" Paige asked. "She's being so…helpful."

"I have her working with the committee
instead of overriding them," Lori explained.
"I told her it was the only way to earn back
people's respect. She seemed to like that idea.
The respect part." Lori shrugged. "I go with
what works."

"How many tables are we looking at?"

"Well, hopefully at least fifty since we

have three hundred on the RSVP list. I need to go over and check with Harvey and Gil. They're setting up the makeshift stage. The audio's been giving them some trouble."

"Sure, yeah, okay. Lori?" Paige caught her arm. "Whatever is going on with Matt, I hope you work it out. He's been really good for you. And I've never seen him happier."

"Thanks. We'll see." She ducked her head and moved off, happy to leave the conversation about Matt behind. As she hiked up Monarch Lane and saw the line of tables begin to take shape, she never felt such pride in her community. In her friends. Not only had they come through for the beautification project, but they hadn't batted an eye when they'd put out the call for tables. Dozens of people had turned up at Calliope's yesterday and again this morning to help harvest all the bounty of her plantings both to transport to Jason and Holly, but also to help with preparation.

The lineup of grills and barbecues paralleled the tables and already the smell of charcoal wafted through the air and mingled with the salty brine of the sea. Jason had called in some favors with local seafood suppliers and had stockpots full of clam chowder and hearty vegetable soups simmering. Holly had begun baking up a storm yesterday afternoon while her cook, Ursula, had joined forces with her sister Matilda in turning out biscuits and rolls and... Lori's stomach was growling at the very idea of the feast that would take place in just a few hours.

They'd blocked off Monarch Lane, so the directed traffic would be filtered in and around the main thoroughfare, which was ideal now that all those streets had been prettied up and were showing off their town's appeal.

Things could not be going better. And yet...

As Lori continued walking, she couldn't help but think the day was incomplete. She missed Matt. She missed his teasing and his dedication and his rational observations mingled with sardonic wit. She missed how he made her feel; as if she could accomplish anything she set her mind to. As if nothing other than her ability and attitude mattered.

She watched as a father and his two teenage boys hurried past her on their way to the grills, where the father started handing out tools and instructing them on how to operate the fire extinguishers in case of emergency. Watching them together, seeing them laugh and work side by side, a unit, a family, tightened the knot in her chest she feared would never loosen.

The way those boys looked up to their dad, the trust and admiration felt like a knife to her heart as she realized what she was standing in the way of.

Not all lies were meant to be cruel. Not all lies were acts of malice. She hadn't made things—any things—easy on Matt. She hadn't given him a lot of choices as to how to deal with what was going on with Kyle. Or with her. Refusing to testify on his behalf, keeping a hold of her anger and pain might seem like an appropriate and maybe an understandable response, but she was doing far more harm than Matt had ever done to her.

He'd been there when she'd needed him. She'd relied on him, trusted him, and he'd expected so little in return. Expectations he'd been too afraid to voice for fear she'd turn him away—and walk away. And because of that, a boy could very well lose out on the father he deserved.

And Matt would fail in keeping his word.

Whatever else might happen between them, she couldn't let that happen. She couldn't let Matt lose his family.

"I can't do this." She searched the street, her mind spinning as she tried to figure out what to do, where to go. "I can't let Kyle pay for something that isn't his fault."

She spun around and nearly slammed face-first into Kendall. "Kendall. Good heavens." She pressed a hand against her chest. "Sorry, I was distracted."

"Seems to be going around," Kendall said. "You and I need to talk."

"Not again. And not now." Lori shook her head. "I have to go. I have to find a car." She shoved her tablet into Kendall's hands and rushed past her.

"Where are you going? Wait! Lori, you don't drive, remember?"

"I know how to. I just prefer not to."

"Would you wait a minute? I need to talk to you about Matt!"

Lori skidded to a halt. "Where do you think I'm going? I need to get to court."

"You mean you're going to testify?"

"Yes." Lori looked down at her watch. "I

only hope I'm in time. It starts at two, right? Maybe I can catch him before he—"

"He's already gone," Kendall said.

Lori swore. She pulled out her cell and dialed her brother. "Fletcher?" She turned a pleading eye to Kendall, who seemed to know what she was thinking. Kendall nodded. "Where's your truck? I need it."

"HEY, KID, how are you doing?" Matt focused all his energy on keeping his voice encouraging and even as Kyle was escorted in to the defendant's table. He was wearing a smaller version of Matt's suit, but he didn't look nearly as uncomfortable as Matt felt. Matt stood behind the banister and laid firm hands on Kyle's shoulders. "Everything's going to be okay."

Kyle nodded, the innocent optimism on his face nearly cutting Matt to the quick.

Chris had suggested, rather strongly, that Matt talk to Kyle before court was called into session, but Matt hadn't been able to figure out what to say. Story of his life these days. He'd already screwed things up with Lori by postponing the inevitable, which was why they were in this situation to begin with.

The only way out of it was through, which meant Matt was going to have to be completely honest with the judge and hope she would see how important Kyle was to him. And that he was responsible enough to admit when he had made a mistake.

Nothing, however, was stopping that ball of anxiety from bouncing around inside of him like a renegade pinball.

"All rise!" the bailiff announced. Matt gave Kyle a firm pat and turned him toward the judge as she emerged from her chambers. Judge Jeannette Harris was younger than Matt expected, not much older than himself. Her robes flowed around a rotund figure, her intense gaze scanned the room with practiced ease. She looked stern but confident and, Matt could only hope, fair. He could practically hear Kyle swallow as they all took their seats.

Matt unbuttoned his suit jacket as he sat, and settled in to listen to the business of the court. Kyle kept glancing back at him, as if needing to confirm he was still there. Whatever happened, whatever decision the judge made, he wasn't going anywhere. If Kyle's sentence needed to be served in total, he'd continue with the visits. If he got handed off to a group home, he'd be there, too.

And if, by some miracle, he ended up taking Kyle home with him, he'd never tell another lie for as long as he lived.

"I understand there's been a change in your witness list," Judge Harris said as she opened Kyle's file. "Is this correct, Mr. Walters?"

"Yes, Your Honor." Chris cleared his throat and stood. "We had hoped to be able to include Ms. Lori Bradley's testimony today, but unfortunately…"

The double wooden doors at the back of the courtroom burst open. "I'm here!"

Matt and the other observers in the courtroom all spun in their seats.

"I'm sorry, Your Honor." Lori darted forward, dropped her bag on the bench beside Matt and smoothed her flyaway hair. She was sweaty and nervous and determined, and Matt couldn't remember a more beautiful sight in his life. "I've been dealing with an emergency back in Butterfly Harbor and I was only just able to get away."

The judge looked down from the bench at her. She turned those piercing eyes on Matt, who tried to erase the look of surprise on his face, but he had the feeling he hadn't fooled her. He saw Kendall step into the court and stand in the back of the room. She had an odd smirk on her face, as if everything was going according to plan.

"Is it your intention to testify on behalf of the petitioner, Deputy Matthew Knight?" Judge Harris asked.

"It is, Your Honor. But I'd much rather make a statement if that would be permissible?"

Kyle gripped the edge of the table and looked back at Matt, then Lori, who walked over and held out her hand. "Hey, Kyle."

He smiled and nodded. "Hey, Lori."

"Miss Bradley?" the judge said. "You're welcome to proceed."

"Cool. Good. Thanks." She smoothed her hands down the front of her torn T-shirt and pushed through the swinging gate. "Do I need to swear on a Bible or something?"

"Would it make you feel better to do so?" Judge Harris's eyes glittered.

"Yes, actually." She approached the bailiff, who held up his hand and came to her. After she'd been sworn in, she stood in front of the judge. "I could stand up here and tell you a lot of things about Matt Knight."

Oh boy. It was all Matt could do not to sink in his seat.

"I could tell you how good he is at his job, how compassionate and dedicated he is. I could tell you about his sense of humor, about his patience and his ability to deal with whatever comes his way. I could tell you he served this country with courage and valor, and despite his physical injuries, he harbors no resentment about it. But I don't need to tell you all that because it's all in his file. It's in the letters of reference from his coworkers, from his friends. Friends who have become his family. What you can't read in that file is the man I know him to be. A man who will do whatever is asked of him, a man who will always, always, live up to his word.

"Most of us have dealt with adversity and pain. But where others might use those challenges as excuses to be less than, he's constantly strived to rise above those circumstances. He doesn't make excuses—he finds solutions. He embraces the struggle because he knows only by overcoming those challenges will he make things better for everyone involved."

Lori stopped, took a slow breath. "No one is perfect, Your Honor. No one is claiming to be, but if your main concern is finding the perfect home for Kyle, there's only one man who can give that to him."

Matt couldn't breathe. His heart picked up speed as the blood pounded through his head.

"I've spent most of my life alone. But when Matt Knight loves you—and he loves Kyle—the last thing you ever feel is alone. And I know, without a doubt, Kyle deserves that in a father."

"Thank you, Ms. Bradley. Just one question," Judge Harris said.

"Yes, Your Honor?"

"I understand that your testimony is to the character of Deputy Knight. I am curious as to your feelings regarding Kyle Winters. Depending on how your relationship progresses with the deputy, is this a relationship you're willing to take on yourself?"

"I wouldn't have come here today if I didn't think that maybe one day soon he could be mine, too. He's made some mistakes, but he's followed Matt's lead and turned his life around. Butterfly Harbor is anxious to have him back. And so am I. I'd happily choose him as part of my family. If for no other reason than to have someone to talk with about comic books." She grinned. "He doesn't get them." Lori jerked a thumb in Matt's direction.

"It sounds like you and Deputy Knight have a bright future together."

"I hope so," Lori said, and looked into Matt's eyes. "I truly, truly hope so."

"I DON'T KNOW what to say."

Lori had never heard Matt sound so uncertain before. Or so shell-shocked. Standing in the hall outside the courtroom, her heart was still racing. Her mouth was dry and all she could do was replay what she'd said in front of a courtroom of people.

In front of Matt. She'd been honest. More honest than she'd ever been in her life, both with Matt and herself. If she was wrong, if there was too much standing in their way, at least she'd put her feelings on the record—literally.

"You weren't wrong. The other night," Lori clarified when his brow furrowed. She was having a tough time concentrating. She thought he'd looked perfect in that uniform of his, but what he did for a blue suit might just cause heart palpitations. "As excited as I was about what was happening between us, part of me didn't believe it was true. I was scared. I didn't want to be hurt again. I shouldn't have taken it out on you. I'm still ticked you lied to me."

His lips quirked as he shoved his hands into his pocket and ducked his chin. "Yeah, I didn't think I was out of the doghouse on that one just yet. I wouldn't purposely hurt you for the world, Lori. I hope you believe that."

"I do. You're a good man, Matt Knight." She touched his cheek. "Maybe the best man I know."

"Why does it sound as if nothing's changed?"

"Because I'm not sure it has. I love you, Matt. And I want to believe you love me, but for now, there's a lot going on that you need to focus on."

"Whether we work things out today, or tomorrow, or next year, it won't change how I feel. I love you, Lori. I'm done. And for the record, I'd marry you tomorrow if you just said the word."

"If only that pesky divorce of yours wasn't getting in the way." Her attempt at humor felt like a wall coming up. "I'm not going anywhere, Matt. We'll see what happens. In the meantime…"

The courtroom doors opened and Chris and Kyle walked out. Chris steered the teen over to them, planted his hand on Kyle's shoulder and held out his other hand to Matt.

"Congratulations, Dad. It's a boy."

Matt turned all his attention to Kyle. "I think it's too late to change your mind. You good?"

Lori blinked back tears as Kyle looked up at Matt. His chin wobbled as he nodded. "I'm good."

"Come here." Matt reached out and pulled him into a ferocious hug. "Lori?"

"I'm going to drive back with Kendall," she whispered. "We'll see you at the dinner, right?"

"We'll be there," Matt said. "And Lori? Thank you."

"EVERYTHING'S ALL SET with Kyle?" Fletcher wrapped an arm around Lori's shoulders as the dinner crowd funneled down Monarch Lane.

Her team, her family, stood near the stage where Gil was going over last-minute notes with BethAnn and the audio expert. The tables were filled with plates and trays of the best food Butterfly Harbor had to offer. Small votive lanterns dotted the walkways and tables as the sun began its slow descent, casting glittering rays against the ocean nearby.

For the first time in a while, Lori couldn't find anything to worry about. Anything to focus on except the growing realization she'd made a horrible mistake where Matt was concerned.

The high school girl who still lived inside, the girl who had been humiliated and betrayed wouldn't let go easily. The past had sharper talons than any bird of prey and could do far more damage. But she'd helped bring Matt the one thing he'd needed most: a family of his own.

"Everything with Kyle is great." She leaned her head on Fletcher's shoulder. "The judge approved the adoption and Matt should be bringing him to the dinner. If we can find them a spot."

"Already reserved. Table's over there." He

pointed to where her friends and family were taking their seats.

"You knew he'd win?"

"Once you decided to forgive him? Of course I did." Fletcher hugged her. "I never bet against my baby sister."

"I was wrong. Matt isn't the best man I know. You are." She patted a hand against his chest. "You and Paige are so lucky. Don't you dare blow it."

"Couldn't if I wanted to. But there's nothing standing in your way of being happy either, sis. Right now I'd venture to guess you could get just about anything you wanted out of Matt Knight."

"Because he owes me for helping with Kyle, right?"

"Because he loves you." He gave her another squeeze. "Looks like they're about to get started. Let's get our seats."

"Abby." Lori hurried over to catch her friend before she sat down. "We can talk about this in detail later, but about your wedding?"

"Uh-huh." Abby's eyes narrowed. "Don't you dare back out on me on those flowers.

Not after all the work you've done the last few weeks."

"Oh no, I'm already working up plans. No, I meant about being a bridesmaid." She took a deep breath. "I've thought about it and, well, if the offer is still on the table, I'd love to stand up for you."

Abby squealed and locked her arms around Lori in a huge hug. "You just made my day! You'll have a total say in your dress, I promise. And the color. Maybe. We'll start talking soon, yeah?"

Lori settled on the edge of the picnic bench across from Charlie having a battle of wills against Simon, who kept trying to snag another cheddar biscuit. As the microphone buzzed and Gil and BethAnn, along with the town council, took their places behind the podium, she looked down the street. And there, making their way toward her, were Matt and Kyle.

"Scoot over." Charlie shoved Simon and everyone moved down. "Hi, Kyle."

Lori watched as Kyle gave the little girl a weak smile as he sat next to her. "Hey."

"It's okay that you scared us all that time

ago," Charlie announced. "Simon and I forgive you. Don't we, Simon?"

"I guess." Simon shrugged. "I have a scar from where you shoved me." He shoved his bangs out of the way to show the older boy.

"Simon Saxon!" Holly looked horrified. "Don't be rude."

Kyle actually grinned. "Scars are cool. But, yeah, I'm sorry about that."

Simon narrowed his eyes. "Sorry I spied on you."

"Now you're friends. Yay!" Charlie raised both her arms and dropped them over the boys' shoulders and rocked back and forth.

Lori watched through misty eyes, but then she looked at Matt who, still wearing his suit, didn't seem interested in anything other than her. "Good drive home?"

"We missed you," Matt said. "Kyle and I decided we aren't letting you off the hook. Just so you know."

"Did you now?" Lori had to admit she liked the sound of that. But something wasn't right. Something felt off, as if there was something...

"Ladies and gentlemen." Gil tapped his fingers against the microphone to get everyone's attention. When the street went as silent as it could, he cleared his throat. "I'd like to welcome all of you to Butterfly Harbor's inaugural welcome dinner to the Butterfly Festival. Before we all dig in to this amazing feast prepared by our very own Jason Corwin and Holly Saxon—"

Cheers erupted up and down the road.

Gil waited for the quiet again. "I'd like to acknowledge a number of people who made this evening possible, beginning with…"

Lori tuned out as Gil called out the businesses and committee chairs and board members and BethAnn. The older woman had undergone a stunning transformation since Lori had dragged her out of her bathroom. But she hadn't returned to the coiffed, buttoned-down professionalism of her politician wife status. Instead, she'd gone for comfort—and community. She was even wearing one of the tourist shirts sold at the Wings & Things Gift Shop, complete with iron-on wings on the back.

Matt was watching her. She could feel his eyes on hers and when she glanced at him, she noticed he'd held out his hand, palm up, on the table. Without hesitating, she dropped hers into it. And squeezed.

"BethAnn Bottomley has a few things she'd like to say," Gil said finally, as Lori's stomach growled. She was so hungry! And that grilled salmon and asparagus less than an arm's reach away was calling her name.

The smattering of applause was stronger than Lori expected and sounded like the first step toward forgiveness for BethAnn. She had a wineglass in one hand, but Lori knew she'd been drinking sparkling cider all day. The board members stepped up behind her, surrounded her; supported her as she took the podium.

"As much as I would like to take even a modicum of credit for this event tonight," BethAnn said, "I'm not able to do that. We would not even be having this event if it hadn't been for the astute planning and preparations made by Butterfly Harbor's own Lori Bradley."

"Oh no." Lori's entire face went hot. "Oh, she is not doing this to me." But as she looked up at the stage she saw her entire table of friends turn smiling faces on her. "You're all in on this, aren't you? You knew?" Lori hissed.

"Of course we did," Calliope announced. "Now hush."

"Lori, I know public speaking isn't your favorite activity, but I would be grateful if you would please join us up here so we can say a proper thank-you." BethAnn raised her glass, but gave Lori that stern look Lori had come to appreciate in recent weeks.

"Go on," Matt whispered. "Time to shine."

"This is all your fault." She got to her feet and, before she thought it through, caught his face in her hands and kissed him. "Before you, I never would have had the courage to do this."

Before he could speak, she walked up to the stage and found herself laughing at the teasing Matt was receiving back at the table.

"Please." BethAnn motioned to the microphone, a hint of nerves on her face, as if she was worried Lori was going to out her failures over the past few weeks. Surprising them both, Lori reached out and hugged her and swore she heard the older woman sob.

"I couldn't have done it without you," Lori whispered. She turned and felt the world drop away. She couldn't count the number of faces staring back at her, or the pairs of hands applauding or the voices cheering. "Thank you, everyone, but I can honestly say this entire event was a town effort." The crowd quieted. "Butterfly Harbor has been my home for most of my life. It's given me the best friends, family, and a loving and caring community that we are so proud to share with all of you." Her pulse began to pound. She could feel the words freezing in her throat as the panic set in.

She looked to the side and there, amidst everything, was Matt. Sitting there, beaming at her with such love in his eyes and pride on his face. Everything she'd ever wanted, ever dreamed of, looked back at her.

"I, um." She paused, tucked her hair behind her ears. "I know we're all anxious to get to this amazing farm-fresh food that's been provided by Calliope Jones and prepared by Jason and Holly, but first… Um." She took a deep breath. "I need to say something to someone and I'm going to do it before I lose my nerve. I'm also going to do it in front of all of you so he can't ignore me. It's not everyone who is lucky enough to fall in love with someone who only has your best interests at heart. Someone who supports and encourages and reminds you that all that you are is enough. I never thought that could happen for me. I never let myself believe it, but now I do. And because it's the absolute last thing he'd ever expect me to do… Matt? Could you please come up here?"

Matt sat up straight, the same panicked look on his face that she was sure she had had only a few minutes before.

Her brother let out a sharp whistle as the cries and cheers erupted from the back of the tables and washed up and over the stage. Kyle reached out and shoved Matt off his seat and she watched, heart pulsing in her throat, as he made his way to the stage.

"I hope you know what you're doing," he murmured into her ear as he wrapped an arm around her shoulders.

"I know I don't have a ring or anything." She turned to face him, took his hand in hers. Smiling into his beautiful brown eyes, she bent down on one knee. "I love you with all my heart, Deputy Matt Knight. Will you—and Kyle—marry me?"

He stared at her for what seemed like hours, as the crowd erupted and her own table was nearly tipped over by her friends jumping to their feet.

"You sure about this?" Matt asked. "Because I have about three hundred witnesses."

"I know." She smiled and laughed. "Makes it hard for you to say no, doesn't it?"

"Never crossed my mind. The answer is yes." He bent down and gripped her arms, pulled her to her feet. "I love you," he whispered before he kissed her in front of the town, her friends and all of their guests.

Lori wrapped her arms around him, hugged him close and sighed. Life settled.

So the girl who never allowed herself to believe in fairy tales embraced her happily ever after.

* * * * *

Get 2 Free Books,
Plus 2 Free Gifts—
just for trying the Reader Service!

Get 2 Free Books,
Plus 2 Free Gifts—
just for trying the Reader Service!

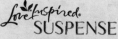

YES! Please send me 2 FREE Love Inspired® Suspense novels and my 2 FREE mystery gifts (gifts are worth about $10 retail). After receiving them, if I don't wish to receive any more books, I can return the shipping statement marked "cancel." If I don't cancel, I will receive 4 brand-new novels every month and be billed just $5.24 each for the regular-print edition or $5.74 each for the larger-print edition in the U.S., or $5.74 each for the regular-print edition or $6.24 each for the larger-print edition in Canada. That's a savings of at least 13% off the cover price. It's quite a bargain! Shipping and handling is just 50¢ per book in the U.S. and 75¢ per book in Canada*. I understand that accepting the 2 free books and gifts places me under no obligation to buy anything. I can always return a shipment and cancel at any time. The free books and gifts are mine to keep no matter what I decide.

Please check one: ☐ Love Inspired Suspense Regular-Print   ☐ Love Inspired Suspense Larger-Print
(153/353 IDN GMWT)   (107/307 IDN GMWT)

Name _____ (PLEASE PRINT) _____

Address _____ Apt. # _____

City _____ State/Prov. _____ Zip/Postal Code _____

Signature (if under 18, a parent or guardian must sign) _____

Mail to the **Reader Service:**

IN U.S.A.: P.O. Box 1341, Buffalo, NY 14240-8531
IN CANADA: P.O. Box 603, Fort Erie, Ontario L2A 5X3

Want to try two free books from another line?
Call 1-800-873-8635 or visit www.ReaderService.com.

* Terms and prices subject to change without notice. Prices do not include applicable taxes. Sales tax applicable in N.Y. Canadian residents will be charged applicable taxes. Offer not valid in Quebec. This offer is limited to one order per household. Books received may not be as shown. Not valid for current subscribers to Love Inspired Suspense books. All orders subject to approval. Credit or debit balances in a customer's account(s) may be offset by any other outstanding balance owed by or to the customer. Please allow 4 to 6 weeks for delivery. Offer available while quantities last.

Your Privacy—The Reader Service is committed to protecting your privacy. Our Privacy Policy is available online at www.ReaderService.com or upon request from the Reader Service.

We make a portion of our mailing list available to reputable third parties that offer products we believe may interest you. If you prefer that we not exchange your name with third parties, or if you wish to clarify or modify your communication preferences, please visit us at www.ReaderService.com/consumerschoice or write to us at Reader Service Preference Service, P.O. Box 9062, Buffalo, NY 14240-9062. Include your complete name and address.

HOME on the RANCH

YES! Please send me the **Home on the Ranch Collection** in Larger Print. This collection begins with 3 FREE books and 2 FREE gifts in the first shipment. Along with my 3 free books, I'll also get the next 4 books from the Home on the Ranch Collection, in LARGER PRINT, which I may either return and owe nothing, or keep for the low price of $5.24 U.S./ $5.89 CDN each plus $2.99 for shipping and handling per shipment*. If I decide to continue, about once a month for 8 months I will get 6 or 7 more books, but will only need to pay for 4. That means 2 or 3 books in every shipment will be FREE! If I decide to keep the entire collection, I'll have paid for only 32 books because 19 books are FREE! I understand that accepting the 3 free books and gifts places me under no obligation to buy anything. I can always return a shipment and cancel at any time. My free books and gifts are mine to keep no matter what I decide.

268 HCN 3760 468 HCN 3760

Name	(PLEASE PRINT)	
Address		Apt. #
City	State/Prov.	Zip/Postal Code

Signature (if under 18, a parent or guardian must sign)

Mail to the **Reader Service:**
IN U.S.A.: P.O. Box 1867, Buffalo, NY. 14240-1867
IN CANADA: P.O. Box 609, Fort Erie, Ontario L2A 5X3

* Terms and prices subject to change without notice. Prices do not include applicable taxes. Sales tax applicable in NY. Canadian residents will be charged applicable taxes. This offer is limited to one order per household. All orders subject to approval. Credit or debit balances in a customer's account(s) may be offset by any other outstanding balance owed by or to the customer. Please allow 3 to 4 weeks for delivery. Offer available while quantities last. Offer not available to Quebec residents.

HRCBPA18

Get 2 Free Books,

<u>Plus</u> 2 Free Gifts –

just for trying the *Reader Service!*

STRS17R2

Get 2 Free Books,

SPECIAL EDITION

♥HARLEQUIN®

Plus 2 Free Gifts—

just for trying the
Reader Service!

HSE17R3

READERSERVICE.COM

Manage your account online!

- Review your order history
- Manage your payments
- Update your address

We've designed the Reader Service website just for you.

Enjoy all the features!

- Discover new series available to you, and read excerpts from any series.
- Respond to mailings and special monthly offers.
- Browse the Bonus Bucks catalog and online-only exculsives.
- Share your feedback.

Visit us at:

ReaderService.com

RS16R